MY FAVORITE SOUVENIR

PENELOPE WARD
VI KEELAND

This book is a work of fiction. All names, characters, locations, and incidents are products of the authors' imaginations. Any resemblance to actual persons, things, living or dead, locales, or events is entirely coincidental.

MY FAVORITE SOUVENIR
Photographer: Davide Martini
Model: Simone Bredariol
Edited by: Jessica Royer Ocken
Cover designer: Sommer Stein, Perfect Pear Creative
Proofreading and Interior Formatting:
Elaine York, Allusion Graphics, LLC
www.allusiongraphics.com

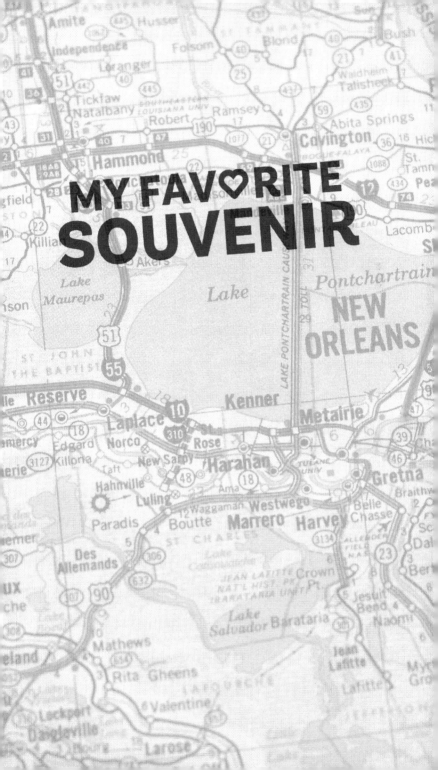

MY FAV♡RITE SOUVENIR

Chapter 1

Hazel

"Good afternoon. You've reached the Four Seasons Resort, Vail, Colorado. How may I direct your call?"

I took a deep breath. "Hi. I checked out early this morning. My reservation was for ten days, but I only wound up staying two nights. Is there any chance you might still have my room available? Or any room, for that matter? My flight was canceled because of the storm."

"Let me take a look. What's your last name?"

"Appleton." I shook my head. "Actually, the reservation was under Ellis. My fiancé's last name." *Or ex-fiancé.* But I'd let her call me Mrs. Ellis at this point if it meant I could have a place to sleep tonight.

"Give me one moment and I'll check."

"Thank you."

I sat down in the lobby of the Best Western, the third hotel I'd been to in the last two hours. It was dumb of me to check out this morning. Though, at least I was consistent. After making the bad decision to go on my previously planned honeymoon alone, I'd brilliantly decided to check out only two days into the trip...*without* looking at the weather report for Vail. When I arrived at the airport, I had no idea that a blizzard was on the way. But the airline had assured me my flight was still scheduled as planned. And they'd kept their word right up until five minutes before we were supposed to board, when they announced a two-hour delay. Two hours turned into three, and three turned into five, and when we hit six hours of sitting on uncomfortable plastic seats outside the gate, they finally admitted it wasn't going to happen. Every other flight had been canceled by then. And now, every hotel seemed to be full.

The hotel operator came back on the line.

"Hi, Mrs. Ellis?"

I cringed at being called that, but answered anyway. "Yes?"

"I'm sorry. After you checked out, your room was rebooked. We're actually sold out for the night because of the storm."

I sighed. *Of course you are.* "Okay. Thank you."

This was just my luck lately. I called four more hotels, until one said they might have a few rooms available. Apparently they had guests that hadn't checked in yet and were in the process of making calls to confirm whether they would still be arriving today. Rooms would be freed up on a first-come, first-served basis. So I decided to take a chance and head on over. It was already seven o'clock at night, and there was no point in sitting here anymore. Surprisingly, Uber was still running, even though the airport had called it quits hours ago.

Out front, the snow was coming down hard. A giant SUV with snow chains on the tires pulled up in front of the door. I couldn't check the license plate or get a look at the make and model of the vehicle since it was covered in snow, so I walked over to the car and motioned for the driver to roll down the window.

"Are you Hazel?" the older woman behind the wheel asked.

I smiled. "Yes."

"Heading over to the Snow Eagle Lodge?"

"Yes, please."

Even though the next hotel was only two miles away, it took fifteen minutes to get there. By the time we pulled up, the conditions were almost white-out. It couldn't be safe driving in this anymore.

"God, it's really terrible out here," I said as I pulled up the hood of my jacket. "Be careful driving tonight."

"Oh, I will, honey. The next place I'm driving is home. I only picked you up because you were on my way. Good thing you're at your hotel now. No one is going to be on the roads tonight anymore."

Great. This place really better have a room for me.

As I climbed out of the SUV, a gust of snow smacked me in the face, despite the fact that we were parked under the building's overhang. The wind made it look like someone had shaken a snow globe, hard. Inside the hotel, I wiped flakes from my eyelashes and glanced around the lobby.

Oh no.

This didn't look good. A line of at least thirty or forty people snaked five rows deep, waiting to get to the reception desk. I sighed and wheeled my luggage to behind the last person. More than half an hour later, I finally reached the front.

"Hi. I called earlier, and the person I spoke to said some rooms might become available, that you were going to contact guests who hadn't showed and see if they were still coming?"

The woman nodded with a frown. "Yeah. I can put you on our waitlist. But we're still making calls, and to be honest, it's not looking too good."

My shoulders slumped. "Okay. Well, I guess please add me to your wait list."

The woman lifted a clipboard and set it down on the counter. She thumbed through a few pages and turned it to face me, pointing at the next available line, which was two from the bottom of the page. "Just add your name and cell phone number."

I scribbled both and let the pages above the one I'd been writing on fan back into place. Noticing the sheet at the top looked just like the one I'd signed, five or six pages down, I glanced through all the papers. There had to be at least a hundred names and telephone numbers.

"Are these *all* on your waiting list?"

The hotel clerk nodded.

"How many people haven't checked in?"

"I think about a dozen."

Oh God. This really wasn't good. But maybe people had just added their names and left, like in a packed restaurant. Maybe the bulk of people ahead of me on the list had found other hotels.

Turning around, whatever hope I'd talked myself into immediately deflated. Every seat in the lobby area behind me was taken. Some were even sitting on the floor, leaning against their luggage. With very few options, I wandered over and found an empty space on a carpeted area of the floor, not too far from the concierge

4

desk. Though I knew it was futile, I took out my iPad and continued to search for a hotel with availability. Even if I found one, getting there would be a miracle on its own at this point.

The nearby concierge desk had been empty while I scrolled and made calls, but now two women walked over. One I recognized as the manager, since I'd spent a half hour staring at the people behind the front desk while I'd waited in line. The other had on a nametag and held a clipboard. I couldn't help but eavesdrop on their conversation from where I sat.

"These seven we still haven't reached," the manager said. "All of the other rooms have been checked in, or we've reallocated them to people from the waiting list."

The employee flipped through the pages and looked around the full hotel lobby. "Jeez. And this storm is supposed to stick around for days."

Out of the corner of my eye, I noticed a guy standing on the other side of the concierge desk. His back was to the ladies talking, but he craned his neck, and I thought he, too, might be eavesdropping. Figuring he was probably just as bored as me, I went back to my iPad search—until a few minutes later when I noticed him scribbling something with a pen on the inside of his hand.

What the hell is he doing?

He wrote for a few seconds and then seemed to go back to eavesdropping. The manager had walked away, leaving the employee to make her phone calls. She hung up from one call and dialed again.

"Hi. This is Catherine from the Snow Eagle Lodge. I'm trying to reach Milo or Madeline Hooker."

The minute she said the names, the eavesdropper scribbled on his hand again.

Catherine continued leaving her message. "I just wanted to confirm whether you'd still be arriving this evening. Your reservation is guaranteed, so we'll hold it as long as you need. However, if the storm has perhaps caused a change in your travel plans, we do have a long wait list of guests who could use the two rooms you have booked. My number here is 970-555-4000, if you could please return my call at your earliest convenience. Thank you."

The same thing went on with the next two calls. Catherine left a message and the eavesdropper scribbled. Curious about what he was up to, I kept my eye on him. After the hotel clerk finished making her calls, she went back to the front desk. Eavesdropper picked up his backpack and casually strolled down a nearby hallway. I leaned to watch where he was going, and he eventually pulled up his hood and exited out a side door I hadn't even noticed was there.

I thought it was odd, but I figured the show was over.

But a few minutes later, a guy with the same ski jacket walked through the front lobby door. He pulled his hood down, and I got a look at his face for the very first time.

Damn, he was handsome. Medium brown hair that was kind of shaggy and needed a cut, full lips, hazel eyes, and tanned skin. His warm skin tone really stood out against the pasty color of most people in Colorado this time of the year, including me. It was a shame I loathed men right now, because he was seriously gorgeous. He dusted some of the snow from the shoulders of his jacket and went to wait in line. It was much shorter now, with only two men in front of him, mostly because people weren't braving the storm anymore. I had no idea what possessed me to do it, but I decided to get up and wait behind the guy. Maybe I was imagining things to keep myself entertained, but I had the distinct feeling he was up to something.

When it was his turn at the front desk, I moved as close as I could to listen without seeming like a stalker.

"Hi. I'm checking in," the man said.

"Great. What's your last name, sir?"

He cleared his throat. "Hooker. Milo Hooker."

I squinted. The guy was totally full of shit. *I knew it!*

The unsuspecting hotel clerk punched a bunch of keys on her keyboard and smiled. "I have your reservation right here. Two rooms for two nights, breakfast included. Is that right?"

"Uhhh..." The guy nodded. "Yeah. I booked two rooms. But it turns out I'm only going to need the one." He looked over his shoulder. "Looks like you won't have a problem filling the other one, though."

She smiled. "No, we definitely won't. I'll just need a credit card and a picture ID please, Mr. Hooker."

I waited. This was the moment of truth. If he wasn't actually Milo Hooker, he was going to have to make up some excuse.

The guy reached into his front pocket like he was going to pull out his wallet. For a second, I thought I might've been wrong, but then he pulled out a wad of cash.

"I lost my wallet on the slopes today. Luckily, I had some cash sent over through Western Union before the storm got too bad. Can I just pay cash?"

The young woman hesitated. "You don't have any ID at all? I'm not supposed to check people in without photo identification."

Fake Milo poured on the charm. He leaned forward and showed off a set of cavernous dimples. "We could take a selfie together?"

The woman giggled. *She actually giggled.* "Let me just check with my manager."

She disappeared into the back and returned with the manager a few minutes later.

A crazy idea popped into my head. *She said there were two rooms...* I made a spur-of-the-moment decision and approached the counter.

"There you are, Milo." I rested my hand on the guy's shoulder. "My flight was canceled. I hope they still have our rooms."

Fake Milo turned and looked at me with his brows furrowed.

He was going to blow it if I didn't do something, so I turned my attention to the two hotel employees. "My brother and I booked rooms here for two nights, but I was trying to get out before the storm. Obviously I had no luck. I spent the entire day in the airport. Please tell me you still have my room? I'm dying for a hot bath."

Milo looked at me, then the hotel employees, then back at me. I smiled and arched a brow. For a second, I almost felt bad for the guy. He looked so bewildered. Since he still seemed to be at a loss for words, I figured I should continue talking. "We went skiing early this morning and had our backpacks stolen. Between that and the storm coming, I figured it was a sign that I should get back home early. Apparently Mother Nature had other plans. We should have two rooms—Milo and Madeline Hooker. Someone actually just left me a message on my cell asking us to confirm. Her name was Catherine, I believe."

The desk clerk nodded. "That was me. The storm has a lot of people stranded here unexpectedly without rooms, so we were checking in with guests that hadn't arrived yet."

The manager looked back and forth between Fake Milo and me. "We'll have to take a hundred-dollar deposit for incidentals on each room since you don't have a credit card."

I smiled. "Of course."

She nodded to her employee. "Check them in. It's fine."

The man next to me still had his mouth hanging open. So I dug into my purse, being careful not to show my wallet, which was supposed to have been stolen, and scooped out all of the cash.

"How much are the rooms?" I asked the clerk.

"Let's see. With tax, they come to three-hundred-and-forty-two dollars each, for the two nights, and then we have to collect the hundred-dollar deposit."

Shit. I didn't think I had that much cash. I counted the money in my hand and slid it over in front of Fake Milo. "Can you spot me forty dollars? You know I'm good for it, bro."

"Uh, yeah. Sure."

After we paid and got the room keys, we walked side by side to the elevator bank in silence. It wasn't until we were alone and the elevator doors slid shut that Milo turned to me. "What the hell just happened?"

I laughed. "We just got rooms, that's what happened."

He shook his head. "But who are you?"

"I noticed you standing near the concierge desk and eavesdropping while she called the guests who hadn't arrived yet." I reached forward and took the man's hand, opening it to display blue ink. "You wrote down the names of the guests. I thought it was odd, so I followed you to the front desk to see what you were up to. When you made up that bogus story about losing your wallet so you could justify not having any ID, I knew you were full of shit." I shrugged. "When the woman said there were *two rooms* on the reservation, I saw an opening and took it."

"How did you know I'd go along with it?"

I smiled. "I didn't. But that's what made it so much fun!" I covered my chest with my hand. "My heart feels like it's trying to ricochet out of my ribcage at this moment. It's been a long time since I did anything risky like that."

His eyes roamed my face. I got the feeling he still wasn't sure what to make of me, even though I'd just explained what I'd done. He looked down at my lips, which were still curved in an excited smile.

"Why is that?"

My forehead wrinkled. "Why is what?"

"Why's it been a long time since you've done anything risky? It looks to me like you enjoyed it."

I blinked a few times, not having expected a question that would tug at my heartstrings, and my smile fell. "I don't know. I guess I kind of turned into a different person over the last few years."

Fake Milo's eyes locked with mine. We'd gone from pulling off a crazy stunt and laughing, to an odd seriousness. His eyes flickered to my lips and back once again. "That's a shame. You have a great smile."

Warmth spread through me, and I couldn't seem to unlock my eyes from the stranger's—at least until the elevator dinged and the doors opened on the third floor.

"This is us," he said. "Rooms 320 and 321."

"Oh. Right. Okay." I stepped out and followed the signs to our rooms. Since we were, of course, family, they'd put us right next to each other. We stood a few feet apart as we opened our respective doors. As my lock unlatched and I turned the handle to go inside, something dawned on me.

"I almost forgot! I owe you forty dollars for the room."

He smiled. "Don't worry about it."

"No, don't be silly. I just didn't have enough cash and didn't want to hand the woman a credit card when we weren't supposed to have ID. I'll just throw my bag in the room and go downstairs to find an ATM. They must have one somewhere."

"I thought you couldn't wait to take a hot bath, or was that part of the act?"

I laughed. "No, it actually wasn't. I wasn't lying when I said I spent the entire day at the airport. A hot bath sounds pretty amazing right about now. But I can grab your cash first. It won't take me long."

Fake Milo scratched at the stubble on his chin. "I'll tell you what. I'm going to take a quick shower and then go downstairs to the bar for a drink. Take your bath. You can find me there afterward to give me the money."

"Okay."

We looked at each other for a moment.

"Alright, well, enjoy your soak, sis."

I smiled. "Thanks, Milo. I'll see you later."

Chapter 2

Hazel

"Hey."

After my bath, I found Milo exactly where he'd said he'd be...at the bar.

He pivoted on his stool and flashed a smile. "What's up, Hooker?"

"Excuse me?"

He chuckled. "It's our last name, Madeline."

I smiled. "Oh. I suppose it is."

He sipped his beer from the bottle. "I think you look more like a Maddie than a Madeline, though."

I laughed. "I'm glad you didn't say I looked like a Hooker."

Milo pointed his eyes to the empty seat next to him. "Join me for a drink?"

"Oh...no. I, uh, just came to give you the money I owe you." I dug the cash from my purse and extended it to him.

He waved me off. "Use it to buy the next round."

I supposed one drink couldn't hurt. My neck was killing me. I didn't like to fly, and an entire day of waiting at the airport had made me tense, not to mention the stress of not knowing where I was going to sleep tonight. Maybe a drink would help me loosen the knot.

I nodded. "Sure. Why not."

Milo motioned to the bartender while I settled into the seat next to him.

"Ed. This is my sister, Maddie. Maddie, this is Ed."

The bartender reached over to shake my hand. "Nice to meet you, Maddie."

"You, too."

"What can I get for you?"

"Umm. I'll take a vodka and cranberry, with lime, please."

Ed rapped his knuckles against the bar. "Coming right up." He looked to my left. "You want another Coors Light, Milo?"

"Sure thing. Thanks, Ed."

I laughed as the bartender walked away. "Is your name really Milo or are you getting into character?"

He shrugged. "I sort of like Milo better. Thought maybe I'd change mine. So I'm trying it on for size."

I couldn't tell if he was kidding or not. "Whatever you say."

"So, Mads, what's your excuse for not having a hotel room tonight?"

I sighed. "It's a long story."

He lifted his shirt sleeve and twisted his arm to look at his watch. "Just what I thought."

"What?"

He shrugged. "I have plenty of time for a long story."

I chuckled. "Well, to keep from boring you to death, I'll give you the abbreviated version anyway." I paused to think about how to explain and decided not to sugarcoat things. "I'm here on what was supposed to be my destination wedding and honeymoon. My ex-fiancé called off the wedding a couple of months ago. Our tickets and hotel were non-refundable, so I opted to make use of them and get out of town for a few days. Lately he's started making contact with me again, telling me he's missed me. So I figured it would be a perfect time to come do some soul searching. But two days into my ten-day trip, I realized it was a bad idea and decided to go home. Only I didn't check the weather before I checked out this morning. So I wound up sitting in the airport all day, and by the time they canceled my flight and I realized everything in the area was sold out, my hotel had already given my room to someone else."

Milo's brows rose. "Whoa. That's a pretty shitty story."

I laughed. "Thanks. That makes me feel a lot better."

"Sorry." He chuckled.

The bartender brought over my drink. "You want to start a tab?"

"Put hers on my tab, Ed."

"Oh, no, that's okay. I'm just going to have this one, so I'll pay for it."

"I insist." He winked at me. "Mom wouldn't like me letting my little sister pay."

I placed the forty dollars I owed him in front of him on the bar. "Thank you. At least take the money I owe you for the room."

Fake Milo nodded. "So what happened?"

Why did I seem to keep getting lost in conversation with this man? "What happened, what?"

"You said your fiancé called off the wedding. Was he always an asshole and you just figured it out now, or is there more to the story?"

"That's sort of a personal question, isn't it?"

He shrugged. "I'm your brother. You can tell me anything. Plus, I'm thinking I might need to go kick his ass for hurting you—defend my sister's honor and all."

I liked Fake Milo. He had a dry sense of humor. But there wasn't an easy answer as to what had led to the demise of my engagement. Though it looked like the man next to me was waiting for one.

"No need to kick his ass. I actually take part of the blame."

His eyes widened. "Say what? You take part of the blame for that asshole canceling the wedding?"

"Well, not for how he handled it, but perhaps for what led to it."

"What could possibly give him an excuse to cancel a wedding? If you're not sure, you don't propose."

How to explain...

"Well, when he first met me, I was a free spirit, fun-loving—the total opposite of him. But you know, opposites attract, right? Even though he was more straight-laced, he was attracted to my wild personality. But over the years, I lost my way. I became...more like him. And I think despite a mutual respect for each other, he woke up one day and realized he needed to step back before he made a lifelong commitment to someone who wasn't the same person anymore."

"How long were you engaged?"

"A year."

Milo frowned. "That's fucking bullshit, and you know it, right? There's no reason to lead someone on

15

until right before a wedding." He took a drink of his beer and slammed the bottle down. "Anyway, you think there was more to it? Like maybe he was fucking someone else and felt guilty? Not that he would've had any reason to do that if he had you at home."

I shook my head. "No, I don't think he would do something like that. I mean, there have been times when I wondered about a couple of his female co-workers. A group of people from his office go out a lot together after work. They drink a little too much. But I don't think he ever did more than flirt with them."

Rehashing anything having to do with Brady was starting to make me feel sick to my stomach.

"How did he tell you...that he didn't want to get married?" Milo asked.

"He just said he wasn't sure it was the right decision anymore. He kept things very vague. It was all so sudden. Even though I probably should've seen it coming, I didn't. I truly believed he loved me, even if our relationship might have changed since the beginning. Like I said, I don't really blame him for his change of heart."

"Well, you should blame him for how he handled things. That's messed up to let you plan a wedding and then pull that shit."

"It definitely seemed like it hurt him to have to do it. I don't think it was an easy decision. He'd probably known about it for a while but was just reluctant to tell me. He was very apologetic."

"Christ! As he should be."

I rolled my eyes. "Yeah."

"But you know what?"

"What?"

He paused. "He's an idiot. He'll regret it someday."

My cheeks felt hot, and our eyes locked for a few moments.

"Well, that's very nice of you to say. You know, if I didn't know better, I'd think you actually *were* my brother," I said in a low voice. "You're awfully protective of someone you don't even know."

He turned to the bartender. "Ed, can you get my sister here another drink?"

Holding out my palms, I said, "I'm not sure I should have another."

"Trust me. You're gonna need it."

"Why's that?"

"Because I'm about to set you straight. You might need something to take the edge off."

I squinted. "Is that right?"

"Yes."

Ed placed another vodka cranberry in front of me. Milo grinned. "Drink up."

I took a long sip. The alcohol burned my throat. "So what is it that I need to be intoxicated in order to hear?"

Milo leaned in. "This guy of yours, he's gonna come back, begging you to give him another chance."

"How do you know that?"

"I just do, okay? Men are fucking dumb, and he's going to realize his mistake and try to get you back."

His tone gave me an inkling that maybe he'd learned that firsthand.

"Speaking from personal experience?" I asked.

"As a matter of fact, yes. The same thing happened with my brother. It was a little different than your situation, because he actually cheated on my sister-in-law with a co-worker. She forgave him, took him back, and he thanked her by doing it again, that time with a different co-worker. My brother has always been a dick, even when we were kids. I love him, but he's just a dick. People don't change, Maddie. They don't. And if this guy could let you go so easily once, he will fuck up again. He doesn't deserve you."

A part of me wanted to believe he was wrong. "Well, I can't help it if I'm still holding out hope that I didn't waste the past few years of my life."

Milo shrugged. "People make bad investments all the time. You chalk it up to a mistake and move on. You don't linger over a dead horse just because you rode the shit out of it." He paused. "Maybe that's not the best terminology. But anyway, dead horse? You step over it and move on. You know what happens if you try to wake that dead horse?"

"What?"

"It bites you in the ass."

I chuckled. "Okay. I get your point. But you know, moving on from a relationship that's lasted several years is easier said than done. But I do thank you for your advice."

He winked. "That's what big brothers are for." He sipped his beer. "Anyway, tell me why you think you're so boring."

I stared down into my glass. "I don't even recognize myself anymore, Milo."

"Aside from the fact that you're impersonating a Hooker, what do you mean by that?"

That made me laugh. "For the record, we're both impersonating Hookers, and it's a long story."

He pretended to look down at his watch again. "Once again, I got time. In case you haven't checked the weather recently, neither of us is going anywhere anytime soon."

"I suppose that's true."

He smiled. "So, talk to me."

I let out a long sigh. "Okay, well, to understand me, you'd have to know that my parents were hippies."

He crossed his arms. "Peace and love—nice."

I nodded. "We moved around a lot when I was growing up. I always resented it—you know, having to change schools and everything. But as I got older, I became accustomed to the lifestyle. After college, I basically turned into my parents."

"You became a hippie?"

"Not exactly. But I was never in one place. I'm a photographer. Years ago, right out of school, I worked for a music magazine and traveled the country shooting various bands. I've definitely seen my share of tour buses. And let me tell you, back then this girl liked to party right along with everyone else. It was fun for a long time, until—"

He finished my sentence. "Until it wasn't."

"Yeah, exactly. It hit me at a certain point that I was definitely becoming my parents, and while that had suited me just fine in my early twenties, it was starting to get old."

"So you quit that job?"

"Not immediately. I met my ex-fiancé at a concert, ironically."

Milo nodded. "The day the music died..."

That made me laugh again. Or maybe it was the alcohol.

"He was everything I wasn't: conservative with roots. And for the first time in my life, I started to believe I wanted that type of a life instead of the one I had. I think I was really in search of a feeling of safety more than anything else."

He leaned back and made himself more comfortable in his seat. "I can understand that."

"His parents have been married for thirty-five years, and he still goes to his childhood home every Sunday night for a family dinner. I had no real home base, so I decided to quit my job to be with him."

"You stopped taking pictures?"

"No. He helped me open a private studio. It's become a thriving school-photography business. I'm the school photo queen of my town."

"Riveting. Do you put those fake blue and pink laser beams in the backgrounds of your photos?"

"Of course not! That's so eighties. I think my mom had a school photo like that, though."

"I think everyone's mom probably did. Don't forget the profile face floating in the upper corner of the picture." He laughed.

"I can proudly say that my photos are a lot classier than that."

"In all seriousness, good for you for finding a way to profit from your talents."

I shrugged. "School photography is far from creative, but it pays the bills and helps maintain the cushy life I've become accustomed to."

He seemed to see right through me. "But sometimes you want to trade cushy for dirty again, don't you?"

The way he said *dirty* sent a chill down my spine. I loved the way it sounded coming out of this guy's mouth.

I could feel how red my face must have turned. "God, we've spent this entire time talking about me. I haven't even asked you what the hell *you're* doing in Vail."

"I'm from here, actually. Grew up in Vail."

That surprised me. "Really?"

"Yep."

"So why are you staying at a hotel?"

"I don't live here anymore. I was just visiting my parents and some friends. They live on the outskirts of town, and I wanted to spend a few days here in the heart of things."

"Where do you live now?"

"Seattle."

"What do you do?"

"I'm a high school music teacher."

Not sure why, but that warmed my heart. I had the best memories of my music teachers, who were part of my early inspiration to pursue a career in music photography.

"Really? That's so cool."

"Well, I try to be *cool*, but generally my students can see through me."

Damn. I could only imagine how many hormonal teenage girls had a crush on this guy. I was starting to feel a little like one of those girls the more I stared at him. He was sexy in a grungy way, his hair a perfect, tousled mess. There seemed to be a permanent glimmer in his eyes when he looked at me, a bit scrutinizing and a lot sexy. And don't get me started on those lips, so full. They were quite distracting.

I shook my head, because the last thing I needed was to start fantasizing about some stranger I wouldn't see after tomorrow.

I cleared my throat. "Wow, okay. So, we've both worked in fields that involve music—you in a much different capacity, of course."

"Well, naturally, when you said you were a music photographer, my ears perked up. Except I chaperone field trips on school buses, whereas you were gallivanting on *tour* buses. The latter sounds much more exciting."

I sighed. "It was."

"I assume you dated some of the musicians?"

"Only one. Herbie Allen. The drummer for Snake. Ever hear of him?"

"Yeah, sure. Whatever happened with that?"

"We dated for a couple of months, and then I decided staying with a musician would ultimately end in heartbreak. I was scared to get hurt, so I broke up with him. Real ironic, considering my conservative fiancé was the one who ultimately broke my heart. I probably would've been safer with Herbie. At least that would have been more what-you-see-is-what-you-get." I shook the thought away. "Anyway, tell me how you ended up becoming a music teacher."

He stared at me for a few seconds. "That might be a story for another time."

I shook my head. "There's not going to be another time. We won't see each other after today."

He winked. "The night is young, sister."

Who is this man and why am I so captivated by him that I almost completely forgot I was snowed in at this damn hotel? Why am I telling him my life story?

I had so many other questions for "Milo," but he soon changed the subject back to me.

"So, who are you really, Maddie?"

Moving the last of my cocktail around in the glass, I answered honestly. "I'm not sure anymore, Milo. I'm really not. I feel very lost right now, like I don't know which direction to take my life." I looked up at him. "But at this moment, I'm quite happy to just be Maddie, to forget about my troubles for a while."

"Then Maddie you shall remain." He smiled. "Whatever makes you happy. Think of our time here as a little adventure."

"I'd like that. Mr. Hooker."

"Very well, Ms. Hooker."

I sighed. "I lost my sense of adventure over the past few years. I have wondered if my fiancé calling off the wedding might have been a sign I was headed in the wrong direction. Every day had become the same as the last. And as much as I appreciated the stability, I don't know if that kind of life is in my nature."

"That's my girl. Look at what happened as your ticket out—on to bigger and better things. I can see the need for adventure in your eyes."

"What does a need for adventure look like? A tired, crazy person?"

He just laughed.

We stayed at the bar, enjoying our conversation for a while longer until we decided to call it a night. Milo left Ed a huge tip before we walked together back toward the elevators.

After arriving at our adjacent hotel rooms, we lingered before entering.

I was the first to speak. "Well…it was nice chatting. Thank you for the drinks."

Despite my essentially saying goodbye, we continued to stay in our spots.

Milo suddenly shook his head. "No."

I was confused. "No?"

"This can't be how it ends—I go back to my room. You go back to yours. We fall asleep and then part ways in the morning. You said you wanted adventure, right?"

My heart sped up. "What do you have in mind, Mr. Hooker?"

"You have your camera with you?"

"Of course. What kind of a photographer would I be without my camera?"

His mouth curved into a mischievous grin. "Good. Grab it. Then meet me down in the lobby in about ten minutes. Wear your coat and dress warm."

Chapter 3

Matteo

She said she wanted adventure; I planned to give it to her.

I wanted to see if I could put a smile on her face. This girl—whoever she was—had gotten a raw deal. Why not make the best of being stuck in Vail? There were worse locations to be trapped. If anyone knew how to make the most of this place, it was me. Though I hadn't lived here permanently for years, I still had a major in at one of the best attractions in town.

The only problem would be getting there in this blizzard.

I was waiting for her in the lobby when Maddie exited the elevators. Damn, she was beautiful. Wild red hair and a dusting of freckles over her nose. She wore a white knit hat that matched her white puffer jacket. She looked like a living snow angel. Despite the obvious pain she'd experienced lately, her whole face still it up when she smiled. Yeah, there were definitely way worse situations to be stuck in. I wasn't minding this at all.

My adventure partner had her camera strapped around her neck inside a leather case. She looked like she'd put some lipstick on. This girl was gorgeous without a drop of makeup, but the fact that she'd done that made me wonder if she was trying to impress me. She hadn't given me any inkling that she was interested. I was sort of sick for even thinking about it since she was fresh off getting her heart broken. Technically, she was supposed to be on her honeymoon. That was so fucked up. I'd had a little rage brewing inside me ever since she'd told me what her ex pulled—definitely a weird reaction to have on behalf of someone I barely knew.

When she was right in front of me, I could also smell that she'd added some perfume.

"You look nice."

"Thanks." Her fair skin turned pink. "So, what's this all about?"

"You'll see. Wouldn't be an adventure if I told you, now would it?"

"Oh boy. What am I getting myself into?"

"You'll be fine. I'd never let anything happen to my sister." I winked.

The first thing I needed to figure out was how the hell we were going to get from point A to point B.

"Stay here for a minute, okay? I'm gonna try to arrange for a ride."

"Good luck with that."

"Questioning my ability to work my magic, eh? Are you forgetting how we got our rooms in the first place?"

She laughed as I walked backwards, flashing her a cocky grin and wriggling my brows. Too bad I nearly crashed my ass into a moving luggage cart.

Her lack of confidence only made me more determined to make this ride happen.

I walked over to the concierge to see if there was any chance in hell he could help. "I'm looking for a ride out of here and back in a few hours. I was wondering if you could help me."

Without even looking up from his desk, he said, "Driving conditions are very poor, sir. It's not advisable to be out on the road, even if I were able to arrange that."

"Let me ask again." I took out my wallet and slammed down a fifty-dollar bill. "Can you help me with a ride to Parkside Resort and back in about three hours?"

He took the fifty. "Give me a minute to see what I can do."

The concierge made a few calls while I waited at the desk. I looked back over at Maddie, who was nervously bopping her legs up and down. She smiled when she noticed me watching her. That smile was worth way more than fifty bucks.

The concierge hung up the phone. "Good news. I was able to find a driver with a Toyota 4Runner who can take you to where you need to go."

"Sweet. Thanks, man."

A few minutes later, the black SUV pulled up in front of the hotel. We exited out the revolving doors and got in the backseat. A large man sat behind the wheel.

"Thanks a lot for doing this," I said to him, blowing hot air into my cold hands. I promptly grabbed my gloves out of my pockets and put them on.

The guy turned to look at us. "They don't call me Crazy Abe for nothing. Makes no sense how people can grow up around here and get freaked out over snow."

"My thoughts exactly."

"You headed to Parkside Resort?"

"Yes."

She looked at me. "We're going to a ski resort?"

"Maybe."

"Wow. Okay. It's funny, here I was thinking I was going to leave Vail without really enjoying the snow. But...are they even open?"

"Don't worry. I got connections."

My aunt and uncle owned Parkside, and I had a key to the gondola. Hopefully my plans would work out.

It soon became apparent that Crazy Abe had earned his name. The guy was driving way too fast, considering the road conditions.

It probably shouldn't have surprised me, then, when he drove right into an embankment.

"Shit!" Maddie screamed.

"Are you okay?" It took me a few seconds to realize I'd thrown out a protective arm and my hand had landed across her chest. Even through her coat, I could feel the softness of her breasts.

"Yeah," she breathed out. "I'm fine."

"Sorry about that!" Abe yelled.

The wheels on the SUV kept turning to no avail as he pushed on the gas. We were officially stuck. Without hesitating, I got out of the car and began to push from the back, trying to help Abe get us moving.

It was clear more manpower was going to be needed, though.

I walked over to the driver's side window. "You mind helping me move this thing? She can get behind the wheel and press on the gas while you work with me."

He shook his head. "Sorry, no can do."

"What do you mean?"

"I got a bad back. Can't risk straining it. I'll end up in the hospital."

This dude was gonna end up in the hospital for another reason if he didn't get his ass out here and help me.

But he wouldn't budge. The next thing I knew, Maddie had gotten out of the car and was right next to me, helping me push.

"I can't believe that guy," she said.

"Thanks for coming out," I said, feeling like a total pussy for not being able to handle this myself.

Despite us both using all of our might, the 4Runner wouldn't budge. And we were both covered in snow.

"This wasn't exactly what I had in mind for an adventure," I said.

"Not your fault." She smiled.

The fact that she was able to smile at a crappy time like this spoke to her character. She was a good egg, this Maddie.

We took a quick breather and started the pushing process again. The back windshield wipers moved the snow off the glass and allowed us a view into the car while we were working our asses off.

We seemed to notice it at the same time.

That's not…

It isn't…

He can't be.

While Abe was mindlessly pushing on the gas, he was watching something on his phone.

Not just anything.

Maddie's mouth dropped open. "Is that porn he's watching?"

"Considering the giant ass on the screen, I'd say that's a safe assumption."

Her eyes went wide. "We've got to get the fuck out of here."

I nodded in agreement. "One huge push. Ready?"
"Yes!"

The grunting that escaped us as we used all of our force probably rivaled the sounds going on inside the vehicle. It was mind over matter because that time, by some miracle, the car pushed free. I could only hope Abe would put his dick away long enough to get us the hell off the road.

"Wow. This is really beautiful." Maddie stared out the gondola window at the fresh coat of snow. "I've never been on one of these before."

"You mean at this resort?"

"No, I mean I've never been on a ski gondola before."

"Really? How come?"

"Umm... Because I don't ski."

I turned to look at her. "What do you mean you don't ski?"

She shrugged. "I've never tried it before."

"But your honeymoon was in Vail? Who goes to the ski-resort capital of the United States when they don't even ski?"

She frowned. "My ex loved to ski."

"But you don't."

Maddie shoved her hands into her coat pockets. "I told you I started to lose myself."

The way her face fell caused an unexpected ache in my chest. "So skiing wasn't exactly your ideal honeymoon then?"

"I liked the idea of a nice fireplace with a big picture window looking out at the snow. Does that count?"

I scratched my chin. "What *is* your ideal honeymoon?"

She thought about it. Because of how long it took her to answer, it was clear her dumbass ex-fiancé had never even bothered to ask. The more I heard about her relationship, the more I started to think him calling the wedding off was a blessing in disguise.

"I've always wanted to go to the island of Mo'orea, in Tahiti—stay in one of those over-water bungalows."

I smiled. I'd grown up in Vail, and skiing used to be as second nature to me as walking, but I'd opt for Maddie in a bikini over her bundled in a snowsuit any day of the week. Her fiancé wasn't just a coward. He was a dope.

"When the right guy comes along, that's where he's going to take you on your honeymoon."

Maddie smiled sadly. "Thanks."

We rode the gondola up to the top of the mountain. I'd programmed it for a one-way trip, so when we reached the exit terminal, it slowed to a halt.

"Get your camera ready."

I still hadn't told her what I was bringing her up here to see, and she'd never asked. That proved she truly did have an adventurous streak. Maddie unzipped her camera bag and took out two lenses.

"Do I need long range or close up?"

"Definitely long range."

She detached the regular lens from the camera and clicked a telephoto zoom into place, then cleaned the viewfinder and zipped her case closed. "I'm ready. Should I tuck my pants into my boots? How deep do you think the snow is up here?"

I chuckled. "Doesn't matter. You're not going out there."

Her forehead wrinkled. "Are you?"

"Just for a few minutes." I leaned over and nudged open one of the gondola's sliding windows so she'd have an unobstructed view. Then I bent to strap a pair of snowshoes on my feet. "You're going to look right out there." I pointed to a dark area of the woods off in the distance. "The gondola is about two feet from the ground because people are usually disembarking with long skis on. I'm going to jump down and go to that control station booth to turn on the lights up here. Then I'll come back and join you."

I could see the excitement in her face. "Okay!"

Halfway back to the gondola, I heard Maddie gasp.

I smiled and rushed into the warm, dry enclosure. Pulling the door shut behind me, I brushed the snow from my shoulders. "You see them? I wasn't sure if you'd be able to or not with the snow. But it's lightened up a lot since we left the hotel. I think we're in the eye of the storm."

The sound of a shutter clicking away responded before Maddie. "What kind of bears are they? They're so adorable."

"They're black bears."

"Are they dangerous?"

"I don't think there's such thing as a safe bear, except maybe Yogi. But the mountains at these ski resorts are filled with black bears. They pretty much learn to cohabitate with the humans. They'll keep out of your way, if you keep out of theirs."

Maddie adjusted her lens and shot more pictures. "I thought bears hibernated for the winter."

"They do. But hibernation doesn't mean going to sleep in November and waking up in June. They just sleep a lot to conserve energy in the months they can't forage food. But they still get up every few days."

"They're awake now. Bears are nocturnal?"

"Not usually, but in ski resort areas like this, many of them adjust to avoid people."

"That's incredible. How did you know they were here?"

"My aunt and uncle own the ski resort. I stopped by the other night, and one of my cousins brought me up to check them out. They had to close this run to skiers, probably for the season, because of how close the bears set up their den."

We stayed at the top of the mountain, watching the family of bears and taking pictures, until Maddie's teeth started to chatter. It was warmer and dryer in the gondola than outside, but not by much with the window open. "You're freezing. We should probably get going."

She nodded. "Okay." Her nose and cheeks were bright red, so I slid the window shut and started to put on my snowshoes again.

"Wait. You're going back out there?"

"If we want to get back down, I am. There's no control in here to start the lift. Plus, I need to shut off the lights."

Maddie's eyes bulged. "But there are bears out there."

"There were bears out there when I went to turn the lights on, too."

"I know. But I didn't know about them then!"

I chuckled and finished strapping my foot into the second snowshoe. "Relax. I'll be right back." I started to open the door, but turned back with my best solemn face. "Just in case I get mauled, there's storage under the seat cushion where you can find a whistle and some flares for an emergency."

She sounded panicked. "Are you joking?"

I laughed. "Yes. There aren't really any flares or a whistle. You'll probably just freeze to death if the bears don't get you after they're done with me." I hopped out of the gondola and ran to shut off the lights.

When I got back to the car, Maddie was at the door, blocking my entrance. Her hands were on her hips, and she did not look very happy. Though I thought her attempt at looking pissed off was sort of sexy. There's nothing hotter than a fiery redhead. I bet she was gorgeous when she was *really* angry.

"I shouldn't even let you back in after what you just pulled."

I smiled. "That's fine. But you should know this gondola is going to take off in less than thirty seconds. It's on a timer after I press start." I held one hand to my ear and cupped it. "Did you hear that? The gear shaft just cranked into place. Less than ten seconds now. Nine. Eight. Seven..."

Maddie's eyes widened, and she leaned forward and grabbed my hand, helping me up and into the gondola. "Oh my God, get in here!"

Once I was safely inside with the door shut, and the gondola still hadn't started moving again, Maddie squinted at me. "You didn't hear any gears shifting, did you?"

"Nope. Though it really would have taken off without me...in seven or eight minutes. I set it to take off in ten."

Maddie shoved my chest, but she had a smile on her face. "You are just like a big brother, teasing and scaring the crap out of me."

34

Once we were moving, she had her nose pressed to the glass, looking out the window. From the top of the mountain, you could see all the different ski trails, as well as the lights from the city in the distance. The snow had tapered off, but the fresh layer on the ground made everything seem to twinkle. It looked like a magical winter wonderland outside. I'd almost forgotten how beautiful Colorado could be.

"It must've been cool growing up here," she said.

"Yeah, it was. People on the coasts live for summer break and sunshine. Most of us here lived for the first snowstorm. I grew up on these slopes."

"So I guess you're a pretty good skier then?"

I nodded. "I was an instructor right here at this resort for six years."

"Oh, wow. Too bad we don't have more time. My brother could have taught me how to ski." She smiled.

I stared out at the slopes. "I haven't skied in years."

"Did you get injured or something?"

"Or something." The shit that had transpired the last time I'd put on a pair of skis wasn't anything I wanted to talk about, so I quickly changed topics. "Do you think you got some good pictures?"

"I definitely did. I can't wait to download them to my laptop and take a look. It's been a long time since I shot anything but grade schoolers. I forgot how invigorating it could be. I feel like I could run up this big mountain right now."

Maddie's eyes were wide and sparkling. Her entire face lit up like a little kid's on Christmas morning. The beauty I'd been appreciating outside couldn't hold a candle to this woman's smile. Not even close. Realizing I was staring at her lips, I forced my eyes anywhere else. "I'm glad you enjoyed it."

"I did. In fact, it was the highlight of my honeymoon," she said with a laugh.

"That's pretty sad." I chuckled. Using my teeth to grasp the end of one glove, I yanked my hand out of it so I could dig into my pocket for the keys to the control station at the base of the mountain as we approached.

After we exited at the bottom, I turned off all of the lights, returned my snowshoes to the rental room, and locked everything up. Our driver pulled up within a few minutes.

I opened the SUV door and whispered in Maddie's ear as she climbed in, "You might not want to touch anything in here."

"Ugh. I'd almost forgotten about that. Did you have to remind me?"

I winked. "That's what big brothers are for."

The ride back to the hotel was luckily uneventful. Vail might get a shit ton of snow, but they definitely knew how to clear the roads. The main thoroughfares had already been plowed once and were much more passable than on our outbound trip. I wasn't ready to call it a night yet, so I thought maybe I'd ask Maddie to have a drink at the bar with me again when we got back. But it turned out the hotel bar was already closed. I felt deflated, though it was probably for the best. The last thing this woman needed was me having a drink or two and hitting on her.

Once again outside our adjoining-room doors, we both lingered.

"Thank you again for tonight," she said. "It meant more than you know."

I smiled. "I'm glad."

Maddie surprised me when she stepped forward and pushed up on her toes to kiss my cheek. "Goodbye, Milo. I hope you have a safe flight tomorrow."

"Yeah. You, too, Mads. Take care of yourself."

She opened the door to her room and turned back to wave one last time. All I could think as I watched her disappear was, *I hope like hell this storm sticks around a while longer.*

Chapter 4

Hazel

Normally, I had no problem sleeping in. But this morning I'd been tossing and turning since six am, even though I hadn't fallen asleep until almost one. I just couldn't stop thinking about the way I'd felt up on that mountain last night—how exhilarated and alive I'd been. My heart had thumped inside my chest, and it made me realize how long it had been since I'd felt that kind of excitement. It was as if I'd been dead the last few years, only no one had told me to lie down and call it a day.

Oddly enough, it hadn't even been Hazel Appleton who had awoken. It was Maddie Hooker. The entire evening, starting with the crazy hotel check-in, had been more excitement than I'd experienced in a long time. And that said a lot.

Two months ago, I'd believed I was perfectly happy. Had Brady not done what he did, I'd likely be on my honeymoon with him at this very moment. That thought didn't sit well with my stomach for so many reasons now. So many questions ran through my head.

Would I have been happy if Brady hadn't canceled the wedding and we'd gotten married?

How could one night—a few hours with a random stranger—make me feel more alive than I'd felt over the last few years with a man I supposedly loved?

Did I love Brady?

Or did I love the *idea* of Brady?

Where did I go from here? Did I move back to Connecticut and slip back into my comfy life, taking pictures of runny-nosed school kids for the next forty years?

A sense of panic came over me at that thought, and I had to sit up in bed and whip the covers off.

God, I felt a little nauseous.

I needed to stop lying in bed and ruminating over my life. I also really needed to figure out what the heck was going on with my canceled flights. The airline had told me to check my confirmation number online, and eventually all passengers would be rescheduled onto new flights. So I reached over to the nightstand to grab my phone. When I signed in, I found they'd put me on a two o'clock flight connecting through Atlanta, instead of the direct one I'd had before. Though it probably wasn't a good sign that the airline's website had a bright red flashing weather alert, warning that there could be delays and cancelations again today.

I sighed and dragged my ass out of bed, off in search of some caffeine.

Downstairs, I grabbed two cups of the complimentary lobby coffee. I thought I might listen at Milo's hotel room door and deliver one to him if I heard any signs that he was awake. It was the least I could do after all the trouble he'd gone to last night.

I didn't even have to put my ear to the door to hear the television blaring in his room. I knocked lightly. After a minute or two went by, I figured maybe he was out already or slept with the TV on. But just as I turned toward my room, Milo's door opened.

"H..." I never made it past the first consonant.

Oh.

Jesus.

Oh my.

Milo stood in the doorway wearing nothing but a white towel wrapped around his waist. Droplets of water ran down his chest...*his very carved chest.*

I swallowed.

"Sorry," he said, running a hand through his wet hair. "I was in the shower."

God, he had the most amazing body I'd ever seen. His shoulders were broad, his chest lean and sculpted, and his skin was perfectly smooth and tanned. Not to mention, that towel hugged the most delicious V.

"Uhh. Shower, right."

I blinked a few times and forced my gaze to meet his before I got caught staring. But the cocky smirk and the glint in his eyes told me that ship had sailed. He'd totally watched me ogle him.

Milo folded his arms across his chest, and his smirk widened to a full-blown smile. "How did you sleep?"

"I...uh...slept."

Seeming amused, he chuckled. He looked down to the two coffee cups in my hands. "Not much of a talker before you have your morning coffee?"

I nodded. "Ah...yeah. That's me."

"Is that why you have two?"

I shook my head and offered him one of the cups. "Oh. No. One is for you. That's why I knocked."

He took the coffee. "Thank you."

At least one of us was completely at ease having a discussion in the hotel hallway with him wearing only a towel. Too bad it wasn't me.

"Did you already have breakfast?" he asked. "I was going to knock and see if you wanted to grab a bite after my shower."

"No, I actually didn't. Just went downstairs for the coffees. I need to take a shower myself."

"How long will that take you?"

"Umm... I don't know. Maybe twenty minutes if I don't wash my hair."

He nodded. "Okay, sounds good. I'll knock in fifteen."

My eyebrows drew together. "Fifteen? Are you telling me to hurry?"

He winked. "I'd like a chance to appreciate you in your towel, too."

I felt my face warm. *Jesus.* I couldn't remember the last time I'd blushed, and now it had happened multiple times in the last twenty-four hours. "Very cute. You couldn't let that pass, could you?"

Milo rocked back on his heels. "Not a chance, sis."

"I'll tell you what," I said. "How about I knock on your door when I'm all ready?"

He shrugged. "Won't be half as much fun, but sounds good."

"I just want to thank you again for last night," I told him over breakfast.

Milo finished off his side order of bacon and wiped his mouth. "It was no big deal at all."

41

I sipped my second cup of coffee. "That's the thing. Maybe it shouldn't have been a big deal, but it was—for me, at least. I had trouble sleeping last night because I was thinking about all the things missing in my life. I've only been going through the motions the last few years. But when I was living the day to day, I didn't realize anything was missing. And now that I do, I'm not quite sure what to do with myself."

He nodded. "I guess that's why they say hindsight is twenty-twenty."

I sighed. "Yeah, it definitely is."

We were seated in the hotel restaurant next to a big picture window. Outside, the trees drooped with heavy snow, and fresh flakes were coming down again. "It really is beautiful here."

"It is. I might've forgotten that over the last few years."

We'd talked so much about me, yet I didn't really know much about Milo other than he grew up here in Colorado. "What made you leave here and move to Seattle?"

Milo's eyes stayed glued to the outside. "I needed a change."

Something about his voice told me there was more to the story. I usually wasn't one to pry, but this time, I did.

"Did you have an epiphany moment like I did last night? That you needed something more out of life and you went in search of it?"

Milo's eyes slanted from the window to meet mine. He seemed to lose focus for a few seconds as he considered my question, then he shut his eyes and shook his head. "I lost someone close to me, and staying here afterwards was difficult."

Oh God. Now I knew why I never pried. I felt terrible for bringing that to the surface. "I'm so sorry. I had no idea."

"It's fine. It was four years ago."

I didn't know what to say after that, so I just kept quiet. Milo called the waitress over and got another cup of coffee, and then a busboy came to clear our plates. The air still felt awkward a few minutes later. Eventually, Milo broke the silence.

"So I guess we both needed to get out of town to find a way to move on."

I nodded. "I'm not sure I found my way, but I've definitely realized I need to make some changes." I looked at the time on my phone. We'd been down at breakfast for almost two hours, yet it felt like ten minutes.

Fake Milo looked at his watch, too. "It's getting late. I should probably go upstairs and pack up to get to the airport for my flight to New York."

"New York? I thought you lived in Seattle?"

"I do. But I'm going to visit a friend after this, so I'm flying into JFK."

"Oh. That's funny. I'm actually flying to New York, too. But LaGuardia airport. It's easier to get a direct flight there than the airport closest to me in Connecticut. I'd rather drive the hour home from New York than get stuck somewhere on a connection. Though my rescheduled flight has a connection now anyway."

"What time is your flight?" he asked.

"Two. Yours?"

"Three."

"Neither of our flights are going to go today," he said.

"What makes you say that?"

"Round two of this storm is starting soon. The airport hasn't even recovered from the wallop it took yesterday. I lived here for twenty-five years. The only local people who don't know all the afternoon flights are going to get canceled are the people who work at the airlines."

Yesterday morning I'd been dying to get home—so much so that I'd checked out of my luxurious hotel early and forfeited the small fortune we'd prepaid for our trip. Yet only twenty-four hours later, I wasn't entirely upset at the notion of having to stick around another day. That is, assuming my *brother* stuck around, too.

"I guess we head to the airport and see what happens then?"

Milo rubbed the stubble on his cheek. "I was actually thinking of pushing off my flight until tomorrow. If we give up our hotel rooms, and our flights do cancel, there's no chance they'll still be available when we come crawling back with our luggage between our legs."

"Oh. Yeah. Crap. I didn't even think of that."

"So what do you say? We both cancel, and I'll take you on another adventure?"

"I don't know..."

"Do you remember how you felt up there on the top of the mountain taking pictures last night?"

Of course I did. My body had an incredible buzz pulsing through it, and my heart had impersonated a runaway train—not that different from how I felt as I considered spending another day with Milo. Plus, I did have coverage at work for the next two weeks since I was supposed to be off, anyway. I really had nothing to rush back to. Maybe another adventure would bring even more clarity.

"You know what? Let's do it. I'm in."

I could see the smile in his eyes. "Excellent."

"But I do have a request for our adventure today."

"What's that?"

"You teach me to ski."

Well, what do you know? Apparently you needed appropriate attire to ski in Vail. Based on what I'd brought with me from Connecticut, I'd come prepared for sipping hot cocoa in the lodge, not actually skiing. Clearly, I'd had no intention of skiing when I'd packed to come here. Milo took me to a local shop, and we picked up items I hadn't even heard of, like ski underwear and ski socks. We bought special trousers, a ski jacket, and a new hat and gloves. I already had gloves and a hat, but I figured they'd be all wet by the time we finished today, so spares were needed. Milo also insisted on buying me a helmet. When I asked whether everyone wore them, he said it was a requirement for beginners.

After our shopping jaunt, Milo took me to a local ski resort he said he used to frequent. It wasn't the same one where he taught.

"Is it even possible to learn to ski in a day?" I asked as we sat on the chair lift.

He winked. "With a good instructor, it is."

Being on a chair lift was scarier than being on the gondola last night. Even though we weren't going nearly as high, it was just so open and easy to imagine I could slip out. Though I sort of wished I'd had my phone to take some more pictures. The view up here was spectacular. I'd left it back at the lodge—probably one of the first times I'd parted with it in ages. I had a feeling I was about to make a huge fool of myself, so I could only hope Milo had a lot of patience.

Once we got out to the slopes, I began to doubt whether asking him to take me skiing was a good idea since I'd underestimated just how green I'd be.

I had to say, though, I didn't exactly mind all the close contact as he helped me put on the skis, something I had no clue how to do.

"Listen for the click."

"Did it click?" I asked.

"Did you hear it click?"

I shrugged. "No."

"Then it didn't click."

Wiseass.

"You think I'm the biggest idiot, don't you?"

He looked up at me and flashed a smile. "Nah. It's kind of cute. I used to teach total newbies like you all of the time."

"That's right. I forgot you're probably used to this."

Once he'd helped me get my skis on, he said, "Okay, so now you're gonna jump up and down to make sure they're on right."

Feeling like a goof, I jumped several times. "They seem good."

"Congratulations. You've passed the first step of skiing, which is getting your damn skis on."

Then I could barely move. "Oh my gosh. How do you walk with these things?"

"That leads into your next lesson, actually. It's called waddle walking."

Milo began to demonstrate what he meant. He was basically teaching me to walk like a duck.

"So, just practice this technique," he said. "It's walking as if you have something between your legs."

Interesting visual.

"This technique will help you get around if you lose one of your poles," he added.

Lifting my legs one by one, I mimicked him. It was awkward. And it certainly had been a while since I'd had anything big between my legs. *Ha!* My mind had been in the gutter ever since I saw Milo in his towel this morning.

After my waddle-walking lesson, he taught me how to properly use the poles.

Once we got moving, I did my best. "It isn't as steep out here as I imagined it would be."

"That's because it's a bunny slope, sweetheart."

I'd always heard that term—*bunny slope*. Come to think of it, there were mostly children around. I was lamer than I thought.

He spent a good deal of time making sure I knew how to stop and turn right and left. I struggled a bit, but managed to finally conquer those basic moves after an hour or so.

"When do we leave the beginner slope?"

"This is it for today. You won't be ready for anything else. I don't want you to get hurt."

While that sounded kind of pathetic, I appreciated that he was being protective of me. And he was right, of course. I stood a good chance of hurting myself.

"It must have been so exciting to be a ski instructor," I said as I waddle walked beside him.

"The perks were fun, but there's also your fair share of dealing with whiny kids and adults. It's not exactly a cake walk."

"The women must have loved you."

I immediately regretted my comment. *What are you thinking, Hazel? Isn't it bad enough you eye-fucked him when he was in that towel?*

"I actually had a girlfriend for the majority of the time I worked on the slopes," he said.

"Oh yeah?"

Almost immediately after he announced that, he changed the subject— almost too quickly, which made me wonder if there was a story there.

"Let's teach you some more turns," he said.

And so he did, and I fell down over and over. But there was an upside to falling: Milo would reach out his hand and help me up. His strength with only one arm was impressive. A couple of times, I might have purposely fallen, pretending to have trouble getting up just so he could help me.

Yes, I'd completely resorted to cheap thrills at this point. I knew nothing would be happening between Milo and me before we parted ways, so I enjoyed the innocent physical contact any way I could.

The contrast of the bright blue sky and white snow was breathtaking, a calm before the next storm was set to roll in this afternoon. Perhaps I should have been paying more attention to where I was going instead of the sky above, because at one point, I crashed right into Milo, who had been several feet ahead of me. We toppled to the ground together. The sunlight beamed straight into his beautiful eyes.

His concern was only for me, not himself. "Are you okay?"

"Yes. I'm so sorry. I still have to remember to lean downhill and not backwards when I feel myself losing balance. Looking straight ahead and not at the sky would help, too."

Once again he helped me to a standing position. "You'll get the hang of it. I wish we had more time. A couple days more, and I think you could've been great."

I smiled. "Have I earned my hot cocoa yet?"

He chuckled. "That's my cue to take you back, huh?"

Later on, after we returned to the hotel, a cloud of sadness lingered in the air.

Tomorrow morning we would go to the airport together, and that would be the end of this little adventure. We'd both been able to change our flights, but even though we were going to New York City, we were still on different airlines and flying to different airports.

We returned to our respective rooms but planned to meet down at the bar after we'd showered. I opted for a bath to soak my sore muscles after the many falls I'd endured today. Once I got dressed, I knocked on Milo's door to see if he just wanted to walk downstairs together.

"Come in," he said.

I thought the fact that he signaled me to enter would have meant he was fully dressed. But instead, I opened the door to find him shirtless, wiping a towel over his wet hair. Once again, I found it hard not to look at his gorgeous body. Seeing as though he'd caught me gawking at him this morning, I didn't want to be caught in the act again. So I intentionally looked away from him as I spoke.

"Is the plan still to head downstairs for a drink?" I asked, staring out the window.

"Are you talking to a ghost outside or something?"

He was fucking with me.

I pretended not to understand his comment as I continued to look away. "What's that?"

"I'm covered. You can look at me now."

I turned to face him and cleared my throat.

He smirked. "How are you feeling?"

"Great."

"I thought you might be a little sore."

"Oh, I am, actually."

"You know what would be really good for that?" he asked.

"What?"

"The hot tub. There's one downstairs by the indoor pool. Wanna hit it?"

The prospect of taking a dip in the hot tub with him gave me mixed feelings.

"You have swim trunks?" I asked.

"No. But I was thinking you could go in alone."

Ah. "I did bring a bathing suit, actually."

"Perfect then."

"What are you going to do while I'm in the hot tub?"

He shrugged. "Watch you?"

"You're gonna sit there and gawk at me?"

"No." He winked. "It would be rude to gawk at someone when they're underdressed."

Nice. Real nice dig.

I felt my face heat up. "I'll go get my suit on."

Downstairs at the pool, I got right into the hot tub while Milo went to the bar to grab a beer and a drink for me. He brought me a white wine and set it on the stone tile just outside of where I was immersed in the hot, bubbly water.

A little girl with floaties around her arms suddenly appeared and entered the hot tub. Her parents were on the other side of the pool area.

"Hello." I smiled.

"Hi," she said shyly.

"What's your name?" Milo asked.

"Georgie."

"Nice to meet you, Georgie," he said. "I'm Milo Hooker, and this is my sister, Maddie Hooker."

I chuckled at his emphasis on our fake last name. I'd almost forgotten about that.

The little girl played quietly as I leaned my head back and let the steam penetrate by achy body.

"Feeling better?" Milo asked, prompting me to open my eyes.

"You weren't kidding. This really does help sore muscles."

"I kind of wish I had my swim trunks now."

Rather than agree with that and get myself in more trouble, I asked, "What's your prediction about our flights tomorrow? Think we'll make it out of here?"

He took a drink of his beer and nodded. "I do think tomorrow we'll actually get out, although we made the right call on today."

"You deserve all of the credit for that decision."

"Well, I figured why not buy us one more day of not having to be our actual selves, right?"

"I have to say, I'm really digging Maddie. She has no worries in the world, aside from what to order off the drink menu. She's impulsive—and she sort of knows how to ski now." I grinned.

He smiled back, and then his expression turned more serious. "You weren't the only one in need of a change. Believe me."

I had to follow up on that. "So...I meant to ask. You said you're a high school music teacher, but you're in the midst of this trip, and now you're going to New York. That seems like a lot of time off. How much vacation do you get?"

He looked down at his beer. "Actually, I took a semester off from teaching."

"Wow. You can do that?"

"Apparently so. They let me."

"You just needed a break?"

He exhaled. "I was starting to feel like my heart wasn't in it. And it really needs to be. So I did something people rarely do: I gave myself a break."

"Do you think you'll be ready to go back after this semester?"

"I do. So many times in life, we just keep going because we feel like the whole world will crumble if we stop moving at a pace like the Energizer bunny. But that's not necessarily how we were meant to operate. The principal at my school really likes me, so that helps, of course. If they hadn't allowed me the leave of absence without guaranteeing I'd still have a job, I suppose I couldn't have taken it."

As much as I admired his philosophy, I was still internally scratching my head. "So, you're...reevaluating your life with this time off?"

"You could say that."

"I really envy that. It does take a lot of courage to know when to stop. I didn't realize this trip would be sort of like that for me until I got stuck here. In just the two days we've been hanging out, I've realized so much about myself—my truest desires, how much I've missed living spontaneously."

"I'd say we accomplished a lot in a short amount of time, sis." He winked.

"Yeah." I smiled.

I knew there was so much more than met the eye with him. He'd said he lost someone. I'd never pried about that, but I certainly wondered what happened. I'd almost asked him just now, but ultimately, I didn't want to spend our last moments together on a subject that might have been upsetting for him.

We'd been so immersed in our conversation that we hardly paid attention to little Georgie, who continued to flap her arms to stay up in the water. A few minutes later, her parents gathered their things and came over to the hot tub.

"Georgie, are you ready? Come on, honey. We're going back to the room."

The little girl suddenly pointed to me and proclaimed, "She's a hooker."

I felt a rush of blood to my head. Her parents stood frozen for a moment before hurrying little Georgie along.

Of course, just as she'd said it, I'd been taking a long swig of my wine with my tits hanging halfway out of my bathing suit.

Milo snorted, then lost it in laughter after they walked away.

He rubbed his eyes. "That was a fucking perfect way to end this night."

With Georgie and her parents gone, the two of us were now completely alone in the pool area.

Milo shocked me when he took off his shirt and began to undo his pants.

"What are you doing?" I swallowed, catching myself admiring his bare chest.

"I'm continuing our impulsive streak with a dip in the hot tub in my boxer briefs. It's to celebrate you being mistaken for a whore."

I barely got a glimpse of his impressive bulge before he immersed himself in the water next to me.

Chapter 5

Matteo

I didn't know why I hadn't thought of this sooner. Boxer briefs weren't all that different from swim trunks.

I took a swig of my beer and breathed in the hot steam. "This is the life, huh?"

Maddie closed her eyes. "Sure is. I'm really glad you convinced me to stay today. Thank you again for taking me out on the slopes."

"It was my pleasure. It had been a really long time since I was out there. It was much needed."

Now wasn't the time to bring up the reason *why* I hadn't skied in so long. Although a part of me wanted to open up to her, I didn't think it was a good idea to darken the mood tonight. We were buzzed and half naked in a hot tub. I needed to enjoy that fact and not bring real life into the fantasy we'd been enjoying for two days. *You're Milo, not Matteo, right now. Remember that.*

She chuckled. "The only bad thing about you joining me in here is that we no longer have anyone suitably dressed to fetch us more drinks."

"I'll dry off and put my clothes on if I have to. Then come back in," I said.

"You're such a good sport."

"Well, you don't seem to mind watching me dress and undress, right?"

Her face turned beet red. *Shit*. I might have pushed it too far with that one.

"I'm just kidding, Maddie."

She blew out a frustrated breath. "You know what? The old me would have denied that I ogled you this morning. But given that I'm supposed to be carefree on this trip, I will say *yes*, I do admire your physique. But it ends there. I'm not looking for anything, certainly not sex with a virtual stranger. Or my brother. I hope you know that."

Ouch. Virtual stranger. I thought we were a bit beyond that.

Things went silent.

Well, this was a downer.

I hadn't meant to make her uncomfortable or defensive. I was a little drunk and loose with my words.

"I apologize for making you uncomfortable. I was just joking with you."

"Okay. Well, I didn't want you to get the wrong idea. I'm just coming off a bad breakup, and maybe a part of me is a little lonely and vulnerable, but not enough to lose my inhibitions with you, in case I insinuated anything."

Man, she was tense all of a sudden. It sort of made me want to kiss her, take her upstairs, and help her properly unwind. But I knew none of that would be happening. Number one, she'd just closed the door. Number two, what would be the point in making a move when we were leaving each other tomorrow? Number three, she kind of hated me right now.

Maddie was clearly not the type of girl you messed around with, despite her alleged desire to be more impulsive. Women give off signals, and from the very beginning, I knew she wasn't the type you have a one-night stand with. She was far too complex. And far too... special. I really did hope she didn't take the asshole back who'd hurt her.

I felt like I was eating crow. "Okay, now that we've clarified that there are no expectations, can we try to relax a little before we have to leave in the morning? Can I go get us another round?"

"I'd like that." She offered a slight smile that didn't quite fix the mess I'd made.

After we returned to our rooms, I had a hard time getting to sleep.

And the following morning, I woke up feeling the same way: like shit.

I'd pushed it, embarrassed her. Instead of teasing her, I should've told her the fucking truth: that I'd felt more alive with her on the slopes yesterday than I had in years.

Later that morning, we met for a quiet breakfast downstairs.

The ride to the airport was even quieter.

When we got there, we found that both of our flights were delayed about an hour, but we were still scheduled to take off today. I was thankful for a little extra time to spend with her before we had to say goodbye.

The mood was still somber. We were standing in front of a bookstand when I said, "We're early. Do you feel like grabbing a coffee and sitting down somewhere together?"

She nodded. "I'd love that."

We stood in line at Starbucks and fought over who would pay on our respective phone apps. I ended up winning and footing the bill.

We then took a seat in one of the waiting areas.

I nudged my head toward an old man sitting across from us. He wore a tweed jacket and was munching on what looked like a head of raw cabbage stuffed inside a Ziploc bag.

"What's his deal?" I said to her.

"What do you mean?"

"Let's play a game. Tell me who you think he is and where he's going."

She pursed her lips, pondering. "I think his wife just died, and he doesn't know how to cook for himself, so he stuffs roughage into plastic bags and snacks on it for sustenance."

"Interesting theory. I'll finish the story."

"Okay." She laughed.

"Archibald..." I turned to her. "That's his name... had been struggling after his wife's death—until he came across Irina in a mail-order-bride catalog. He's currently on his way to Moscow to meet her." I nodded, prompting Maddie to continue the story.

"Much to his future chagrin," she said. "Irina will be nothing like his late wife. She can neither cook nor keep a house. While he originally felt Irina would be the right choice for him, it turns out the entire trip was a mistake. She's young enough to be his daughter, and they have nothing in common." She sighed dramatically. "So, Archibald decides to return to the US alone."

"But not before he lets Irina go down on him behind the Kremlin."

She rolled her eyes. "You had to go and ruin it!"

I laughed and pointed to a new set of targets, a woman and man who were currently ignoring each other with their heads buried in their smartphones. "What about them?"

"They're going to visit their daughter at college in Boston. Things have been touch and go ever since she left home. The empty-nest syndrome is hitting them hard, and they're finding they spend more time ignoring each other than interacting."

I nodded. "So that's why he's currently sexting her here in the airport. He's trying to spice up an otherwise dismal situation by sending her a dick pic he took moments earlier in the bathroom."

Maddie cracked up. "She hasn't reacted yet because, unbeknownst to her husband, he accidentally sent the photo to his mother-in-law."

"Ouch!" I bent my head back in laughter. "That's bad—but so very good. Now you're getting the hang of this."

She smiled, but then a bout of silence replaced the jovial mood.

"Milo, I have to apologize to you," she said after a moment.

I turned to her, perplexed. "For what?"

"I...got really defensive last night, and I'm sorry. That's not me. You were just teasing, and I took it to heart, because I was feeling emotional and a little insecure, maybe. You're a beautiful man, and while

59

I wasn't looking for anything more than a friendship with you, I'm not blind. I had admired you physically and should've just owned up to it instead of acting so defensive."

Shit. She shouldn't have been apologizing. It should've been the other way around.

"Maddie, please don't waste another second thinking about that. I'm just really comfortable with you, and that makes it easy to tease you. When you shut down last night, I felt like shit. That was the last thing I wanted—not only because you seemed upset, but because I didn't want to waste one minute of our final hours together." My walls started to crumble a little. "You told me when we first met that you were feeling lost. That hit me in my soul because I was feeling the exact same way...until we met. The last couple of days—being Milo to your Maddie—have been amazing and much-needed for me, too. Believe me."

The smile that spread across her face made my admission worth it. "I'm glad it wasn't only me."

"It wasn't. And I want to go on record saying... that guy who hurt you? He's a damn fool. You are as smart as you are beautiful. Creative and adventurous. Everything a man could want. And I'm not saying this as some guy who's trying to make you feel good or get into your pants. I'm saying this as your friend."

"Or brother." She winked.

Then she pulled me in for a hug, one I definitely wasn't expecting. I could feel her heart beating against my chest.

"Thank you for reminding me what it feels like to be alive," she said.

We let go of each other, stood up, and began the long walk to our respective gates. With each second that passed, my feeling of dread got more intense. I didn't want to go back to my pre-Maddie life, mainly because I'd been dealing with things in a very solitary manner. I enjoyed her companionship. She wasn't even gone yet, and I found myself longing for what we were walking away from.

We got to a point where she would turn left for Terminal A, and I would turn right for Terminal B.

We stopped and faced each other.

"Well, I guess this is it," she said.

Don't ask me what came over me in that moment, but a voice inside me just said: *The fuck it is.*

"This doesn't have to be *it,* Maddie."

The words flew out of me so fast I wasn't sure if I'd said them or thought them.

"This doesn't have to be it?" she said. "What do you mean?"

"Do you really want to go back to Connecticut right now?"

Her eyes flitted back and forth. "Honestly? No, not in the least."

"Can I ask you a question?"

"Yeah."

"What's the craziest thing you've ever done?"

"I don't know offhand..."

"It doesn't matter. Because I want the answer to be: said yes to a pseudo-stranger who asked me to go on a blind adventure with him."

"What are you saying?"

"I'm saying I'm not ready to say goodbye to Milo, if you're up for playing Maddie a little longer."

Her breathing quickened as she seemed to be considering my proposal. "Where will we go?"

"Wherever the wind takes us? Wherever the hell we want? As long as it's not Connecticut or New York or Seattle."

She wiped sweat off her forehead. "Would I be totally crazy if I said yes to this?"

"Not if it's what your heart is telling you to say."

"Then...yes." She nodded. "I say yes. I want to go."

Relief washed over me.

"Let me ask you a question," I said.

"Yeah?"

"What's the craziest thing you've ever done?"

"Said yes to a pseudo-stranger who asked me to go on a blind adventure with him."

"Maddie, welcome to the craziest day of your life."

She grinned. "Hookers Part Two?"

I lifted my hand and high-fived her. "Hell, yeah."

Chapter 6

Matteo

"They're on a first date. He's worried his credit card is going to get declined because he overspent this month on his webcam-girl porn addiction."

Maddie looked at me like I had two heads. I lifted my chin and pointed to the couple standing at the counter. The guy was rubbing his hands down the sides of his legs like his palms were sweaty, and he really did look pretty pale. Of course, that could've been because he was about to rent a machine that goes a hundred-and-fifty miles an hour with only a helmet for protection. But I liked my story better.

Maddie caught on to that I was playing our game again and leaned toward me. "He met Candi, his webcam girl, a year ago online. They never talk. He's into voyeurism, so he sends her messages about different things he wants her to do, and then when he signs on, they both pretend he isn't paying her to watch. The girl he's with today, her name is Emily. She lives a few blocks from him. She thinks they met at the gym by chance. Poor thing has no idea that the new guy she's seeing has been climbing a tree across the street from her for over a year. He watches her get changed through her bedroom window at night."

My eyebrows jumped. "That's a little creepy. I freaking love it. I didn't think you had it in you, Madeline Ophelia Hooker."

She chuckled. "Ophelia? That's my middle name?"

I shrugged. "Our mom was a huge *Hamlet* fan."

After Maddie and I decided to continue our adventure, we'd rented a car at the airport, and I drove us up to Steamboat Springs. Maddie had said she'd never been snowmobiling, and the trails here had some of the most gorgeous scenery. I figured we could incorporate her photography into our day exploring the beautiful Colorado mountains. Plus, the idea of spending the day with her body pressed up behind mine...well, that didn't suck.

"Mr. and Mrs. Hooker?" A man yelled from behind the counter. Sweaty man and his date had disappeared somewhere.

Maddie looked at me. "Did you tell them we were husband and wife, instead of brother and sister this time?"

"Nope. Just registered us as Maddie and Milo Hooker. I guess they assumed."

We walked up, and the guy who'd helped us with our paperwork took us outside to our machine. I'd rented a two-person Ski-Doo Grand Touring model, which had great suspension and a place to store Maddie's camera equipment. It sat one passenger in front of the other, motorcycle style, and I had Maddie get on before I saddled up.

"We're going to go about a half hour before our first stop," I said. "These things are loud, so it will be hard to talk. Give me a tap if you need me to stop for any reason." I'd come here enough times to know the best trails, and I was looking forward to seeing her reaction when I got to the place I had in mind. "Are you scared?"

She flashed a huge, toothy smile. "I am!"

I chuckled. Normally people who were scared looked like they were about to shit their pants, but not Maddie. She seemed to channel fear into excitement, and it had an exhilarating influence on me. Like yesterday, for example. I'd been avoiding going skiing for four years. If it were up to me, I'd never have clicked into a binding again, but she'd inspired me to turn the bad memories into new, good ones.

I finished packing her camera equipment into the rear storage bin and tucked away the Thermos of hot chocolate she had no idea I'd bought for our ride. Then I straddled the snowmobile in front of her.

"You comfortable?" I yelled.

"I am. But where do I hold on?"

There were grips she could grab attached to the sides of her seat, but luckily, the guy who gave us the equipment overview hadn't mentioned that fact.

"You wrap your arms around me."

"Oh. Okay. I need to move up then."

"Yeah, you do."

She'd been sitting with a gap between us, which she could've maintained if she'd known about the handles. Instead, her thighs wrapped around mine, and I reached down and gave one a squeeze. "You good?"

"Yes. I'm comfy."

Yeah, I couldn't agree more—*definitely* more comfy this way. Too bad we were both bundled with heavy winter coats. Note to self, steering this adventure to a warmer climate to shed some of these layers might not be a bad idea.

I started the snowmobile, and Maddie tightened her grip around my waist.

She shrieked, "Eeep! I'm so nervous," and I couldn't stop smiling as I hit the gas.

The trek through the trails was gorgeous. Huge evergreens blanketed in thick snow outlined the perimeter of the path. On more than one occasion, Maddie yelled and pointed things out. Even though I'd ridden here a hundred times, everything seemed new today, like I was seeing it through her eyes instead of mine. We wound through the mountains until we were almost at the top, and then I slowed down.

"Hold on tighter, okay? We're going off trail for a few minutes."

"Okay!"

I loved that she didn't ask if it was allowed or what we were going to see. Maddie trusted me to keep her safe, even though we'd only known each other for a few days. Once I got close to the overlook, I parked and climbed off, removing my helmet and hanging it from the handlebars.

Maddie climbed off, removed her helmet, and proceeded to rub her butt. "I think my ass is a little numb from the vibration."

"Think how my nuts feel."

She laughed. "I guess I should be glad you're not rubbing them then."

"What did you think I took you up here to show you?" I winked.

I unpacked her camera equipment from the back of the snowmobile and grabbed the Thermos of hot chocolate. "Come on. This way."

Leading her over to a giant rock about twenty feet from the edge of the mountain, I climbed up first, then extended a hand to pull her up with me.

She turned and got her first glimpse of the winter-wonderland view down below. The landscape was truly magnificent. The forest was turned white, the sky was bright blue, and smoke hovered over a geothermal spring in the center of the valley. "Oh my God. It's gorgeous."

I looked at the giant smile on her face. "Yeah, it really is."

Maddie couldn't unpack her camera fast enough. She stood and took pictures, lost in her own world for a solid ten minutes. When she sat down and sighed, I figured it was the perfect time for a warm drink, so I poured some of the steaming cocoa into the plastic cap that doubled as a mug and passed it to her.

"Oh wow. This is just perfect," she said.

We passed the hot chocolate back and forth a few times, taking turns sipping.

She shook her head and sighed. "I can't just take pictures of kids for the rest of my life."

"No?"

"There has to be a middle ground somewhere. I loved my job for the music magazine, but I was never home. I want to have a family someday, and there's no way I want to drag my kids around the globe nonstop like my parents did to me. But the last few days have really made me realize how much I also need to fuel my soul."

I nodded. "I get it. That's how I found my way to teaching."

"You know, when I asked you the other day how you got into teaching, you blew me off. You said it was a story for another day." She bumped shoulders with me. "Well, it's another day, Mr. Hooker."

I stared out at the sky for a moment, not sure where to start. Eventually, I closed my eyes and figured it might be easiest to get the worst part of the story over with first. "I met Zoe my first semester in college—not in class, but at a bar where I was playing a gig, though she was a student, too. She was four foot eleven and weighed a hundred pounds, if that. But she walked up to the microphone and just started singing with me— 'Some Kind of Wonderful' by Grand Funk Railroad."

I shook my head and pictured her that night. It was the first time in a long time that I'd actually smiled thinking about Zoe. "She had the craziest deep, raspy voice. It sounded like it belonged to a three-hundred-pound, forty-year-old gospel singer. I used to tell her I fell in love with the woman stuck inside the young, pretty girl. She really was an old soul." I paused. "Anyway, that was the last gig I ever played alone."

"Zoe and you became a duet?"

I nodded. "She couldn't sing if she looked out at the audience. So we sang to each other. We were students, so we played mostly local places during the week. But we branched out some on the weekends, and we started to gather a big following. Our senior year, a record label came to see us play and offered us a deal."

"Oh wow. I had no idea."

"That's because we never recorded the album. Zoe and I were set to take a semester off of school. We were scheduled to go to LA to record in January. The night before we left, I had the bright idea to go skiing one last time before we went to the land of sunshine. Zoe was a decent skier, but she didn't ski double-black-diamond trails like I did. Rather than stick to the regular trails with her, I told her I'd meet her at the bottom because I wanted to do one last run down the doubles. She insisted on coming with me. I didn't fight her on it hard enough, so she came. Halfway down, she hit an ice patch landing a mogul and went off course." I took a deep breath and swallowed. "She hit a tree. Broke her neck. She died instantly."

"Oh my God, Milo." Maddie reached out and pulled me into a hug. She held me tight. "I'm so sorry."

I nodded. "Thank you." After a few minutes, she loosened her grip, and I finished my story. "Anyway, yesterday was the first time I'd skied since that day. And I decided to go into teaching to stay within music, which I loved. But I couldn't bring myself to sing without Zoe after that."

"Wow. I can certainly understand why. But, Jesus, Milo. Why didn't you tell me how monumental a day yesterday was?"

I didn't know the answer to that question. "I guess I needed it to *not* be a big deal for me. Making it about you helped me keep my mind off of the reason I'd stopped skiing."

"And here I am telling you all my problems. What I went through isn't half as traumatic."

"We both suffered a loss of someone we loved. Just in different ways."

Maddie slipped off her glove, then reached over and gave one of my gloves a tug. Once our hands were free, she laced her fingers with mine and squeezed. "I think we were supposed to meet, Milo Hooker. Life brought us together for a reason." She rested her head against my shoulder and let out a big sigh. "We're here to help each other find our new paths."

I nodded. "I think you might be right, sis. I think you really might be right."

After we finished riding, we found a little hotel off of Main Street in downtown Steamboat Springs to stay for the night. Again, we got adjacent rooms.

"I'm starving," Maddie said as we stood in front of our respective doors and swiped the keys to unlock them. "When we drove through town, I saw a cute place where I'd like to eat."

"Oh sure. What place?"

She smiled. "It's a surprise."

I smiled back. "Okay. How long do you need to get ready?"

"Forty minutes?"

"Sounds good. Knock on my door when you're done."

I took a shower and got dressed, then kicked my feet up on the bed to rest my eyes for a few minutes. A knock at the door woke me sometime after.

I opened the door, still in a sleepy fog, and found Maddie all dressed up in a slinky silver slip dress with spaghetti straps. Her red hair was blown out into soft waves, and she had on more makeup than I'd ever seen her wear. I had to blink a few times to make sure I wasn't dreaming.

"Wow. You look great. I guess I need to change."

She took a step back and looked herself up and down. "Is this too much for downtown? I brought so many nice clothes. I'm not sure where I planned on going all dressed up since I came by myself, but I figured, why not use them? Though look at the back of this. Is it too much? Obviously I need to grab my coat before we go outside."

She turned and showed me the low-cut back of her dress, which showcased creamy white skin and dipped to just above her ass. I salivated at the sight of the silky material hugging her perfectly round cheeks.

I cleared my throat. "Ummm... It's definitely not your typical snow gear, but damn, you look sexy as hell. I don't think we should tell people we're brother and sister tonight, because they might think it's fucked up when I drool looking at you."

She blushed. "You're sweet. But should I change?"

"Absolutely fucking not." I nodded toward my room. "But come inside so I can at least put a collared shirt on."

It had seemed like a perfectly innocent request when I made it, but the moment the door clanked closed behind her, that all changed. Maybe it was her being inside a room that was pretty much all bed, coupled with the way she looked in that dress, but suddenly I really wanted to see her gorgeous red hair fanned out all over my pillow.

Needing a distraction from that thought, I went to my suitcase and dug around while Maddie took a seat on the edge of the bed. She crossed one leg over the other, and I lost my battle with staring.

Damn, she has great legs, too.

And I hadn't even noticed her sexy-as-fuck shoes. They were sparkly, with a thin strap that wrapped around her ankle and a tall, skinny heel. Never had I been so thankful for the stupendous job Colorado did clearing the walkways in these touristy areas before. Those things were a hell of a lot better than snow boots; that was for damn sure.

I'd been wearing a pair of black pants and a thermal, but I pulled off the thermal to change into a nice, gray dress shirt. As I pulled down the hem of the T-shirt I'd put on underneath, I caught Maddie checking me out again.

The feeling's mutual, Mads. Totally mutual.

Out on the street, I offered her my arm. "I don't want you to hit a patch of ice in those shoes."

"Oh. Thank you." She gripped my bicep, and together we strolled two blocks. I had no idea where we were going, but Maddie seemed to. Following her adventurous lead, I didn't ask.

She stopped in front of a local bar. "This is it."

The place had been around for years and was kind of a shithole. I was surprised she didn't want to go somewhere fancier with the way she was dressed.

"I think they only have a bar menu, burgers and stuff. There's a steak house on the next block, if you want something nicer."

She smiled. "Nope. What I want is right here. You got to pick the last two adventures. Tonight it's mine."

I chuckled. "Whatever you say."

Inside, a waitress told us to sit anywhere we wanted, so we grabbed a booth. I looked around. It had probably been eight years since I'd been here, but the place hadn't changed a bit. It was dark, with wood-paneled walls and a concrete floor. Music played overhead from what sounded like a pretty decent sound system for such a crappy bar, and there was a small stage in one corner where two guys were working to set up equipment.

"Did you want to come listen to music or something? I can't imagine you picked this place for the food."

"I did come for the music."

I nodded. That made a little more sense. Though I hadn't noticed a sign in the window about a band. "Who's playing tonight?"

Maddie smiled. "You. It's karaoke night. The sign outside said it starts in ten minutes."

I hated to be a buzz kill when Maddie had been so up for anything whenever I directed our adventures, but there was no way I was singing.

"I'm sorry, Mads. I appreciate that you wanted to come here for me. But I just can't." Skiing was one thing, but getting up on that stage without Zoe was another thing all together. It's where she belonged.

"Okay. But I hope you don't mind that I'm going to."

"I didn't realize you could sing."

She grinned. "I can't."

I drank a beer, and Maddie had a glass of wine, which I noticed she downed pretty damn fast. When she was done, she stood. "I'm going to go sign up. Any special requests?"

I lifted my arms to the top of the booth and spread them out. "Surprise me."

She said she couldn't sing, but I assumed she was exaggerating. Who signs up for karaoke unless they can at least carry a tune? At least while sober. Although when she returned to the booth and ordered a wine *and* a shot, I realized her goal might be to get drunk before they called her name.

"Do you do karaoke often?" I asked.

She sucked back the shot and made a face like she'd sniffed a dead fish before slamming the glass down on the table. "I've never done it before."

My brows shot up. "Seriously?"

"Seriously. I've never sung in public before. Well, unless you count my first apartment. I lived in a studio that had thin walls. Apparently my shower wall was next to the neighbor's bedroom. I used to sing in the shower at night. Sometimes I'd even rock the shampoo bottle microphone when I got really into it. Then one day my sweet, elderly neighbor knocked on my door. Mrs. Eckel handed me a pie and smiled politely before she told me her dog cried every time he heard me singing. She asked if I could refrain from crooning in the bathroom from then on."

I chuckled. "You're full of shit. That didn't really happen."

Her finger traced a cross over her chest. "Swear to God." She motioned for the waitress and ordered another shot.

"Umm... You're sucking back vodka like it's water. How often do you do shots?"

"As often as I sing karaoke."

Shit.

Luckily the guy running the karaoke called her name before the third shot arrived at the table. "Next up is Madeline Ophelia Hooker. She'll be singing a song by CeeLo Green—the original, not the PG-version they play on the radio."

Maddie stood and smoothed down her dress. "Oh my God. I can't believe I'm doing this. How do I look?"

"Honestly, hot as fuck. No one is even going to notice if you can't sing for shit. Though, there's still time to back out, if you don't want to go through with it. I appreciate what you were trying to do whether you get up there or not."

Maddie leaned down and kissed my cheek. But instead of pulling away after, her mouth moved to my ear. "You know how you got undressed in front of me earlier?" Her hot breath tickled my ear.

"Yeah."

"If you join me, I'll return the favor at some point before we part ways."

I blew out a deep, ragged breath. God, this woman was as unpredictable as she was gorgeous. But not even that could get me up in front of that microphone.

"Break a leg, beautiful."

I watched as Maddie strutted to the stage. That dress really looked phenomenal on her ass. I was pretty sure my head rocked back and forth in unison with the sway of her hips as she walked. The waitress brought the shot Maddie had ordered to our table just as she got up on stage. I took it from her hand before she had a chance to set it down and immediately sucked it back. "I'm gonna need another one of these, please."

The karaoke host came over the sound system. "This was an interesting song choice, Madeline. Is there anyone you want to dedicate this song to?"

Maddie cleared her throat and tilted the microphone to her mouth. "Yes. To my ex-fiancé, and all the other asshole men of the world."

The host chuckled. "Alright then. Here we go."

The music started to play, and I immediately recognized which CeeLo song she'd picked. "Fuck You," though most radio stations called it "Forget You" and bleeped out half the lyrics.

Maddie started to sing, and Jesus, she really hadn't been lying. Some people had a bad tone, some people couldn't hold a tune, and others just had no rhythm when they sang. Poor Mads was afflicted with all three.

It was bad.

So, so freaking bad.

At first the bar was quiet. I think most people were probably stunned at how such a horrible sound could come out of such a gorgeous woman. But eventually, the bar snapped out of it and people started to grumble. A few assholes even booed and heckled her. Maddie looked like she wanted to crawl into a hole somewhere.

Fuck.

I raked a hand through my hair.

Fuck me.

The booing from the crowd grew louder, but Maddie kept going, trying to push through it.

I couldn't let her stand there and make a fool of herself.

I growled *fuck* and slid out of the booth, marching toward the stage. She'd been there with me every step of the way, and I couldn't let her do this alone.

I stopped at the karaoke host's station and asked the guy to do me a favor and put on a different song. There were two microphones on the stage. I followed the cord of one and yanked the plug out of the wall. Just as the host turned off CeeLo, I told Maddie to slide over to the mic that was no longer on.

"What are you doing?" she whispered.

"Growing some balls. Now move over a mic before the next song starts."

Chapter 7

Hazel

I couldn't stop staring at Milo.

He had the most amazing voice. It was raspy and deep, and the moment he started to sing, it felt like he'd wrapped it around me like a warm blanket. He sang Lady Antebellum's "Need You Now," which was a duet, though he didn't need anyone to sing with him at all.

I stood at the microphone for a long time just watching him, in awe of how effortless his singing sounded and how comfortable he was standing there. When he got to the chorus, he looked over and smiled at me and pointed to my mic. I joined him, though luckily no one could hear.

When the song ended, we got a standing ovation. Well, let's be real. Milo got a standing ovation. He waved to the crowd and offered me his hand as he stepped off the stage. Our eyes locked.

"Thank you for saving my ass," I said.

"No, Mads. Thank you for saving mine."

I woke up with a huge smile on my face the morning after Milo's performance.

My mood only got better as we checked out of the hotel in Steamboat and packed into our rental car, headed to the next leg of our adventure.

"Where are we going now, Mr. Hooker?"

"You know the answer to that question."

"Wherever the wind takes us?"

He pointed at me. "Bingo."

"Does the wind have any inkling of where it wants to push us?" I chuckled.

He put his seatbelt on. "The wind was thinking maybe we could slowly make our way southeast and then up north, eventually. I assume you want to end up in Connecticut when this is all over."

The thought of going back to reality made me a little uneasy, even if it was a little ways away.

"That sounds perfect. The Southeast is one part of the country I'm pretty unfamiliar with. I'd love to see Texas...New Orleans."

We hit the open road, and seven hours later, we found ourselves in Santa Fe, New Mexico.

What a beautiful place. The mountainous terrain, the architecture. There was a peacefulness here that was instantly welcoming.

I rolled down the window to breathe in the clean air. "I used to sing that song 'Do You Know the Way to Santa Fe'," I told Milo.

"I believe it's San Jose." He glanced over at me. "Do you know the way *to San Jose...*"

"Same difference." I winked. "By the way, did I give you PTSD just now when I mentioned my singing?"

Milo grinned. "Maybe a little."

I bounced in my seat. "I am not leaving this place without some funky cowboy boots. Can we go shopping tomorrow?"

"Sure. We should actually get a souvenir from every place we stop."

"Well, crap." I pouted. "We didn't get anything from Steamboat."

He winked. "We did, actually."

"What?"

"I got my balls back. I'd lost them, and now I have them again."

I slapped his leg. "Well, that's true."

"Actually, I did pick something up," he said. "A souvenir."

I perked up. "Really?"

"Yeah." He took it out of his pocket and handed it to me.

It was a little Snoopy pin that said *Steamboat* on it. Snoopy wore a hat, sweater, and skis.

"This is adorable. Where did you get it?"

"I actually found it. When I said I picked something up, I meant off the ground. It looks vintage, doesn't it?"

Rubbing my finger over it, I said, "It's precious. Can I keep it?"

"Of course."

I happily pinned Snoopy to my jacket.

We finally arrived at our destination, a beautiful hotel and spa that had a stunning view of the Sangre de Cristo Mountains. The sun was just starting to set, and the scenery here was a stunning sight to behold.

After we checked in, as we were walking to the elevators, we noticed the hotel workers setting up some type of event in one of the function rooms. The décor was especially flamboyant, with bright yellow linens, and it sparked my curiosity.

"I wonder what's happening in there."

"Maybe a wedding," Milo said.

"Could be. But did you see all that yellow? And the giant disco ball they were putting up? Also, there weren't any flowers. I feel like it might be something else."

Milo's expression spelled trouble.

"What?" I asked.

"Feel like getting dressed up tonight and crashing it?"

"Are you serious?"

"Sure." He shrugged. "Why not. It will give us a good chance to put our recently acquired imposter skills to use."

"So, the Hookers are going to a party, and we don't even know what it's for?"

"Does it really matter? Have any of the destinations we've hit mattered? It's the experience, the thrill of the unknown. It's never the destination."

He had a point. Crashing some mystery party sounded kind of fun.

"You're so right." I nodded. "Let's do it."

Milo and I checked into our respective rooms and vowed to meet up in an hour after we'd showered and gotten dressed. He'd once again insisted on paying for the hotel rooms, but I told him he'd better let me cover the rooms in the next city, or at least the cost of my own room. As a high school music teacher, he likely didn't have an endless stream of funds. He wasn't even currently working.

As I let the warm water pour down on me in the shower, I couldn't help thinking about our time in Steamboat, and his confession about Zoe and her tragic accident. It broke my heart to think about it, and it explained so much. He'd lost his partner and soulmate. That was far worse than what I'd been through. It certainly put everything with Brady into perspective. I could move on or choose to forgive Brady. I had choices. But Milo had been forced to part with his love. He'd had no choice in the matter, and it was terribly sad. I wiped my tears and exited the shower.

Selecting one of the sexiest dresses I'd brought with me, I got myself all dolled up for our mystery party. Were we about to crash a wedding? A corporate party? A bar mitzvah? Who knew? Either way, the Hookers were ready to turn on the charm.

I looked at myself in the mirror. The dress I'd chosen was black sequined, strapless, and short. I wore the same sexy, strappy heels I'd worn out to karaoke and decided to leave my hair down.

Once dressed, I felt antsy, so I went to knock on Milo's door.

When he opened, I exhaled upon the sight of his shirtless body. *Again.* This always seemed to happen. I almost had to wonder if the prick was doing it to me on purpose, waiting to put his shirt on until I had a chance to ogle him. How long does it take a guy to get dressed? He always seemed to be running "late," and was therefore half-naked when I knocked.

He gave me a onceover. "You look even more amazing now than you did in the dress back in Steamboat. This one really takes the cake, Maddie. Damn."

"Why, thank you. I have it on good authority that I'm attending a party tonight, so I wanted to look my very best."

"Well, mission accomplished." He sighed. "I, on the other hand, am wearing the same shirt from Steamboat, because unfortunately, I don't have another suitable one."

"Well, we're going shopping tomorrow. We can buy you another dress shirt."

"You're really angling to shop, aren't you?"

"Yup. Funky boots, remember? And maybe a nice wool blanket with a southwestern pattern."

I noticed his shirt hanging in the closet. "Your shirt's all wrinkled."

"I know. I was gonna iron it."

Grabbing the shirt and unfolding the ironing board, I said. "I got it."

"You don't have to do that."

"I don't mind."

I got to work pressing. The smell of his cologne on the shirt emanated through the steam. I definitely didn't mind ironing a shirt that smelled like him.

When I'd managed to get all of the wrinkles out, I held it open behind him as he slipped his arms inside. I then faced him and slowly buttoned it from bottom to top as Milo watched every movement of my hands. It was unintentionally sensual, and I could feel the energy of his stare until I buttoned the very last one.

Our eyes lingered until he said, "We'd better go. We'll be late for the…"

I finished his sentence. "Whatever it is."

"Yeah." He smiled. "Promise me one thing, Maddie."

"What?"

"Whatever we're getting ourselves into tonight, you'll stick it out. No running away if things get awkward. We play it till the end—or until we get kicked out." He laughed.

I couldn't believe I was agreeing to this, but I felt myself nodding. "Did you not see my crazy ass get up on that stage and belt out a song called 'Fuck You' with my terrible voice last night? I'm not the one who needs convincing to do crazy shit."

"That's true. And that's one of the things I love about you."

His word choice sent a shiver down my spine as we headed out the door.

Once downstairs, we entered the packed function room, still completely clueless as to the nature of this event.

In looking around, I confirmed once again that it definitely wasn't a wedding, because there were still no flowers in sight. The centerpieces were interesting, though: fresh pineapples.

A woman standing at what looked like a hostess station near the door asked, "Are you registered?"

"Yes," Milo answered.

"What's the name?"

"Milo Hooker." He turned to me. "And this is my sister, Madeline. Or as I like to call her, Maddie."

She pursed her lips as she checked the list. "Hmm. Hooker. I don't see your names on here."

Milo pretended to be outraged. "Well, there must be some kind of mistake then. I registered weeks ago."

She seemed frustrated that she wasn't able to find our information.

Leaning in she whispered, "Honestly, I don't think any woman here is going to complain that I let you in. In fact, they might kill me if I let you walk out that door. So, how about I just add your names now?"

"That sounds excellent." He smiled. "Thank you."

She asked him to confirm the spelling of our names before she said, "It's rare to see siblings coming to our events together. I have to say, that's a new one."

Hmm...

Was this a singles mixer?

"What's the itinerary for tonight?" Milo asked her.

"Well, we have a cash bar. And everyone is ready to mingle. Should you decide you've made a match, we have a certain number of rooms blocked upstairs. You'll come to me, and I can provide you with a key. If you decide to use one of our rooms, you'll just need to provide a credit card to claim it. They're on a first-come, first-served basis."

She handed us each a badge to clip onto our clothing. They had a single pineapple on them.

Milo nodded. "Got it. Thank you."

As we walked away, I clipped the badge to my chest and said, "You told her you got it? Way to play it cool. What the hell is this? Some kind of pineapple-lovers convention?"

Milo ducked his head in laughter. When he calmed down, his expression turned serious. "We're at a fuck fest, Maddie."

Huh? A fuck fest? My eyes went wide. "What?"

"This is a swingers event."

"Oh my God. What?"

"The first dead giveaway was the goddamn pineapples."

I wrinkled my forehead. "Pineapples?"

"Yeah." He chuckled. "You didn't know that?"

"No! What do pineapples have to do with swinging?"

"They're a universal symbol to identify...like-minded people. I used to have neighbors who always had a pineapple flag hanging outside their house. I had no clue what the fuck it meant until the woman asked me to one of their parties. She seemed to think her husband would like Zoe, and she made it clear she wanted to fuck me. When I told her we weren't into that kind of stuff, she made it sound like I should've known what they were insinuating—because of the pineapple. So I never made that mistake again. I see a pineapple now? I know what's up."

Still trying to make sense of it all, I asked, "Wait... You noticed the pineapples on the way up to our rooms when we first got here? You *knew* about this when you asked me to crash it?"

He shook his head. "No. I swear. I didn't notice the pineapples until we got down here just now."

My jaw dropped as I looked around. "Holy shit." So many eyes were on us—like almost every set of eyes in the room.

"You look like you want to flee," he said. "Remember our promise. We said we'd follow this through until the end—no matter what."

"This is a pretty big 'no matter what'! And what exactly does 'the end' mean under these circumstances? My name might be *hooker*...but I'm not a hooker, if you get my drift."

"We won't be partaking, crazy girl." He laughed. "But it will be fun to mess around with these people." He tilted his head. "Come on."

Milo went to the bar and got us a couple of drinks while I stayed a few feet behind and continued to peruse the room nervously. I was definitely going to need alcohol for this.

Not to boost my own ego, but we were the best-looking people here. I suspected it would be no time before we were approached.

Sure enough, soon after Milo returned with our drinks, a man and a woman who looked to be in their late thirties came over to where we were standing.

"Hello," the man said.

Milo smiled, looking cool and confident. "Hi."

The woman sounded kind of tense. "I'm Carolyn, and this is my husband, Troy."

"Nice to meet you," Milo said.

My pseudo-brother gave me a challenging look, like he wanted me to say something to them.

I cleared my throat. "So...do you do this often?"

"Actually, no," the woman said. "This is my first time. It's my fortieth birthday, and I told him I wanted to try this at least once."

"Ahhh." I breathed out. "Well, happy birthday."

Her husband took a sip of his drink. "I've been many times before. My ex and I used to like to frequent these things. Carolyn is my second wife and not quite as adventurous. Probably why we've lasted, though."

After several seconds of awkward silence, the woman asked, "How about you two? How long have you been together?"

"Actually, we're not together. Maddie is my sister."

"Oh, wow. You're both...single?" she asked.

"Yes," I said, taking a long swig of my drink.

Troy leaned in to whisper in my ear. "You know there's a name for women like you at these things."

"What's that?" I said, taking a long step away from him.

He wriggled his brows. "A unicorn."

"Is that so?"

"Yes." He grinned. "No strings attached. That's a hot commodity."

After several minutes of small talk, Troy finally got to the point. "So, what are the chances you two would like to...play?"

No chance in hell.

I looked at Milo and let him do the honors.

He took my cue. "Thank you. But we're already committed to another couple. We're...supposed to be meeting them here."

Carolyn looked super disappointed to not be getting a piece of my hot *brother* tonight. "Ah...well...worth a shot." She smiled.

"In any case, it was nice meeting you two," Troy said before they walked away.

Sayonara.

After they left, I felt like I needed a shower. But also, oddly jealous. Which was ridiculous because Milo wasn't my boyfriend. But somehow the thought of him having sex with that woman—her even wanting him— made me feel stabby.

He sensed something. "You okay?"

I surveyed the room. "Yeah. I'm fine."

There were several couples lurking around us. Women were checking out Milo, and I could see some of the men staring at me.

While my inclination was to flee, we'd agreed to see this through. But what was the end exactly if it didn't involve "playing" with these people?

At one point, someone came up to us and announced in a low voice, "The penthouse suite is open now, if you're interested."

After the guy walked away, I turned to Milo. "What's going on in the penthouse suite?"

"I'm supposed to know?" He laughed. "But let's check it out."

Well, we've come this far. Might as well see what that's all about.

As we headed upstairs in the elevator, all I could think was: *What the hell am I getting myself into now?*

Once at the penthouse suite, we showed our pineapple badges at the door and were given access to the room.

The lighting was red tinted and muted. Soft jazz music played. Because of the dim lights, you couldn't very easily make out faces. There were air mattresses strewn all over the floor and people lying about.

Next to where we entered was a bowl of condoms. Next to that, a bowl of wet wipes.

A man standing just inside the room took our cell phones before we could go in any farther, giving us numbered tickets and noting that we should pick our phones up on the way out.

Within a few minutes, there were people all around us, undressing and going at it on the mattresses. The smell of alcohol mixed with pungent cologne filled the air. This was literally, as Milo had put it earlier, a fuck fest.

There were plenty of people standing on the sidelines watching, too. I suppose we were part of that group. I noticed the couple we'd spoken with earlier also standing in a corner on the opposite side of the room. They were probably wondering where our "friends" were—you know, the ones we were supposed to be meeting in lieu of having sex with them.

The room was eerily quiet, compared to what I would have expected. As much as many of these people were not what you would consider typically attractive, I was surprised to find that the longer I watched them having sex, the more hot and bothered I became—not because of my attraction to anyone here, but because of my attraction to the man standing beside me. And when I turned to look at Milo, he was staring right at me.

Our eyes stayed fixed on each other for a while until he leaned in and said, "I think we've now seen this through to the end. You?"

Feeling flustered, I nodded and followed him toward the door. We retrieved our phones and left. My heart beat rampantly, and I wondered if that was because for a split second, I'd thought he was going to ask me if I was interested in joining in with him. *But that would've been crazy.* Milo would never do that. That wasn't the type of relationship we had. Not to mention, those people were under the impression that we were brother and sister, so you could imagine what they would have thought.

The fact that I'd even thought for a millisecond about Milo asking me to do that with him was pathetic. Yet, it seemed to be all I could think about as we walked together back to our rooms. What would it have been like down on one of those mattresses with Milo hovering over me—inside of me?

Wow. *I really need to get laid.*

We found ourselves alone in the elevator. I looked down and could've sworn he had an erection. Thank goodness the wetness between my legs wasn't visible. The vibe between us had somehow been altered by that voyeuristic experience.

"Well, that was interesting," he finally said, his eyes hazy.

In that moment, it all seemed to hit me. I burst into laughter. Then Milo did, too. We laughed until the elevator dinged open on our floor.

I wiped my eyes. "I'll never look at a pineapple the same way again."

Chapter 8

Matteo

It surprised me that she asked me to come to her room for a drink.

After our outings thus far, Maddie had escaped to her room and never invited me in. I was always fine with that, because it made it easier not to blur things between us. I knew she wasn't interested in crossing that line with me. She'd made that crystal clear. And as attracted to her as I was, it was better for both of us if things stayed platonic, uncomplicated. That's what we both needed right now: to have fun and make a clean break when we parted ways. Having sex would ruin that plan.

But the fact that she'd asked me to her room tonight—of all nights—was ironic. That whole experience upstairs had made me horny as fuck. I hadn't realized just how hard up I'd been. And it had nothing to do with anyone there, but instead the idea of sex and Maddie put together. So given that, tonight would have been the one night I preferred to go to my room alone, so I could rub one off in the shower and put myself out of my misery. Instead, I was left sitting on the chair across from Maddie as she lay splayed out on the bed in that sexy dress. It was basically a form of torture.

Maddie sipped her hard seltzer and surprised me with a question. "If I wasn't there, would you have given Carolyn her fortieth-birthday wish?"

I laughed. "No. No interest in Carolyn, or anyone else there, for that matter." I took a sip of my drink. "You?"

She shook her head. "No. Troy wasn't my type."

My brow lifted. "Anyone else there your type?"

She hesitated. "Nope."

I decided to admit what I was feeling. Pretty sure she'd noticed my dick was hard in the elevator anyway, so maybe it was better to be honest. "There was no one there who interested me, but somehow collectively, the idea of everyone so turned on—it got me worked up, I guess."

Maddie looked flushed. Her voice was low when she said, "I thought I was the only one."

Even though I'd suspected she was turned on up in the penthouse suite, hearing her admit it only made the situation in my pants worse.

I needed to change the subject. *Stat.*

"Any idea what you want to do tomorrow besides shop?"

She shrugged. "Just see some of the sights. Walk around, maybe check out the Santa Fe Plaza."

"That sounds good."

When she yawned, I took that as my cue and opportunity to escape this tense conversation. I needed a release.

I stood up. "Well, I'll let you get some shut eye."

As I moved toward the door, she suddenly got up off the bed. "Wait."

My heart started to beat faster. "What's up?"

She looked like she wasn't sure what she'd planned to say. Until she muttered, "Can you unzip me?"

Fuck. What is she doing?

A man can only take so much.

"Sure." I walked back over to her.

She turned around so her back was to me.

I slowly lowered the zipper on her dress, swallowing hard as I gazed at the soft skin of her gorgeous back. She hadn't worn a bra. Her tits were so perky, apparently she didn't need one.

Unexpectedly, her dress fell to the floor, showcasing nothing but a red lace thong over her flawless ass. I felt my pants tightening by the second. This wasn't good. She kept her back to me, lingering there, seemingly wanting me to suffer. And then it dawned on me what she was doing. She was giving me that fucking show she'd promised me. My reward for performing in Steamboat.

The devil inside of me silently begged her to turn around, to show me everything, to take her thong off, lie back on the bed, and spread her legs wide so I could see her glistening pussy. The devil wanted her to beg me to fuck her.

Instead, she covered her breasts as she turned around and blushed. Then, she escaped into the bathroom.

I was wrong. The devil wasn't inside me. She was behind that bathroom door.

And my gut told me she wasn't intending for me to follow. She'd already made her intentions clear. This was simply a cock tease of epic proportions.

Don't get me wrong. It was a cock tease I'd gladly accept.

I heard the water in the bathroom.

With my raging hard on, I headed for the door and retreated to my room alone.

The following day, we did not speak of her little peep show or the sex party we'd inadvertently attended. The vibe was back to platonic as we shopped for her boots. *Thank fuck.*

She didn't need to know I'd spent the better part of an hour after I returned to my room last night whacking off to thoughts of her body, which morphed into fantasies of fucking her on those air mattresses in the penthouse suite. I couldn't remember the last time I'd jerked off so much.

I'd slept with a few women since Zoe, but all of those experiences had been gratuitous and forced. I hadn't been genuinely turned on in ages. Too bad it happened with a woman who was more interested in fucking *with* me than fucking me. Maybe I should've been thankful that Maddie and I had already set boundaries between us, because things would have gotten complicated real fast without them.

But if things were clear, why was I still overthinking everything when I was supposed to be helping her look for ugly cowboy boots?

Maddie lifted her foot. "What do you think?"

We'd been in the boot shop for the better part of an hour. Every pair she selected featured a mish-mash of bright colors.

"Those are pretty hideous."

"This is what I'm going for, though. Bright and colorful."

"You mean tacky?"

"You're no fun, Hooker." She winked.

I got the sudden urge to smack her ass.

Good job putting last night out of your mind, Matteo. Milo. Whatever the fuck your name is.

Several minutes later, when she came back from the register, she carried two large boxes.

Standing up from the bench where I'd been ruminating, I said, "Couldn't decide, eh? You opted for two obnoxious pairs?"

She grinned. "Sure did! But not both for me. One pair for me, one pair for you."

I narrowed my eyes. "What did you do?"

"Put on your new boots, brother." Maddie opened the box, showcasing men's boots that were completely covered in American-flag print.

I shook my head and chuckled. "I guess we have our souvenirs from Santa Fe."

"Do you have a lot of friends?"

I glanced over at Maddie in the passenger seat before returning my eyes to the road. "That question came out of the blue."

She smiled. "I was just thinking of the things I would miss if I packed up and left Connecticut. I've become good friends with a woman there. She's also a photographer. Her name is Felicity. I'd really miss her."

We'd been on the road for seven hours already today. Our next stop was New Orleans. It was about a sixteen-hour trip, but we planned to do ten today and the rest tomorrow morning. I knew from experience that road trips were conducive to deep thinking. There was nothing but you and your thoughts for hours on end. So it didn't surprise me Maddie was contemplating life during our drive.

"I have a few friends in Seattle. I go out with a group of teachers for happy hour every once in a while. And I play two-on-two basketball with these guys at the gym every other Tuesday night."

Maddie nodded. "I had a few good friends when I was little. But every time we would move, I'd be so upset about losing them. After a while, I figured out that if I didn't get too close to anyone, it was easier when my parents picked up and left."

I frowned. "That sucks. Though, to be honest, I think I've been sort of doing the same thing the last couple of years. I had a lot of friends in high school and college, mostly because I played sports. But things have changed since I moved to Seattle. I chalked it up to relocating. Though looking back now, I'm not so sure that's all it was. I've pretty much kept to myself since Zoe."

Maddie sighed. "Yeah." After that, she went quiet for a long time again, staring out the car window, seemingly deep in thought. When she broke her silence, she said, "Can I ask you something personal?"

I chuckled. "You mean all the shit we've talked about over the last six days wasn't personal?"

She smiled. "I guess it was. But I don't want to be too prying."

"How about this? Nothing is off limits from here on out. Everything is on the table for the rest of our trip. You have a question, just ask it, and I'll do my best to answer."

Her face lit up. It was so freaking adorable. "Okay! And same here. I'm an open book."

"Sounds good. Now that we've settled that, what was your question?"

"Oh yeah..." She bit her lower lip. "Do you...ever have trouble...you know, getting excited?"

My brows jumped. "Are you asking me if I have difficulty getting an erection?"

She nodded.

"No, that's not happened to me as of yet. In fact, the last few days I've had the opposite problem. Especially after that little stunt you pulled last night, by the way."

She covered a devilish smile with her hand. "I told you I'd return the favor if you got up and sang with me. I owed you."

"Yeah, well, you're definitely no welcher. In fact, I'll have to remember that and make a few little wagers over the duration of our trip. There's a lot more to see." I winked.

Maddie laughed.

I really did love what our relationship had grown into. It was pretty crazy to think I'd only known her a little less than a week. Especially when I felt like she knew me better than anyone else these days.

"Anyway, getting back to your question," I said. "I'm curious where all of this is coming from? First you asked if I had a lot of friends, and now you want to know if I suffer from erectile dysfunction. Your mind seems to be jumping all over the place."

She shook her head. "Believe it or not, they're actually related. I was thinking how I would miss my friend Felicity if I moved. Growing up, I never really had a friend I could talk to about boys. And she's been a lifesaver ever since my engagement ended. Anyway, this morning I woke up and thought of something really random that happened with my ex. A few months ago, he came over after going out to happy hour with some people from work. He'd had too much to drink, and he couldn't, you know...perform. That had never happened before, and I chalked it up to the alcohol and never really gave it another thought—until this morning. For some reason, I woke up remembering that night and something Felicity told me—that maybe his issue was caused by something more than just the liquor. Maybe Brady had done something he felt guilty about, or perhaps he was hiding something. She told me not to worry too much and assured me the truth would come out eventually, that I'd see it when I was no longer looking through love goggles. I was going to text her this morning and tell her I'd finally taken off my goggles, but then I remembered the time difference and didn't want to wake her."

"And you just *randomly* woke up thinking about that night?"

She smirked. "Well, maybe it wasn't so random. I might've noticed your pants were fitting a little snug after we left that party last night. And you'd had a few drinks. So I guess it got me thinking..."

I knew what I'd done to alleviate that problem when I got back to my room. But I was curious as hell if

Maddie had done the same thing. Since we'd just agreed no question was off limits, I figured, why not ask? Though I wanted some reassurance that she'd meant what she said.

"So...no question is off limits, right? That works both ways."

Maddie raised a brow. "Oh, this is going to get interesting, isn't it?"

I tapped my fingers on the steering wheel. "It most certainly is, Mads. It most certainly is."

She laughed. "What's your question?"

I had about a quarter of a tank of gas left and could probably make it to our planned stopping point for the day without filling up. Yet I decided to pull off the highway when I saw a sign for gas. If I was going to get to ask a good question, I wanted to be able to watch her face when she answered, not have to keep my eyes on the road.

So I waited until I'd parked at the pump before shifting in my seat and turning to face Maddie head on. "It might not be as obvious with a woman, but I'd venture to guess you went to bed a little turned on last night, too. Am I right?"

She nodded with a coy smile. "Yeah. I was definitely a little riled up."

Fuck. I was getting turned on just thinking about her being turned on. Now I *needed* to know. My eyes dropped to her lips. They were so full and pink. I had the strongest urge to lean in and take the bottom one in my teeth and give it a good, firm tug.

Maddie giggled, almost nervously. "If there are no other questions, I'm going to use the restroom since we stopped."

Forcing my eyes to meet hers again, I cleared my throat. "Oh, that wasn't my question, Mads. That was just me clarifying what I already knew. What I really want to know is, what did you do about it once you were all alone in your room?"

Chapter 9

Hazel

How the hell did I answer?

With the truth? That last night I'd imagined the two of us had gone at it like wild animals while I laid in the tub with the showerhead pressed between my legs? Or did I lie and say I hadn't come so hard I saw spots for a solid five minutes after I opened my eyes?

"Mads..."

My eyes jumped to meet Milo's. He flashed a crooked smile. "Sorry. Maybe I took things too far."

"You didn't."

He reached over and twirled a lock of my hair around his pointer finger and gave it a tug. "Come on, let's go get some sugary snacks and hit the bathrooms."

I nodded.

I walked the aisles of the gas station convenience store lost in a fog. The thought of admitting to Milo that I'd masturbated really didn't bother me. I wasn't a prude. Lord knows my days of following rock bands for employment had made me immune to being shy about anything sexual. I'd seen and heard it all over the years. The thing that freaked me out was that I'd done it while thinking about *him*. And if I were being honest, I could shut my eyes and do it again right now. I was that attracted to him. And that wasn't the only thing that freaked me out.

It was that I was starting to want more than just his body.

Milo walked up the aisle carrying a giant package of Twizzlers and a big box of M&M's. He held them up. "I got chewy and chocolate. What's your pleasure for salty?"

I stared at the packages of candy for a solid thirty seconds, then looked up at Milo. Blinking a few times, I blurted out, "I used the showerhead to masturbate after you left. I came so damn hard that I was literally dizzy. And it still didn't satisfy me. It took me two hours to fall asleep after that, and then this morning, you called my room to ask if I was ready for breakfast. You thought you woke me because I sounded so hoarse. But I was awake. *Definitely awake.* My fingers were inside of me when the room phone rang, and it scared the crap out of me. I hadn't yet found my voice. And, since we're being totally honest, I'd use the damn gear shifter that's sitting between us in the car if I wouldn't get arrested for indecent exposure in the parking lot." I took a deep breath and my voice rose. "Because I'm still *that* damn horny!"

Milo's jaw fell open, and the Twizzlers and M&M's dropped to the floor with a loud clank.

The sound snapped me out my head. I'd been so caught up in my answer that I hadn't stopped to look at my surroundings. Which I now became painfully aware of. A mother stared at me in disgust, holding her hands over her daughter's ears. She rushed the little girl out of the store. And a man who was probably in his seventies leaned over from the aisle next to ours. He thumbed toward the parking lot.

"I got a five speed with a fat wooden gear shifter. I can park it around back if you want."

The next morning, I was the first one down at the free hotel breakfast. I scooped some eggs onto my plate and added a sausage patty before making some toast. Since it was only six thirty, I had the small dining room all to myself. I sat staring at the TV mounted on the wall and pushed my eggs around mindlessly with my fork, lost in thought.

Things between Milo and me had gotten weird after my gas station confession. He'd laughed off my outburst before we drove another two-and-a-half hours and checked into the hotel, but the awkwardness that had set in had never been there before, not even the first day we met.

At almost seven, I went to get a second cup of coffee, and when I turned around to walk back to the dining room, Milo was sitting at my table.

"How did you get in here without me seeing you?"

He sipped a cup of coffee. "A herd of elephants could've come through, and you wouldn't have noticed them. You were staring at the TV like you were waiting for it to give you the answer to all of life's important questions."

I sighed and sat down across from him. "Yeah. I guess I was lost in my head."

He drank more coffee and looked at me over the rim of the cup. "You want to talk about it?"

"What?"

"Whatever is on your mind?"

I frowned. "No...not really."

Milo's eyes roamed my face. "Okay. How about if I talk about a problem that's been on my mind instead?"

I shrugged. "Sure. Of course. What's up?"

"Well, I met this beautiful woman."

I felt a pang of jealousy in my chest. He met a woman? When? Last night?

Milo smiled and looked down at my coffee on the table. "You can loosen your grip on that cup. It's not what you're thinking."

My brows furrowed. "I'm confused. Who did you meet?"

"I met an amazing woman. She's adventurous and gorgeous. And has a spitfire personality that matches her fiery red hair."

Oh. *Oh!* I smiled. "She sounds pretty awesome."

He chuckled. "She is. I sort of love everything about her...except one thing."

My smile fell. "What's that?"

"She just got out of a long relationship where she was hurt. It's left her in a pretty vulnerable state. Because of that, I need to be a friend instead of pushing to a place we could both *really use* visiting right now." He paused and searched my eyes. "You see, I really like her, and I don't want her to regret me later."

I closed my eyes and nodded. "I get it."

Milo reached out and took my hands in his. "Do you, Mads? Because I don't want you to think me keeping my distance after what you told me last night at that gas station has anything to do with not wanting you."

I shook my head, looking down, though I still felt weird about what I'd admitted. "Okay."

Milo lifted my chin. "You're completely, out-of-my-league gorgeous, and your ex is a giant fucking idiot for not locking you down. I would love nothing more than to be with you, be inside you, Maddie. You have no idea how many times I've fantasized about it since the minute we met. But using sex to get over your relationship is like doing shots to get over your hangover. The only way to truly feel better is to keep off the sauce for a while so you can see things clearly again." He paused, and his eyes dropped to my lips. "Don't mistake me trying to do the right thing for not wanting to do all the wrong things to you."

I smiled sadly. "You're really a good guy, Milo Hooker."

He winked. "That's because our mother raised us right."

"I'm sorry." The hotel clerk shook her head. "We're completely booked. There are two big conventions in town this weekend."

"Yeah, we heard," Milo said. "Thanks anyway."

That was the third hotel we'd dragged our luggage to after parking the rental car at a lot in New Orleans. We walked away from the front desk still roomless. Milo lifted his chin to a bar in the lobby. "Why don't we have a drink and figure out our game plan?"

"That's a good idea. I'll check online for some nearby hotels."

At the bar, Milo ordered us two hurricanes and asked the bartender to point him to the men's room.

While he was gone, I pulled up a list of local hotels and started making some calls. The first two were sold out, but the third said they had two rooms left. They were both suites, though, and pretty expensive, so I figured I'd check with my partner in crime when he came back before booking anything.

"There's a hotel about three blocks away, on the corner of Bourbon and Orleans, that has two suites available. But they're a little over three hundred a night, plus tax. It's sort of steep, so I didn't book it yet."

Milo straddled the barstool and picked up his hurricane. "I think anything available is going to be expensive. I'm okay with it, if you are. We can just stay the one night."

I nodded. "Yeah, it's fine with me. Let me give them a call back."

"Why don't we take our drinks and walk over?"

"Take our drinks? Like, out on the street?"

"Yeah. Everyone does it here. That's why they gave us these plastic glasses. It's not like the Northeast where you can't walk around with alcohol. Walking around with alcohol is part of the charm of this city."

"Okay!"

Milo and I walked to the Bourbon Orleans Hotel drinking our hurricanes. Even though they were pretty big cups, I'd guzzled mine down, since it tasted like candy and I'd been thirsty. It had gone straight to my head.

"What's in these things?"

"I should have warned you to be careful. They're loaded with rum, but the grenadine makes it taste like there isn't any alcohol in them."

"Wow. Yeah. I'm a little buzzed from just the one."

The doorman at the Bourbon Orleans welcomed us and opened the door. Milo and I walked straight to the front desk.

"Hi. I just called a few minutes ago to see if you have any rooms available. We'd like the two suites, please."

The woman shook her head. "I'm sorry. I just reserved one over the phone two minutes ago. So I only have one suite left. It's a busy weekend for conventions."

"Oh. Shoot."

She looked back and forth at Milo and me. "Our suites are one bedroom, but they do have a pullout couch, if that might work for you." Before we could discuss it any further, the front desk phone rang. "Excuse me for just a moment, please." The hotel clerk stepped away, leaving Milo and me standing there.

"What do you think?" I asked. "Would it be weird if we shared a suite? It has a separate bedroom."

Milo looked as hesitant as I felt. His eyes dropped, and he did a quick sweep over my body before raking a hand through his hair with a laugh. "Does the bedroom door have a strong lock?"

The woman came back. "I'm sorry, I have someone on the phone who wants to book that last suite. You guys are here in person, so if you're going to take it, I'll let her know it's not available."

I looked at Milo. "What should we do? This is the fourth hotel we've called or stopped at. And it looks really nice. I can take the couch, and you can have the bedroom, if you're okay with sharing."

He shook his head. "No. You'll take the bedroom. And barricade yourself inside if we have too much to drink."

The French Quarter is an interesting place. At a tiny restaurant that only seated about ten people, Milo and I shared amazing jambalaya for two, and then we hit a few small bars with live music. Strolling down bustling Bourbon Street, an older woman wearing a flowy black dress and colorful headdress with gray dreadlocks sticking out stepped in front of Milo.

She took his hand. "I'll do you for free."

I laughed. "Sounds like an opportunity you shouldn't pass up."

The woman turned to face me. She closed her eyes and held her hands in the air. "You've been scorned. But you don't need to be so lonely."

I blinked a few times. "Excuse me?"

Milo laughed this time. He pointed to the sign on the building next to us. *Psychic and Chakra Balancing.*

"I'm thinking she works there."

The woman nodded. "I am Zara." She waved her hand around in my direction. "And you are dimming your aura. Come inside. Let me read your cards. Special for you tonight, only twenty dollars."

I scoffed. "You just told him you'd do him for free."

The woman looked Milo up and down. "His aura is very vibrant. Very red. He's passionate." She winked. "Very sexy, too."

"So let me get this straight, he's vibrant red and free, and I'm dark and twenty bucks?"

The woman shrugged. "Even psychics need to make a living, honey."

I chuckled. "I think I'll pass." I started to walk away, but Milo grabbed my elbow and stopped me.

"Not so fast." He looked at Zara. "Can you see the future?"

She nodded with an indignant look on her face. "Of course."

Milo scratched the scruff on his chin. "Twenty bucks, huh? Might be worth it to find out where we're going next." He dug into his pocket. "You know what, we'll take it."

I laughed. "You're really going to pay her to read your cards?"

He grinned. "Nope. She's going to read yours."

Chapter 10

Matteo

Incense filled the air inside Zara's little den. It reminded me of how my college dorm room used to smell. Tapestries in various colors hung along the walls. And a furry cat meowed from the corner of the room.

We took our seats across from her. *This is going to be good.* Maddie and I watched as our fortuneteller dealt the cards in front of her, then arranged them on the table.

"Your names?" she asked.

Maddie looked at me, then back at Zara. "I'm Maddie, and this is my brother, Milo."

If this lady could really read people, wouldn't she be able to figure out that our names weren't legit—or that we weren't brother and sister? Something to ponder.

Zara flipped over three cards in a row. One of them featured a woman with wings, and another had an evil-looking man on it. The last image was hard to make out, but there was a gigantic sun in the background.

She pushed her dreadlocks behind her back. "This three-card spread is known as The Three Fates. The first card represents the past, the second signifies the present, and the third, the future."

Maddie looked nervous as she licked her lips. "Alright."

Zara ran her fingers over the first card. "You were very adventurous in the past, yes? I don't sense that's the case so much now. What happened?"

Maddie looked over at me, seeming a little freaked out. "I lost my way," she said. "But I'm in the midst of an adventure as we speak. So trying to rectify that."

Zara moved to the second card. "This card represents indecisiveness. You're experiencing a lot of uncertainty right now when it comes to your personal relationships." Zara looked up. "Is this making sense to you?"

She nodded. "Yes. Very much so."

Zara's hand touched over the third card. She seemed to contemplate the meaning as she scratched her chin and said, "Ohhh."

Maddie leaned in, looking worried. "What?"

"This card on the right here, which represents the future, is showing me conflict. A big conflict. Something is looming, and it could be soon. You need to be wary."

Is she serious? This seemed like bullshit to me. Any one of her statements could be applied to some aspect of a person's life. I could take those same things and apply them to myself.

I felt the need to say something. "With all due respect, how is she supposed to believe that any of this holds significance? I mean, everything you just said is very generic."

Zara narrowed her eyes at me. "I am merely reading what I am seeing. The cards are meant to act as visual cues to help me understand the energy surrounding her. I can't help that the information seems generic to you. I'm the messenger, and *she* needs to figure out how it applies to her."

"So you can't tell me anything more about this... conflict?" Maddie asked.

Closing her eyes, Zara took Maddie's hands. "Listen...there's someone you know...who's not who you think he is."

A look of alarm crossed Maddie's face. "What?"

"His name begins with M." Zara closed her eyes again and paused. "I'm getting the name Matthew or something similar sounding."

I gulped.

She said Matthew—not Matteo. Relax.

Then Maddie took things in a whole different direction when she announced, "Well, my father's name is Matthew. Is something going on with him?"

No, no, it isn't, Maddie. Because Zara's probably referring to me.

"I'm not getting a father energy. But if your father is Matthew, then perhaps this complication could pertain to him."

I wasn't about to offer up that Zara could have been warning Maddie about *me*. First off, I had no clue what "not who you think he is" even meant. The Matthew thing could've been a coincidence, too. The bottom line was that Maddie and I hadn't exchanged our real names, and it would've been really fucking weird to suddenly announce mine under these circumstances. So I was going to stick with my gut. And it was telling me to shut up and not interfere in this crazy shit.

"The future is not always written," Zara said. "It's fluid and can be changed based on the decisions you make. So just be forewarned when it comes to Matthew. I'm sorry. I'm not seeing anything else that can guide you in this area."

Maddie looked tormented. "Okay. I will." She turned to me and whispered, "I think I'll call my dad soon, maybe remind him to go for his physical if he hasn't already."

I nodded. "Good idea. Can't hurt."

"Watch out for the birds," Zara added.

Maddie squinted. "The birds?"

"Yes."

"What do you mean?"

"I can't be sure. I just received a visual cue that prompted me to warn you. I can't always know what the messages mean, just that they are there and seem to be meant for you."

She sighed. "So, Matthew and birds. Great. Okay."

Zara suddenly placed her hands on her temples. "Okay...this is unusual."

Maddie looked alarmed. "What?"

I was starting to regret bringing her in here.

"Someone is coming through. This doesn't always happen, but it's happening now. Now that she's here, I likely won't be able to get rid of her."

Maddie glanced over at me, then back at Zara. "Someone? Coming through? What does that mean?"

"I'm clairvoyant as well. I don't sell those services, as I typically don't enjoy being a mediator for the dead. But occasionally a spirit can be pesky. This girl is definitely pesky—and loud." She paused for a long time. "She wants the man to know that when he was singing the other night, she was with him."

I got chills. My eyes, which had been focused on the cards still strewn about the table, flew up to meet Zara's stare.

I froze.

It can't be. I wanted it so badly...but it couldn't be her.

"Is there a Z name that means something to you?" she asked.

Holy shit.

"Yes," I answered.

She nodded. "Yeah. She's showing me a Z." Zara closed her eyes. "And David Bowie." She laughed. "Why is she showing me David Bowie?"

Z

Bowie.

Zoe.

"Because her name is Zoe," I said softly.

Maddie's mouth dropped.

"She's also showing me lots of snow. Does that have meaning to you?"

Speechless, I nodded. My heart began to pound faster.

Maddie placed her hand on my knee. I couldn't see her face because my eyes were still on Zara. I waited with bated breath to see what she would come out with next.

Zara cocked her head to the side. "Did she die in a ski accident?"

I let out a long, shaky breath. "Yes."

"She says you suspect this already, but she wants to confirm that she wasn't in any pain when it happened—not even for a split second."

Relief coursed through my veins. That's what I'd always figured, but I appreciated that confirmation.

Then, to my shock, Zara started to cry.

She wiped tears from her eyes. "I'm sorry. I hate when this happens. But sometimes a spirit makes me cry when they get emotional. Their feelings manifest through me. This is why I don't like doing this."

A tear fell down my cheek. I couldn't remember the last time I'd let that happen, especially in front of people. But I couldn't help it. If this was Zoe coming through—and it seemed it was—it was the most amazing thing I'd ever experienced. My emotions were all over the place: happy and sad, relieved and scared, all at once.

"She's making me cry because she's so sad that you blame yourself. She says what happened with her could not have been stopped, that it was her time to go. Her story was written that way. So even if you had done something different or tried to stop her, she would have left this Earth anyway. She needs you to understand that what happened wasn't your fault."

I had to take a moment to grab my bearings. With my face in my hands, I let those words sink in.

"Do you understand that?" Zara asked.

I looked up. My lip trembled as I nodded silently while Maddie squeezed my knee.

I had always blamed myself for Zoe's death, because I'd let her ski the double- black-diamond trail with me, even though it was too advanced for her. To this day, I'd still been ruminating about the what-ifs. If only I'd told her not to come with me, she'd still be here.

"Wow. She's passionate. She really loved you," Zara said.

And with that, I could feel more tears forming.

She smiled. "Ah...she's playing music. Was that an important part of her life? Was she a musician?"

I wiped my eyes. "Yes. She was."

Zara nodded to herself a few times as she concentrated. "She wants you to know that you have no choice but to move on, and that it's okay to do so, alright? That's why she came through today. She needs you to know that."

There was a long moment of silence.

What felt like a couple of minutes passed before I finally asked, "Is she gone?"

"I haven't been able to figure out her last message. She's showing me hazelnuts. Do you understand what that means?"

Hazelnuts?

After several seconds of reaching for meaning in that, I shook my head. "Not in the least."

Maddie looked between Zara and me.

"Sometimes a spirit sends me messages auditorily and sometimes through images that might sound like certain words they are trying to convey. Perhaps I'm misinterpreting what she's showing me. But I believe the image is hazelnuts."

I sighed. "Okay."

Maddie looked utterly freaked out. This had to have been too much for her. It was supposed to have been in good fun. Instead, we got more than we bargained for; we got a séance.

But for me? It was a gift. To hear Zoe tell me that what happened wasn't my fault and couldn't have been stopped was something I would only have believed coming from her. And it seemed it *did* come from her. At least at this point, I had to believe it was real.

"Anything else?" I asked.

Zara's eyes moved back and forth. "No. I think she's gone."

I exhaled, feeling a bit sad that Zoe had left, but also relieved. Anticipating the messages had been intense.

Zara reached into her pocket for her phone and checked the time. "We are actually ten minutes past your allotted time. I hope you've found this reading helpful."

I stood up. "You can't even imagine. Thank you for going outside of the box to let me hear Zoe's message."

She smiled. "She gave me very little choice."

Maddie stood up, and we headed out the door together.

The mood was completely weird as we walked in silence down the road.

"That was intense." Maddie put her hand on my shoulder. "Are you okay?"

I blew out a long breath. "That was... I don't even know what to say."

"It was amazing. Totally and utterly amazing. And meant to be, Milo. So meant to be. We were meant to find this place so Zoe could get that message to you. In fact, that might have been the universe's entire reason for this trip. We were brought together to find this place, to find Zara, and to get Zoe's message."

That was wild. I was starting to get emotional again. Seeing as though I'd done enough crying for one damn day, I tried to lighten the mood.

I wrapped my hand around her back. "So you mean to tell me we've gone to a sex party, bought godawful boots, and you've been caught talking in public about masturbating all so I could hear from Zoe?"

"Yes!" She laughed. "Yes! That's exactly what I'm saying."

"You might be right." I smiled. "I wish I knew what the hazelnut thing was about, though."

She stared off for a moment. "Well, if it really does mean something, and you're meant to figure it out, I suppose you will in time."

I nodded and ruffled her hair. "This day has been way too crazy. We need to do something chill. Where should we go tonight?"

"To be honest, I'm sort of bushed. I kind of just want to go back to the room."

Shit. I was hoping we could avoid having to be alone in that room a little while longer. But what was the point of putting it off? We had to go there eventually.

"Alright. Sounds good. Want to grab some food and take it back?"

She rubbed her stomach. "I'm still full from that jambalaya earlier."

"Yeah. I'm not too hungry either."

Not for food anyway.

But I'll keep that to myself.

"Although..." she said.

"What?"

She grinned. "I could go for some ice cream."

"Ice cream sounds really good."

We ended up finding a little ice cream shop within walking distance. I got a double scoop of chocolate chip with chocolate sprinkles while Maddie opted for a single scoop of cherry.

As we walked in the direction of our hotel, the sun was setting. It was a gorgeous, breezy evening. I was still thinking about everything that happened over at Zara's. Somehow I could feel Zoe's presence with me now, when it had seemed so out of reach before today. I had no doubt she'd been guiding this journey. Although, how did Maddie play into it? It was kind of weird to think

Zoe might've orchestrated my meeting another woman. Maybe I was reading into it too much.

My thoughts were interrupted when Maddie screamed. It took me a few seconds to figure out what was happening. A pigeon had landed on top of her ice cream cone. It flapped its wings and proceeded to take a big chunk of the ice cream into its beak.

Then it flew away.

"What the hell was that?" she asked.

I was too busy laughing to answer.

Then it hit me. "Don't say Zara didn't warn you about birds."

Chapter 11

Hazel

As soon as I locked myself in the bathroom, I breathed a sigh of relief. It was the first time I'd been alone in a while. Though I loved being joined at the hip with Milo, sometimes I needed to process my thoughts without him being able to read them all over my face.

I turned on the shower and got in. As the water rained down, I thought about what had happened today. Zoe's coming through was one of the most incredible things I'd ever experienced—not only because it helped prove there was something out there beyond this life, but because it served as a reminder of the kind of love that transcends this universe. Milo and Zoe's love had been authentic and based on respect. Milo wouldn't have done to her what Brady did to me.

On the other side of the coin, what happened to Zoe was a reminder that life was short. We may not have forever to forgive the ones we cared about. Did that mean giving Brady a second chance was something I should consider? And then there was Zara's warning about a conflict and the name Matthew... I reminded myself to call my dad tomorrow from the road.

After about a half hour, there was a knock at the door. Then Milo's voice registered.

"You still alive in there?"

Shit. I had been in here a long time.

Shutting off the water, I yelled, "I'm fine." I squeezed out my hair. "Just got a little carried away."

"Don't stop on my account. Just making sure you're okay."

Maybe subconsciously I'd been taking my sweet time in here to avoid being alone with Milo. He'd looked so sexy when he emerged from the shower earlier. I'd only gotten a quick glimpse of his wet, shirtless body as he walked past my room in our suite with a towel wrapped around his waist. I knew it was going to be hard to avoid wanting to be near him tonight. How I would love to cuddle next to him, at the very least. Falling asleep next to Milo tonight sounded really good. But I was certain that would lead to other things, so it had to remain a fantasy.

After I dried off and slipped into my cami and sleep shorts, I found my small tub of facial mask. It was the kind you rubbed over your face and slept with all night. That could be my armor, an additional layer of protection. No one can get frisky with green muck on their face, right?

I tied my hair up and began spreading the mask over my face. It quickly hardened. When I looked at myself in the mirror, I saw some kind of monster. *Perfect.*

After I opened the door and walked out into the common area, Milo's eyes widened.

"That's a good look, Mads."

"Well, thank you. I figured since we're bunking together tonight, why not show you what happens behind closed doors?" I teased. "I don't wake up looking like I do, you know. It's hard work."

"And here I was thinking you were just naturally gorgeous."

His words heated my body.

"I'm surprised you put a shirt on before I had a chance to admire you this time," I joked.

"Yeah, well..." He sighed and put his legs up on the ottoman. "You have nowhere to run tonight, so I figured it wouldn't be fair." He winked.

"Thanks for sparing me." I sat down on the far end of the couch, away from him. "How are you feeling?"

He turned to me. "You mean because of Zoe?"

"Yeah. I haven't been able to stop thinking about that whole thing. I can only imagine what you're feeling."

He rested his head back and stared up at the ceiling. "It was surreal. I never imagined something like that could happen. It definitely brought me a sense of peace. I'm not sure how Zara could have been making all of that up. If it were just one thing, I'd still have doubts, but the name, the skiing accident reference, and the fact that Zoe said she was with me when I was singing the other night? All those things? Too much to be a coincidence. And believe me, I was the biggest skeptic about this kind of stuff before today."

"I totally agree. I might have thought the same thing, that it was all baloney. But what happened today seemed real as could be. And that's beautiful."

"Thank you for going along with my crazy idea to go in there. Otherwise, it might never have happened."

He reached toward me. I took his hand, and our fingers intertwined. I knew it wasn't meant to lead to anything. It was just a kind gesture, his thanks for my support. But the contact sent shockwaves through my body.

I instinctively let go. "Well...no need to thank me," I said. "That's what I'm here for, to go along with your crazy ideas. Some of them just happen to lead to beautiful things." I smiled. "Speaking of which, any idea where we're headed next?"

"Let's see what we feel like tomorrow. I think hanging out here another day might be fun. I'm nowhere near done with seeing this city. You?"

I nodded. "I don't think I'm ready to leave yet either."

"Good." Milo got up. "Hang on. Be right back." He headed for the bathroom.

I turned on the TV and settled into the couch. Milo took a while to come back.

When he returned, I did a double take. His face was green—just like mine. He'd put on my face mask.

"What did you do?"

"I wanted to see what all the hype was about."

I cackled. "And?"

"I can no longer feel my cheeks. How can this be good?"

"It's busy doing its job, sucking out all of the clogged pores."

He returned to his seat at the other end of the sofa. "That's not its only job, though, right?"

"What do you mean?"

"If you think putting that shit all over your face makes me want to kiss you any less, you're wrong. Nice try, though."

Well, good thing my face was covered in mud, because I'm sure I was turning red underneath.

We were both quiet for a while after that. Eventually I took a deep breath. "You said you were keeping your distance because using sex to get over a relationship wasn't healthy, and I agree with you. But did you ever wonder...what if? What if you met the right person at the wrong time? All along, the two of us have been thinking we met to help each other move on. But what if we met for another reason?"

I watched Milo's Adam's apple bob up and down. "Like what?"

"Maybe...we met because..." I laughed nervously. "This is probably stupid, but what if the reason we met wasn't just to help each other move on, but because we're supposed to be together?"

My gaze caught with Milo's, and we shared the most intimate moment. It felt like we were in a tunnel, just the two of us. I couldn't see or hear anything but him.

"I would love for that to be true. You're an amazing woman, Maddie, on the inside and the outside, and I'm freaking crazy about you. But can you honestly tell me you didn't think about your ex at all today?"

The hopeful smile I'd been wearing wilted, and I shut my eyes. I shook my head. "I get it. I haven't fully ended the last chapter of my life, so it's not the right time to start writing a new story."

He nodded. "That doesn't mean what you said isn't true, though. Maybe we are supposed to be together. I think it's very possible to meet the right person at the wrong time. In fact, that would be just my damn luck." He looked away for a while and then turned back. "I have an idea."

"What?"

"What if we book this hotel for three months from today? We'll both go back home and fall into our lives. Ninety days from today, if you're not thinking about him anymore, get your ass on a plane and meet me right here." He tapped his hand on the couch. "Right here, just like tonight—except maybe without the green shit on our faces and a fuck of a lot less clothes."

I smiled and felt the mud mask on my face crack. "I love that idea."

"Good." Milo reached out and weaved his fingers with mine. "Then we have a deal."

The next morning, Milo was gone when I woke up. Panic came over me when I opened the bedroom door and found the living room empty. I walked around the room feeling really damn anxious until I saw his bag tucked away behind the couch. I let out a big sigh of relief and went to splash some water on my face to calm down. I'd just finished brushing my teeth in the bathroom when the sound of the door clanking open and closed in the other room caught my attention.

"Milo?" I called.

"Yes, dear."

I smiled and finished my morning routine. When I walked out, I found Milo with his feet propped up on the coffee table and a giant cup of coffee in his hand. He leaned forward and lifted a second cup. "For you, sis."

"Thank you." I plopped down on the couch and tucked my legs underneath me. Peeling back the plastic tab on the cup, I said, "You were up early this morning."

He nodded. "I had a few things on my mind that I needed to get done."

I sipped. "Like what?"

Milo pulled some folded-up papers out of his back pocket. "Well, for starters, I talked to the front desk about extending our room for another night. They said no problem. I also got us tickets to the hop-on-hop-off tour bus. You know the big, red double decker you see around town?"

"Oh. Okay. That sounds like fun."

"I walked over to the tourism office a few blocks away and asked if they knew any good areas to take pictures. The woman I spoke to happened to be into photography as a hobby." He unfolded a map. "She circled a bunch of places she thought you might like. Most of them are not too far from different stops along the bus-tour route."

"That was really thoughtful. Thank you. I can't wait to check out the city some more. But what about you? If we're doing an afternoon of photography for me, we should do something you like to do, too."

Milo wiggled his brows. "We'll do that when we're back here in three months."

I laughed. "I'm serious. This is both of our adventure."

"I did make some plans for me, too. On my way home from getting the coffees, I passed a bar that had a sign hanging in the window about an open mic night tonight. So I signed up."

"You're going to sing again?"

He smiled. "I am. As much as I enjoyed our duet, I think it's time I got up there on my own. It's been a long time coming."

I smiled. "You're full of shit that you enjoyed our duet. But that's okay. I'm excited you're going to sing again. Sounds like you had a productive morning while my lazy ass was in bed."

"I made one other plan for us."

"What's that?"

He locked eyes with me. "I booked a room for us, three months from today."

My heart started to race. "Oh wow! That's so exciting. What's the date?"

"You're never going to believe it. I had to count ninety days from today three times to make sure I'd gotten it right."

"Why? What's the date?"

Milo deadpanned. "Valentine's Day."

"Oh my God!" I clapped my hands together. "That's totally perfect."

"I thought so, too. Unless of course you stand me up in three months. Then that would be just sad."

"Valentine's Day. It's…" I shook my head. "It's…I don't even have words for what it is."

Milo smiled sheepishly. "I do. Too damn far away."

"If we get off in the Garden District…" Milo held up the city map he'd picked up this morning at the visitors' center and pointed to an area. "The woman said there are a lot of places to take pictures. There's a neighborhood with big, old Victorian mansions, and she said there are a few cemeteries people like to photograph in, too."

"Ooooh. That sounds good. I was looking at the welcome book in the hotel yesterday and saw some pictures of those mansions, and I love cemeteries."

After two more stops, we hopped off the bus and walked a few minutes through the Garden District. The area was gorgeous. Lots of ornate period homes with tall oak canopies draping over the streets and colorful hibiscus and crepe myrtle dotting manicured lawns. Some of the mansions had plaques outside, and the houses dated back almost two-hundred years. I could feel the history as we walked around.

"When I was a kid, I wanted a Victorian dollhouse more than anything," I said. "It was the first item at the top on my Christmas list from ages five to eleven."

"Oh yeah? Did you finally get one?"

I shook my head. "My parents didn't buy me large or fragile toys because we'd have to leave them behind when we moved. I mentioned it to my ex once, though, and he bought one of those kits to make me one. It was actually really sweet."

"He bought one of those kits? Did he build it for you?"

"No. But I guess it's the thought that counts."

Milo made a face. "Anyone can swipe their credit card to buy something, Mads."

"I know. But..." I shrugged. "Whatever."

I realized it had been dumb of me to bring up Brady. Yet again, I'd proven Milo's point that I still thought about him. I guess I had three months to stop that from happening. A change of subject was definitely in order.

Looking around at all the beautiful architecture had me wondering what type of lifestyle Milo led at home. "Do you live in an apartment building or a house back in Seattle?"

"An apartment. It's a two-story walk up."

"What does your living room look like?"

Milo's forehead wrinkled. "My living room? What do you mean? It's square. Has a couch and some other furniture, I guess."

"What's on the walls?"

"On the walls?"

"Yeah. Like, what kind of art do you have hanging?"

He seemed to give it some thought. "I don't have anything on the walls."

"Nothing at all? How come?"

He shrugged. "I don't know. I guess I never thought of my living there as permanent."

We stopped in front of a stunning Victorian home. The entire house was whitewashed in a soft yellow with tons of ornamental blue trim. An old man sat on a rocking chair on the wraparound porch.

I waved and called to him. "Your home is beautiful. Would it be okay if I took some pictures of it?"

"Help yourself. What's the point of beauty if you don't share it with others?"

I smiled. "Thank you."

While I snapped pictures, Milo must've been doing some thinking.

"What does your living room look like?" he asked.

I finished shooting and lowered my lens. "The usual—a couch, love seat, coffee table, area rug, and sixty-eight framed photos of smiles on the wall."

Milo chuckled. "You have sixty-eight framed photos of smiles?"

"I do."

"Not whole faces? Just smiles?"

"Yup. They're all black and white, and I cropped in on the smiles. Each one is framed in matte black."

"Who do the smiles belong to?"

I shrugged. "All different people. Some adults, some kids. Mostly people I don't know. I honestly don't even remember what the rest of the face looks like on some of them. I took them over the last fifteen years at various places."

"Do you have a favorite?"

"I do, actually." I laughed. "How did you know that?"

Milo flashed a crooked smile. "Just a hunch. What's it look like? Your favorite smile, I mean."

"It's a little girl I shot while on assignment years ago. I was covering a Jonas Brothers concert, during the first time they were popular. She must've been about five or six. When the concert started and the three brothers walked out on stage, she started to cry. She was really sobbing, yet she had the biggest smile on her face. Tears were streaming down her cheeks, but her smile was big enough to count all of her little teeth. I've never been so happy I cried like that, and I find the photo inspirational." She sighed. "What about you? Have you ever cried and smiled at the same time?"

We started walking again, and Milo shook his head. "Not that I can recall. What else is in your living room? Do you have any family pictures on display?"

I shook my head. "No, I don't."

"Growing up," he said, "my parents always had a ton of family photos hanging on the wall."

"We didn't have any. Oddly enough—since I'm a photographer—my parents weren't big on taking photos. And they definitely didn't decorate any of the places we rented. The house I'm in now is the first place I've ever lived that has any sort of personality."

"So, let me get this straight." Milo rubbed his bottom lip with his thumb. "I grew up with family photos all over the place, and my walls are now bare because I don't feel like where I am is permanent. And you, on the other hand, grew up with empty walls and have plastered your place with photos for the first time in your life. We were definitely in pretty different places a few months ago, huh?"

I smiled sadly. "I guess so."

Milo stopped walking. "Hold up for a minute. Get your camera back out."

I looked around while unzipping my bag. We were still in the pretty Garden District, but I wasn't sure what, in particular, I was supposed to be taking a picture of. "What am I photographing?"

Milo dragged a hand through his hair and stood taller. "Me."

I laughed. "You?"

"Yeah. I want to be on your wall."

I lifted my camera, still chuckling. "Okay, crazy man. Smile pretty."

He held up a hand up. "Wait. Give me a few seconds. I want to think of something good so you capture the right smile."

Milo looked away for a moment. Then he turned back and flashed the sexiest damn grin I'd ever seen. "I'm ready now."

"Do I even want to know what you're thinking about with that devilish smile?"

"Probably not. But I'll tell you what, in ninety days, I'll *show* you what I was thinking about."

Oh my.

I snapped more pictures than necessary, glad to hide my blush behind the camera. "All done."

Milo winked. "That's number sixty-nine."

131

I laughed. "I do currently have sixty-eight photos hanging, so I guess you're correct."

He leaned down and kissed my cheek, then moved his mouth to my ear. "Wasn't talking about the number of photos on your wall. That's what I was thinking about when I smiled for your photo."

Chapter 12

Matteo

I must be out of my damn mind.

Maddie walked out from the bedroom wearing a bright green dress. It didn't have a plunging neckline or almost show the cheeks of her ass, yet it was the sexiest thing I'd ever seen. She looked Drop. Dead. Gorgeous.

Why did I keep telling this woman having sex wouldn't be a good idea? At the moment, I was thinking there had never been a more brilliant plan in the world.

I shook my head and blew out an audible, jagged breath. "You look...that dress... Wow, Mads, just wow."

She looked down, as if she had to remember what she had on. "Oh. Thank you."

"You ready? We should probably get going." *Because a man only has so much willpower.*

She picked up her purse. "I am. I'm excited to watch you sing. When we were up on stage together, it was kind of surreal, and I didn't get to enjoy your performance fully. How many songs do you get to do?"

"Usually it's three songs or fifteen minutes, whichever comes first. But I didn't ask the rules when I signed up this morning, so I'm not actually sure."

"Do you know what you're going to sing?"

"I have an idea, yeah."

She tilted her head. "Well, what are the songs?"

I tucked my wallet into my back pocket. "I can't tell you. It's bad luck."

Of course I was full of shit and just made that up. But Maddie bought it.

"Oh. Okay. Well, whatever it is, I'm sure I'll love it."

Out on Bourbon Street, the nightly party seemed to have already started. The streets were filled with people drinking and different music blared from each bar we passed. When I caught the second guy checking Maddie out, I started to feel a little possessive and grabbed her hand.

She looked over with a questioning face, though she didn't try to pull away.

"You're attracting a lot of attention in that dress," I explained. "Not that my holding your hand will keep 'em from looking, but it should prevent the drunk, aggressive assholes from approaching."

Maddie tilted her head with a coy smile. "What if I want to be approached?"

"Approached by who?"

She looked around. A big, muscular guy wearing a tank top and jeans leaned against a stool outside a bar. His hair was slicked back, and he had his arms folded across his enormous chest. He must've been the bouncer.

"Him," she said. "He's not bad looking."

"You want that juice head to hit on you?"

She shrugged. "Maybe."

I felt my blood pump faster at the thought. "What the hell for?"

"Well, a woman has needs."

"And you want that guy to take care of those needs for you?"

"Maybe not him. I don't know. I'm just saying."

"Saying what?"

She shook her head. "I don't know. Forget I even said anything."

"Ummm... You just told me you might not want me to hold your hand so you can pick up some random guy off the street. Considering you'd be bringing him back to a room we're currently sharing, I think forgetting might be a problem."

"Jeez. I was just teasing. Relax, Milo."

I scratched the day-old scruff on my chin. "Just teasing, huh?"

Maddie nodded.

"Alright." I looked around. It didn't take more than a few seconds to find a woman with a lot of skin showing. We were in the Big Easy, after all. Dropping Maddie's hand, I said, "Do you mind if I go talk to that woman?"

Maddie's forehead wrinkled. "Who?"

I lifted my chin to point out the scantily clad blonde. She had double Ds, at least. "Her."

Maddie's eyes narrowed. "Is that your type?"

"Depends on what I'm shopping for."

Her lips pursed. "Well, maybe I should just go home if you're out shopping."

I chuckled and grabbed her hand again. Tugging her close, I said, "Not a good feeling, is it? Thinking of me picking up some stranger?"

She pouted. "No, it's not."

"Good. Because I'd much prefer to hold your hand and go home and sleep on the couch than bring someone who isn't you home with me anyway."

Maddie's face softened. She leaned her head on my shoulder as we walked. "You know the right things to say to a woman."

I leaned down and kissed her forehead just as we arrived in front of the bar for open mic night. "This is the place."

A bunch of people were milling around out front smoking cigarettes...or weed. I was certain I smelled marijuana mixed in with the tobacco. One of them was Druker, the guy I'd signed up with this morning.

He lifted his chin as I walked us over. "Hey, what's up, man?"

"Not much. Excited to get on stage tonight. I know you said there'd be a piano available to play, but any chance there's a guitar laying around I could borrow for my set, too?"

He tossed the remnants of a cigarette on the ground and covered it with his foot to put it out. "I'm sure I can rustle one up. You want acoustic or electric?"

"Acoustic."

"Give me ten minutes."

"Awesome. Thanks."

Inside, Maddie and I found a booth off to the side of the stage.

"So you're going to play guitar, too?"

"If they can find me one, yeah."

"Do you play any other instruments?"

I smiled. "Well, I'm a music teacher, so I know how to play most of them. But guitar is my instrument of choice."

"I've always wanted to learn how to play."

"I can teach you, if you want."

She smiled. "I'd like that."

"What do you want to drink? Your usual wine?"

"Yeah, that would be great."

"Be right back."

I went to the bar and ordered a beer for me and a glass of white wine for Maddie. When I came back, some old dude was sitting in my seat. Even though he had to be at least sixty, I felt a pang of jealousy.

Maddie smiled when I approached. "Milo, this is Fretty—with two Ts, not Freddy with two Ds."

I nodded. "Nice to meet you."

Fretty held his hands up. He had the raspy voice of a guy who had smoked two packs a day for forty years. "I wasn't trying to make time with your girl. Druker told me someone was looking to borrow a guitar. He said to find the prettiest girl in the room and give it to the lucky bastard by her side."

I winked at Maddie. "I guess it wasn't too hard to find me then."

Fretty stood. "I got an old Rosewood Martin, if you'd like to take her for a spin."

"Yeah. Incredible guitar. That would be great. Thanks."

He held up one finger. "I have one condition."

"What's that?"

"You let me play while you sing one of your songs." He reached up and touched his throat. "Damaged my cords and can't belt 'em out anymore. But I still love to get on stage."

"Sure. Of course. I picked out three songs. But if you don't know any of them, we can swap one out."

The old man smiled. "Trust me. I'll know 'em."

Maddie and I listened to four performers, all of which were pretty damn good, before the host called my name—well, he called Milo Hooker anyway.

I met Fretty at the host station, and we decided he was going to join me for my first song. So I got up on stage and walked over to the piano to play while Fretty took a seat toward the back with his guitar, out of the limelight.

"Good evening, everyone." I adjusted the microphone up a little. "My name is Milo. I'm going to play you a few songs. My buddy Fretty will be joining me for the first one. This song goes out to a very special Hooker in the audience tonight. It's a song I've sung for years, but tonight it seems to have new meaning for me. I hope you all enjoy it."

I stretched my fingers a few times before playing the first notes of Lenny Kravitz's "I'll Be Waiting." It wasn't really a song to get the crowd going, because most people weren't too familiar with it. But that wasn't what tonight was about. I finally felt like being on stage again, after four long years. To me, singing is an opportunity to say all the things most of us are too chicken shit to spout off in real life. Words are all puzzle pieces, and music clicks them into place to show the big picture. Pretty soon, I knew my time with Maddie would be coming to an end, and I wanted her to know how I was feeling. The lyrics started off explaining how a guy broke a woman's heart and she needed some time. But the chorus was all about how he'd be waiting for her to be ready.

When I was done, I looked up from behind the piano for the first time and found Maddie smiling wide, but she also had tears streaming down her face.

It made my heart so full. I pointed to my own smiling lips and traced imaginary tears down my cheeks. Her eyes widened when she caught on, and her smile grew bigger, if that were even possible.

If nothing else came out of what we'd started on this trip, I'd at least given her a souvenir to remember from New Orleans—the smile she'd longed to have from her favorite photo.

Chapter 13

Hazel

While Atlanta was supposed to be our next stop, the flashing lights of a carnival off the highway caught our attention somewhere in Alabama. And since our mantra was that we go wherever the wind takes us, it seemed the wind had a craving for funnel cakes.

And I did also.

Turns out the event was called the Applewood Fair. We'd already spent a few hours here, eating greasy food, playing games, and even enjoying a few of the rides. Milo and I acted like a couple of kids. I couldn't remember the last time I'd had so much fun. Well, yes, I could. Every moment spent with Milo was the last time I'd had fun.

I stuffed a piece of pink cotton candy into my mouth. "I think it's funny that we don't even know the name of the town we're in. Is Applewood the town or just the name of the fair?"

"Maybe we should ask someone." Milo tapped the shoulder of a woman in front of us. "Excuse me?"

She turned. "Yes?"

"What town is this?"

"You're in Bumford, son."

"Not Applewood?"

"No. Applewood is Rusty Applewood, the man who started this fair some fifty years ago."

He nodded. "Got it. Thank you."

"Did she say we're in Bumfuck?" I joked as the woman walked away.

"Basically. Bumford."

A little while later, the sun had gone down, and we'd pretty much had our fill of the carnival. I yawned. "It's getting late. Want to just find a place to crash here in Bumford tonight?"

"I don't mind driving, if you want to keep going toward Atlanta."

I shrugged. "Eh, I kind of just want to stay, if you don't mind?"

I was starting to fear the looming end of our adventure. If there was an opportunity to stall, I'd take it. Staying overnight here would mean an extra day in the end. It wasn't about Bumford. It was about getting to spend time with Milo.

I wasn't about to admit any of that, though, so I tried to come up with an alternate explanation. "This place reminds me of something out of a Hallmark movie. You know, the small town where the heroine always gets sent to by her corporate job to fix some problem or raise money. Then she falls in love with a Christmas tree farmer who drives a red truck, and she somehow ends up settling in the town at the end. This is that kind of place."

"Yeah. Of course I know exactly what you're talking about because I sit around watching Hallmark movies on the weekends." He snorted before stopping a man next to us. "Excuse me. Do you know of any nice place to stay in town?"

The man laughed. "Wyatt Manor."

Why did he laugh?

"That's a hotel?" Milo asked.

"A bed and breakfast." He pointed. "You'll see it about a mile down the road on the right." He smiled. But the look on his face seemed like he might have been kidding us.

After the guy walked away, I asked, "Why did he give us that look with the recommendation? Was that my imagination?"

Milo shook his head. "I don't know."

Hmm...

He gestured with his head toward the parking lot. "Wanna check it out?"

"Yeah. Sure. Always up for an adventure."

After only a few minutes, we arrived at our destination. We parked right in front of the property. There were no other cars in sight, so I wondered if we would be the only guests. It looked like a typical bed and breakfast from the outside—a yellow house surrounded by a series of large oak trees. A porch wrapped around the entire thing, and mounted to it was a sign that read *Wyatt Manor*.

We approached the front door, and Milo knocked.

An old man answered. "May I help you?" He looked to be in his nineties.

"Yes," Milo said. "We were told this is *the* place to stay in town. We were wondering if you had two rooms for the night."

The man's mouth hung open. "Who told you that?"

Milo pointed over his shoulder. "A...man at the carnival down the road?"

"Wow." The old guy's mouth curved into a huge smile. "Wish I could thank him. I haven't had a guest here in months. This is far from the most popular place in town." He stepped aside to make room for us to enter. "But come in. Please. My home is your home."

Milo and I exchanged suspicious looks before we stepped inside. I really wished we could have turned around and gone to a normal hotel, but I felt bad leaving now. The man seemed so happy to have us.

The interior of the house was dated, with dark wood paneling and furniture upholstered in mismatched floral patterns. There were clocks everywhere—cuckoo clocks, grandfather clocks—and also a plethora of figurines on shelves.

But perhaps most notable were the dead, stuffed animals hanging throughout the place. A deer, a fox... and one particularly scary-looking raccoon.

Milo's breath grazed my ear as he whispered, "Is this a dead-animal museum or a bed and breakfast? Say the word, and we can beat this joint."

"So, two rooms will be one-hundred eighty even," the man said.

Milo looked at me, and I shrugged, giving him the okay to pay for the rooms.

He reached into his pocket. "Do you take credit cards?"

"Sorry, no. Cash only." He grinned. "I'm Wyatt, by the way."

Milo opened his wallet and emptied it.

After the man took the cash, he asked, "What brings you two to Bumford?"

"Just passing through town on our way to Atlanta. We saw the fair off the highway and had to stop," I said.

"My wife used to work the ticket booth there years ago. She's been gone now five years."

I frowned. "I'm so sorry."

"It's okay. She's still with me." He walked over to one of the clocks. "See this time, one o'clock?"

I stopped in front of it. "Yes?"

He wandered over to another clock. "See this time? What does it say?"

"One o'clock as well."

He moved to the clock next to it. "What about this one?"

"One."

"My wife passed away at one o'clock on the dot. And wouldn't you know, every single one of these clocks, at some point in time, stopped at one o'clock and never moved again."

Wow. If he was telling the truth, that was certainly amazing.

"A lot of people, including my kids, think that's a bunch of malarkey. But I know the truth. I know it's my Bernadine. I just know it is."

Milo looked at me, and I knew exactly what he was thinking. Then he turned to Wyatt. "I might have been doubtful myself if it weren't for something that happened to me recently. But I definitely think your wife is still with you."

Chills raced through me.

Wyatt led us through the house for a little tour.

As we entered a second living area, I jumped at the sight of more dead animals. These weren't hung on the wall. They were standing on tables. *What the hell?* It

144

quickly became apparent that Wyatt's taxidermy hobby wasn't limited to just preserving animals. Apparently, it involved some theatrics, too. These animals were... dressed in clothing and posed.

What on Earth?

"What is all this?" I asked.

"Well, first of all, I want you to know that no animals were harmed. These guys all died accidentally or naturally. Same goes for my boys hanging up in the other room."

He walked over to three stuffed gray mice lined up on a table. They were wearing suits, ties, and sunglasses.

"Want to take a guess what this is called?"

"Three Blind Mice?" Milo answered.

Wyatt smiled. "Very good."

"They look more like rats," I whispered to Milo.

"What about this one?" Wyatt pointed to three stuffed cats. "The clue is on the ground." On the floor, there were several pairs of mittens by their feet.

Milo cleared his throat. "Uh, the three little kittens who lost their mittens—or whatever that one is called."

Wyatt snapped his fingers. "You got it!"

"Who knew you were an expert in nursery rhymes, Milo?" I laughed.

Wyatt went over to a single stuffed owl. "What about this guy?"

Neither of us knew the answer to that.

"A wise old owl," Wyatt finally said.

"What got you into this interesting hobby?" I asked.

"Well, since the Mrs. died, I have a lot of time on my hands. I always collected taxidermied animals, but I got the idea to create these scenes one day out of the blue. Started laughing to myself in the kitchen when it came to mind—even startled the cuckoo clocks. Now it's my favorite hobby."

This place definitely has its fair share of cuckoos.

He clapped his hands together. "Well, let me get y'all set up in your rooms."

We followed Wyatt upstairs. As weird as this house was, he took good care of it. A nice oriental runner lined the stairs leading to the second floor. I hoped he had some help cleaning this place. At his age, it couldn't be easy to vacuum these stairs.

He opened the doors to two adjacent bedrooms. Each had heavy floral wallpaper and a four-post bed. Other than the differences in color themes, they looked identical.

"You know, it's a shame you don't get more business," I said. "These rooms are really nice."

"From your mouth to their ears, darlin'." He walked to the top of the stairs. "I'll let you two be. How about you come downstairs for some stew in ten minutes?"

After the old man left, Milo and I faced each other in the second bedroom.

"Oh my God." I whispered. "We definitely walked into *The Twilight Zone.*"

"More like *Animal Farm*, maybe?" He snorted, and I couldn't help cracking up. "Do you have a preference on a room?"

I shook my head. "They both look exactly the same. I'll take this one."

"Are you sure you want to stay here?"

I sighed. "It's a mix of sweet and creepy. But harmless."

Milo looked around. "This stop is definitely one for our memory book. You think I can bum one of the dead animals off him for a souvenir?"

146

"Please don't. I'll have nightmares about it attacking me in the car."

Milo pointed to me. "You should've seen your face down there when he was showing us the animals."

"You were looking at my face in the midst of all that?"

"Yeah. I look at your face a lot," he muttered. "Habit, I guess."

My cheeks heated. Milo looked so handsome right now. It had definitely been a few days since he touched a razor. The more rugged and dirty he looked, the more I loved it. My attraction to him was at an all-time high. Too bad we were getting closer and closer to parting ways. That meant with each passing day, it was more dangerous to do anything about these feelings right now.

Still, as he lingered before me, I got the sudden urge to kiss him. I'd had many urges like this, but never as strong as this one. Maybe it was because the bedroom was cozy and welcoming. It made me want to let loose all of my inhibitions, push Milo down onto the bed, and curl into him while I tasted his luscious lips.

That wouldn't be happening, but it was a nice thought.

Milo reached out and cupped my cheek. *Had he been reading my mind?* Crazier things had happened on this trip. The feel of his warm, calloused hand against my face felt amazing. I closed my eyes to relish it.

And then...

"Yoohoo!" the old man's voice startled us. He peeked in. "Dinner's ready."

My heart pounded, and Milo's hand returned safely to his side. I was both pissed and relieved that Wyatt had interrupted our moment. I would never know where it could have led.

We followed Wyatt downstairs and sat at the dining room table. He served us bowls of piping hot beef stew and poured us some root beer. That was an odd combination, but the root beer brought back nostalgia from my childhood. I used to make floats with vanilla ice cream.

I took a spoonful of the stew into my mouth. "This is delicious."

"It was Bernadine's recipe. Never cooked for myself when she was alive. But I've been working my way through her recipe cards."

As weird as he may have been in some ways—okay, in many ways—Wyatt was quite sentimental and sweet.

"I can only hope whomever I choose to spend the rest of my life with remembers me as fondly when I'm gone as you remember your love, Wyatt."

He looked between Milo and me. "So, you're already writing off this guy you're with?"

I looked at Milo. I was just about to tell Wyatt the usual lie, that Milo and I were brother and sister, but Milo interrupted me.

"Unfortunately, I'm not the lucky guy who gets to have her heart. We're just friends. But even if my intentions were different, she's mending a broken heart right now. Only a fool would mess with that."

Wyatt seemed to ponder that. "Well, sometimes there's no way to mend a broken heart by yourself. But you can give it to someone else. Then it heals slowly, because that person helps you forget about the damage." He winked.

Milo and I exchanged a quick look.

Wyatt waved his hand. "Well, I suppose I should've guessed you two weren't romantic, given that you asked for two rooms. But I wasn't gonna pry. Bernadine used to like to sleep in her own room after we did the deed. Said my fartin' kept her up all night. I thought maybe y'all had your reasons, too."

We had a good laugh at that.

I smiled at Milo. "We may not be together romantically. But I feel really lucky to have his friendship and to be here with him right now."

Before Milo had a chance to respond, Wyatt got up from his seat. Our attention turned to him as he walked over to a set of apothecary drawers.

He opened one before taking out something encased in glass. "See this lock of hair?"

I tilted my head. "Yeah?"

"It belonged to Shirley Temple. She was before your time. Ever hear of her, though?"

I remembered my grandmother talking about her. It came up once when I asked why non-alcoholic drinks were called Shirley Temples.

"Oh. Yeah. Cute little actress, right?" I said. "But why do you have her hair?"

"I had a crush on her when I was a boy. My father took me to a meet and greet two states away. And well, when she leaned in, I snipped off a piece of her hair."

What? I knew this man was crazy—in a good way. But this news might have taken the cake.

I wasn't sure what to say. "Wow. That's...cool?"

"Or creepy," Milo whispered.

Genuinely curious, I asked, "How did Shirley react?"

Wyatt flashed a wicked grin. "She didn't know."

My eyes widened. "What? How did she not know you cut a piece of her hair off?"

"Had a pair of those kiddie scissors stuck between my fingers when I went in for a hug. Made my move nice and quick." He winked. "It was all innocent fun."

"It's all innocent fun until someone gets arrested, yeah," Milo said.

"I have some other hair samples in the drawer if you want to see 'em?"

Milo and I looked at each other. I could tell he was just as freaked out as I was.

I pretended to yawn. "I'm feeling kind of tired, actually. Think I should turn in."

There was one bathroom down the hall from our bedrooms. I took a shower, which was badly needed after our long day. The water pressure was good and the temperature hot.

As I settled into bed, Milo peeked his head inside my room.

"Just checking on you. You still feeling okay here?"

I sat up a little. "Well, Mr. Hooker, I think this detour definitely takes the cake."

"I couldn't agree more. At least the rooms are nice. The sheets smell good."

I was certain his sheets smelled amazing—because they now likely smelled like him.

"Last chance, Mads. I'll sneak us out of here right now if you're not comfortable."

I honestly loved how protective Milo seemed, how considerate he was about whether or not I was happy.

"This bed is really comfortable. I'm good. I might have nightmares about stuffed mice, but I'm good."

There was a moment of silence, and I wondered if he was thinking about our moment earlier, when he'd put his hand on my face. It was the closest we'd come to crossing the line. Well, aside from that striptease I'd given him.

Even though I knew there was no point in fantasizing about his touch, I couldn't help it.

After he left, I fell asleep quickly. Today had been an active day, so that was no surprise.

But sometime later, something woke me in the middle of the night. When I opened my eyes, I could've sworn I saw the door to my bedroom move. Was someone leaving my room?

What the hell?

Was it Milo?

Old Man Wyatt?

Am I hallucinating?

Not knowing was starting to freak me out. So, I got out of bed and went to Milo's room.

He turned at the sound of the door opening.

"What's up?" he asked groggily.

"Did you just come into my room?"

"Can't come into your room if I'm asleep. You woke me up. Anyway, why would you think I was in your room?"

"I could've sworn someone was in there. I saw my door close."

"Not me, babe."

His calling me babe made me tingle inside.

Snap out of it, Hazel.

"Okay. Well, sorry to wake you."

"It's okay. Try to get some sleep and not worry," he said. "I'm right next door if you need me."

Back in my room, I spent the next several minutes tossing and turning.

Milo must have heard my bed creaking, because no more than ten seconds later, there was a knock at the door.

"Mads, can I come in?"

I straightened in the bed. "Yes."

Milo entered, and I sat up against the headboard as he took a spot on the corner of my bed.

"How did you know I needed company, Milo?"

"I don't know. I guess I'm starting to know you. We've spent every waking minute together for days."

"Can you stay here with me for a bit?"

He didn't immediately answer. "Yeah. Of course. I'll stay on the floor."

"No. This bed is big enough. We're both adults. We can handle it."

As soon as he laid next to me, I started to feel like something was brewing. Given how close we'd come to kissing earlier, that was a safe assumption. As much as I needed him here in order to be able to sleep, I knew if I slept next to him I would end up in his arms. And then he would end up inside me.

I flipped around so my head faced the foot of the bed. If I turned my head now, I only saw his big feet. Since I was short and my legs didn't reach the top of the bed, the only thing he'd see if he turned his head to kiss me was an empty space.

The following morning, Milo and I got dressed in our respective rooms and prepared to hit the road.

It seemed Wyatt was a late sleeper, because he was nowhere to be found when we ventured downstairs.

"I say we grab coffee and breakfast on the road and skip it here. At this rate, it'll be noon by the time we get out of this place."

"Yeah. That's a good idea," I agreed.

We were just about to head out when Milo's expression changed. He bent down to pick something up off the carpet. "Holy shit."

"What is it?"

"It's a piece of hair. But it's the same color as yours."

I approached to examine it. That wasn't just a random piece of hair. *It was my hair.*

Milo raced to the set of apothecary drawers where Wyatt had kept the Shirley Temple hair sample. He opened every drawer and searched through various Ziploc bags.

He finally lifted one and said, "Bingo."

It was labeled, *Jessica Rabbit* and had yesterday's date on it. Apparently, Wyatt must have thought I resembled that fictional redhead from *Who Framed Roger Rabbit?*

"I think I know who entered your room last night."

Frantically, I ran my fingers through my hair in search of the spot where strands were missing. It wasn't a very big chunk so I might never figure it out.

Milo put the bag of my hair in his pocket as we rushed out of the house together.

He started the car, and we took off down the road.

As he drove, he lifted the baggie from his jacket pocket. "I guess we have our souvenir from Bumford."

Chapter 14

Hazel

"Hazel, I'm so sorry!"

My face scrunched up. No name had come up on my cellphone's caller ID, so I wasn't even positive who was apologizing.

"Felicity?"

"Yes."

"What's going on? Is everything okay?"

I'd taken over behind the wheel for a few hours so Milo could grab a nap. Apparently, once he'd joined me in my bed last night, he'd had trouble falling back asleep. He'd been out cold in the passenger seat for about a half hour now. But he blinked his eyes open and looked over at me on the phone.

"I'm in the hospital," Felicity said.

"The hospital? What happened?"

Seeing the look of concern on Milo's face, I covered the phone and whispered, "It's my friend back home. I'm going to pull over to talk to her. I don't like driving and talking on the phone." I put my blinker on and moved into the right lane.

"I'm so sorry to bother you on your trip," Felicity said. "But I had a car accident."

"Oh no. Are you alright?"

"I'm okay now. It happened last night. Some jerk blew a stop sign and hit the passenger side of my car. My Toyota took the brunt of the impact, but, unfortunately, I took the brunt of the airbag. My husband is always telling me I sit too close to the steering wheel and it's dangerous. But I'm so short that it's hard to sit too far back. Well, turns out he was right, and I should have tried harder. I fractured my neck and broke my wrist—all from the airbag."

After getting off at the next exit, I pulled over to the side of the road and put the car into park. "Oh my God! A broken neck!"

"The doctors said I'm lucky I'm not paralyzed."

"Wow, Felicity. I'm so glad you're okay."

"But I feel awful. Even though I'll probably only be in the hospital another night or two for observation, between my neck being in a collar for who knows how long and my right wrist being in a cast, there's no way I'm going to be able to cover the upcoming shoots for you. I feel terrible about it."

"Of course you can't. Don't even think about it. That should be the furthest thing from your mind right now. What's important is that you're okay, and you get the proper rest and treatment you need. I'm so sorry this happened."

"Thank you. But listen, yet another doctor just walked in, so I have to run."

"Go. Good luck. I'll call and check on you in a day or two. I hope everything goes well."

When I hung up, Milo was looking at me, waiting to be filled in. I shook my head. "That was my friend

Felicity. She was in car accident and fractured her neck and wrist."

He reached over and took my hand. "I'm sorry. That sucks. But she's going to be okay?"

I nodded. "Yeah. It definitely could have been worse."

Milo nodded. "You mentioned her the other day. Is she a good friend?"

"We're pretty close. We met in an underwater photography class, actually. She's a photographer, too. She sometimes covers for me in my school portrait business when I'm in a pinch or need to take some time off."

"You do underwater photography?"

I smiled. "I took a class with hopes to. But I've never gotten around to it."

Milo frowned and nodded. "Well, I'm glad your friend is okay."

I'd been so concerned about Felicity's accident that I hadn't fully realized what her being out of commission meant for me. My stomach suddenly dropped, and it felt like someone reached into my chest and squeezed my heart. "This...sort of puts a wrench in our plans."

Milo's eyes caught with mine. "You need to head home?"

I nodded. "She was the one covering for me while I've been gone and was supposed to do all my school shoots next week, too. Now she can't, obviously."

His eyes looked as panicked as I felt. "When do you need to be home?"

"Monday. Which means I'm going to have to fly home from Atlanta tomorrow."

When we got to Atlanta, Milo navigated through the city and pulled up in front of the Four Seasons. We hadn't yet discussed where we were staying. Just like every other city we'd been to, I'd thought we were going with the flow.

I looked out the passenger window. "Wow. This place is beautiful."

"I researched the nicest hotels in the area while you were driving. Since it's our last night together, I figured we deserved something special."

Just hearing him say *last night* made my chest tighten again.

The valet came around and opened my door while Milo took our bags out of the trunk. The attendant handed him a ticket.

"Hang onto it for a few minutes," Milo told the valet. "We don't have reservations, so we might be leaving if they have no rooms."

The guy bowed. "No problem, sir."

Milo and I walked into the opulent lobby. It was, by far, the nicest hotel we'd been in. The lobby had sky-high ceilings, a massive crystal chandelier, and sun streaming in from floor-to-ceiling windows on two of the four walls. The room literally sparkled. I was pretty sure the marble floor was clean enough to eat off of, too.

"This is so fancy," I said. "I sort of feel like a movie star coming in here."

Milo linked his hand with mine. "These rooms are on me."

"I can't let you do that. They'll be a fortune."

"I insist."

We walked up to the front desk, which had no line. "May I help you?"

"Hi, yes," Milo said. "We don't have a reservation. Would you happen to have any rooms available?"

The woman nodded and smiled. "We do. What kind of rooms were you looking for?" She punched a few keys into her computer and said, "Our regular rooms are four hundred seventy-five dollars a night, or we have a suite for five hundred ninety-five a night."

Milo looked over at me and winked. "Two suites, please."

"Okay. And how many nights will you be staying?"

Again my heart sank. Milo's face was glum when he answered, "Just one."

"Very well. I'll need a license and a credit card."

As the clerk clicked away, the reality of this as our last night sank in. If we had less than twenty-four hours left, I wanted to spend every last moment next to Milo. He handed the woman his credit card and license and strummed his fingers on the counter.

"Actually, ma'am," I said. "Could we change our reservation?"

The woman's brows knitted, and she looked up. "You want to stay more than one night?"

"No. But we only need one suite." I turned to the man standing next to me and lowered my voice. "Would that be okay with you?"

Milo's eyes washed over my face, and he looked into my eyes for a few, very long seconds. He nodded. "Yeah. Definitely."

Linking our fingers together on the counter, I smiled at the clerk. "One suite instead of two, please."

The woman looked amused. "No problem."

After she finished checking us in, she put two plastic key cards into a small holder and looked around the lobby. Leaning in, she said, "I ordered a bottle of champagne and some chocolate-covered strawberries to your room. If the manager happens to ask, your bathroom wasn't working, so I sent it as an apology for the inconvenience. It's also why you've been upgraded to our deluxe suite."

Milo took the keys with a giant smile. "You're the best."

She looked at us with a coy smirk. "Enjoy your evening."

Our suite was gorgeous. We had a view of downtown Atlanta, a separate living room and bedroom, and a bathroom that was bigger than most decent-sized hotel rooms. After I went online and made my flight arrangements, I decided the big bathtub was too irresistible to ignore. Plus, the hotel had a bevy of spa products lined up on a glass shelf in the bathroom that I couldn't wait to try, including a coconut and sea salt bath bomb.

So I filled the tub, told Milo I'd have my ear buds in, and climbed into the warm water. Shutting my eyes as I settled in, I put on classical music and tried to relax. I'd had a tension knot the size of a golf ball in my neck ever since Felicity called.

It seemed unimaginable that tomorrow at this time I'd be back home in Connecticut. Obviously, this trip had to come to an end sooner or later, but I wasn't ready for tonight to be the last one. Milo and I had been together less than two weeks, yet the thought of going home and not seeing him left a hollow feeling in the pit of my stomach. I'd grown so attached to him.

Deep down, however, I did know I needed to figure things out with Brady before starting anything new. Milo had been right about that from the very beginning. And it made me so much more attracted to him to know he put my emotional needs above his own physical ones. Because a lesser man might not have. It would've been so easy for Milo to get me into bed, to take advantage of my neediness and vulnerability, especially because I was so attracted to him. But he didn't. And while not quite two weeks might not be that long to know someone, the way he'd handled things between us had really shown me the type of man he was.

My effort to relax in the tub turned out to be an epic failure, though it wasn't for lack of trying—my skin was pruney by the time I stepped out of the bath. I twisted my wet hair up in a towel, slathered on some of the free body and face lotions, and wrapped the hotel's luxurious bathrobe around myself. Slipping into monogrammed, matching plush slippers, I finally returned to the living room.

Milo was standing at the windows, drinking a glass of wine. He seemed lost in thought—so much so that he didn't notice me walking over, until I slipped the wine glass from his hand so we could share it.

I sipped. "Penny for your thoughts…"

He looked me up and down. "Well, that answers that question."

My brows furrowed. "What question?"

"Could we ever just be friends?"

"That's what you were thinking about while looking so serious?"

Milo nodded. "I was trying to convince myself we could—that regardless of what happens when you go back home, the two of us could still be friends."

"Were you successful? I mean, at talking yourself into it?"

Milo smiled. "I was until you walked out with your hair wrapped in a towel, your body hidden beneath ten pounds of cotton bathrobe, and without a lick of makeup."

I laughed. "So we can't be friends because I don't look so hot after a bath?"

Milo took the wine from my hand and downed the rest of the glass. "Just the opposite. I think you're beautiful without any fancy outfit, makeup, or hair." He lowered his head and stared down at the floor. "I was trying to talk myself into being able to stay friends if you decide to get back with your ex. But the truth is, I can't be friends with you because you're so much more to me already, and there's no going back from that. It's fucked up that this might be the last time we're together."

He looked up at me, his eyes brimming with unshed tears. I could see he was struggling, and I swallowed, trying to force down my emotions. But I wasn't as strong as him. A big, warm tear rolled down my cheek.

Milo wiped it away with his thumb and opened his arms. "Come here."

I snuggled into the warmth of his embrace. It felt so good. *So right.* Like this was exactly where I was meant to be. Yet...it wasn't the right time, and we both knew it. We held on to each other for the longest time, clinging like it was the very end, though we still had a whole night ahead of us.

Eventually, Milo pulled back. He brushed the hair that had fallen from my towel out of my face. "What do you want to do tonight? It's your call. Whatever your heart desires. I looked through a book on Atlanta, and this city has a lot to offer. There's an entire underground area with shops and restaurants and an improv comedy club we could go to. We could go to Centennial Park and take a ride on the SkyView Ferris wheel. It's supposed to have a great view of the city from the top. They also have a haunted pub tour, or there's a hotel not too far away with a rooftop bar and restaurant. You name it, and we're there."

I tossed around the things he'd mentioned, and while they all sounded like fun, there was really only one thing I wanted to do tonight. I looked up at Milo.

"Would it be okay if we just stayed in? Maybe order room service and watch a movie or something?"

He smiled. "Yeah, that sounds perfect."

A little while later, Milo emerged from the bathroom wearing one of the plush hotel bathrobes and slippers. I cracked up when I saw him.

"Are you making fun of me?" I said.

He rubbed the arm of his robe. "Fuck no. This thing is like being wrapped in a cloud. I put on some of the fancy moisturizer you left on the counter, too. Why should women be the only ones with soft skin?"

I'd been checking out the hotel menu and held it up for him. "I'm going to get the deluxe burger with onions and avocado and a side of truffle fries."

Milo took the menu, but set it down on the table. "That sounds good. I'll get the same."

While he ordered, I poured us two glasses of champagne. Handing one to him when he hung up, I sat on the couch and tucked my feet under my butt. "So what are you going to do when I leave tomorrow? Will you head to your friend's house?"

He shook his head. "I think I need a few days before I go to New York. The buddy I'm going to see just got dumped. If I show up feeling the way I think I'm going to feel tomorrow when you get on that plane, I'm pretty sure the two of us will do nothing but get drunk and wallow. I'm probably going to hang here in Atlanta for a few days. I've never been, and it'll give me some time to clear my head."

"Okay. That sounds nice."

"So what's the first thing you're going to do when you get home?" he asked.

"Well, I'll probably dump my bags in the house and run next door to my neighbor's, Mrs. Green. She has Abbott."

"Abbott? You have a dog?"

I sipped my wine. "Nope."

"Cat?"

I grinned. "Nope."

"A kid you forgot to mention?"

I laughed. "Definitely not. Abbott is my pet rabbit."

Milo's eyebrows jumped. "You have a rabbit named Abbott."

I laughed. "Yup. Abbott the rabbit. A blue Angora."

"He's blue?"

"Well, *he's* not anything. Abbott is a girl. And she's more like a gray, but the color is called blue."

Milo looked amused. "Does your blue bunny with a boy's name know he's a gray girl, or is he just as confused as me?"

I smacked his abs. "She's the cutest thing. Abbott has big floppy ears, and she's really fat and round. Sometimes when she's curled up in a ball and someone comes over, they get scared when she moves because she looks more like a stuffed animal. Did you ever watch old *Star Trek* reruns? She sort of looks like a tribble when she sleeps. Oh, and I walk her on a leash."

"You walk a rabbit on a leash?"

"Yeah. She thinks she's a dog."

Milo shook his head. "Well, I can't wait to meet her."

I got excited at that thought, but then his smile fell.

"*If* I get to meet her, I mean."

Again, it felt like the bottom dropped out of my belly. But I forced myself to ignore it so our last night didn't turn depressing. "Do you have any pets?"

He nodded. "I have a cat. Had a black lab growing up, but I've never had a dog on my own. Someday, though."

In many ways I felt like I knew Milo so well, yet I realized we didn't know some very basic things about each other—like if we had pets. For some inexplicable reason, that bothered me. I didn't want to leave and look back and start to second guess whether I'd ever known Milo at all. Suddenly I wanted to ask him a zillion questions.

"Did you go to public school or private growing up?" I began.

"Public. You?"

"Same."

"What was the name of your first crush?"

Milo chuckled. "Julia. You do know your questions are jumping all over the place, right?"

"I know. I just—there are so many things I want to know about you before…"

Our eyes caught and our faces fell once again.

Milo drank his champagne. "Before we never see each other again?"

"No, that's not what I meant at all. It's just that I feel like I know you in a very deep way, yet I don't know some surface things. I want to know everything I can."

Milo lifted one leg up onto the couch and spread his arm over the back of it. "Alright. Shoot. What other questions do you have?"

"Let's start from the beginning. How old were you when you met Julia, your first girlfriend?"

"I was nine. She was fifteen."

My eyes bulged. "Your first girlfriend was six years older than you?"

"No. You asked my first crush. Her name was Julia, and she was my babysitter."

"Oh." I chuckled. "How old was your first girlfriend then?"

He thought about it. "Sixth grade. Lisa Carlisle. She was a redhead. Totally forgot about that. Guess I knew what I liked early." He winked. "What about you?"

"Eighth grade. Eddie Paxton. He was a year older."

"How long did it last?"

"A few months. He was my first kiss. His breath was horrible, so I dumped him."

Milo lifted his hand to his mouth, blew out a few short breaths, and sniffed. He smiled. "All good. Still minty fresh from when I brushed."

I tilted my head. "Does that mean you're planning on kissing me?"

I'd said it kidding around, but the moment suddenly got serious. Milo looked into my eyes. "There's absolutely nothing I'd like to do more. But I know that once I tasted you, I'd never be able to stop at a kiss, Maddie."

Oh my.

He was essentially blowing me off, but my body got all tingly. It made my mind wander to dirtier questions.

"Do you have a favorite position?"

Milo's eyes darkened. "You sure you want to go there?"

I swallowed and nodded.

"Alright. I usually like to be in control—against the wall or doggy style. But something tells me with you, my favorite position would be you riding me so I could watch your face every minute I'm inside of you."

My mouth hung open. I imagined Milo sitting on the couch exactly where he was at this very moment, and me straddling him. Lord, I wanted that in the worst way.

I vaguely heard a knock in the distance, though I didn't register what it was.

Milo leaned forward and whispered in my ear. "Better shut that mouth. Because you're reminding me of another favorite position I've imagined you in a time or two during my showers." He grazed my bottom lip with his thumb. "I think my second favorite position might be you on your knees in front of me—that gorgeous red hair wrapped tight around my hand and those big blue eyes looking up at me while I fill this beautiful mouth."

He stood and chuckled. "Sorry you asked now?"

I swallowed and shook my head.

"At least we're saved by room service," he said. "I'll get the door."

For the rest of the night, we steered away from the road we had started down before dinner. Without discussing it, we both seemed to know it was for the best. However, I was certain the vision of me riding him would be seared into my brain for a long time. We talked for hours, and around midnight, after I'd yawned and caused Milo to yawn, we decided to watch a movie.

He laid on his back on top of the covers with one hand behind his head. Crawling up next to him, I rested my head on his chest. "Is this okay?"

He ran his fingers through my hair. "Yeah. It's perfect."

I thought I would have trouble falling asleep while lying so close to him on the bed. But listening to the sound of Milo's heartbeat as he softly stroked my head was better than a rocking chair and lullaby.

Morning came too soon. My flight was at nine, which meant I needed to be at the airport by seven, and on the road by six thirty. When the alarm on my phone went off at five thirty, Milo rustled in the bed, but didn't wake up. So I shut the bedroom doors and let him sleep while I got ready. He'd offered to drive me, but there was really no reason for him to run out so early in the morning. Calling an Uber was just as easy.

I packed the last of my things into my suitcase and looked around for anything I forgot. Taking a deep breath, I checked the time on my phone and called up the Uber app. Thirty seconds after punching in the airport as my destination, a message popped up that a driver had been located and would arrive in six minutes.

Six minutes.

I broke out in a cold sweat as I opened the door to the bedroom. Milo looked so peaceful sleeping that I was tempted to leave a note and not even wake him. But I knew how I would feel if he did that to me—robbed of the opportunity to say goodbye. So I walked to his side of the bed and gently shook him.

"Milo," I whispered. "I have to go."

His eyes fluttered open and came into focus. Leaning up on his elbow he said, "What time is it?"

"It's six thirty-five. Don't get up. I called an Uber already. It will be here in five minutes, so I need to head downstairs."

His eyes were so expressive. Pain lanced through me, seeing how he felt.

"Why didn't you wake me? I wanted to drive you."

"I thought it would be easier this way." I shook my head. "For so many reasons."

"Fuck." Milo dragged a hand through his hair. "I need more time to say goodbye."

I smiled sadly. "But we're not saying goodbye. I'm going to see you in a few months, remember?"

He blew out a deep breath. "Yeah, okay. But just give me one second."

Milo hopped out of bed and jogged to the bathroom. He came out a minute later and took me into his arms. I smelled mint on his breath, so he must've brushed his teeth while he was in there.

"We didn't get souvenirs from Atlanta," he said.

I smiled. "It's okay."

"No. It's not. I want you to have something to remember every stop we've made."

"I can pick something up at the airport."

He cupped my cheeks with both hands, and his eyes dipped down to my lips. "I think I have something better."

I licked my dry lips.

Milo groaned. "God, I've wanted to do this for so damn long."

Before I could respond, he tilted my head and sealed his mouth over mine. His lips were surprisingly soft, but his touch was firm. He nudged for me to open and wasted no time dipping his tongue inside when I did. All hell broke loose after that. The coat that had been in my hand fell to the ground, and my arms wrapped around his neck. Milo growled and lifted me up. I wrapped my legs around his waist, and I didn't realize we were moving until my back hit a wall.

Milo pushed his hips into me, and I could feel his steely erection even through our clothes. Unable to get enough, I moaned into our joined mouths and threaded my fingers through his silky hair, giving it a good, hard yank to bring him even closer. I could feel the rapid beat of his heart through my chest...or maybe it was my heartbeat raging out of control against his. I couldn't be sure because in this moment, there was no him and no me—there was only us.

We went on that way for a long time; minutes passed as we were lost in our own intimate universe— until the sound of a cell phone ringing broke through and burst our little bubble.

With a groan, Milo pulled back. We were both panting. I dug my cell out of my pocket and saw what I suspected was a local number. I swiped to answer while attempting to catch my breath.

"Hello?"

"Yeah, I'm parked out front of the Four Seasons to pick you up."

My heart sank, and my eyes found Milo's. "Sorry. I'm on my way down now."

I ended the call and whispered, "The Uber driver is here. I have to go."

Milo leaned his forehead against mine. "Don't say goodbye. I can't hear you say that word."

I looked into his eyes. "I won't. This trip has meant everything to me, Milo. I hope you know that."

"Me, too, babe. Me, too."

I forced a smile. "I'll...see you in New Orleans on Valentine's Day?"

He nodded. "You bet your ass you will."

I walked to the door and looked back one last time. Milo was still rooted to the spot where we'd kissed.

"In case you're wondering, I got my favorite souvenir in Atlanta. Take care, Milo."

PART TWO

Chapter 15

The doorbell rang, and I jumped.

God, why am I such a nervous wreck? Ever since I'd agreed to meet Brady to talk, I'd had this looming feeling of dread hanging over me. I'd been so anxious yesterday that it took me forever to fall asleep last night.

At the front door, I took a few deep breaths and smoothed my blouse before reaching for the door handle.

"Hey," I breathed out as I opened the door.

Brady's smile was luminescent. "Hey, beautiful." He leaned in toward me, and it looked like he was going to kiss me on the lips.

I pulled back.

"Shit." He shook his head. "Sorry. I wasn't even thinking. I just... It's been a long time and...habit, I guess. Can I at least give you a hug?"

I forced a smile. "Sure. Of course."

Brady stepped forward and wrapped me in a tight embrace. I relaxed a little as he held me, the familiarity of his scent and touch giving me comfort. But then the fact that I'd started to grow comfortable in his arms began to freak me out, and I pulled away.

"It's cold out there. Why don't you come in?"

I'd been on blind dates that felt less awkward than inviting the man I was supposed to marry only a few months ago into my living room. Brady followed me into the kitchen. Wine was definitely going to be needed tonight. Though alcohol tended to make me emotional, so I planned to have only a glass or two. I wanted to take the edge off, not lose sight of what had happened between us—or what I'd learned about myself.

"Would you like a glass of white wine?"

"Sure. Thanks."

I already had a bottle open, so I took down two glasses from the cabinet and poured us each one. Brady hadn't said much since he walked in, and when I looked up, I found him staring at me funny.

"What?" I offered him a glass.

He took it. "Nothing. I just really missed you. I hope that's okay to say."

My lips pressed together. "Why don't we go sit in the living room?"

Brady followed me, and we sat a polite distance apart on the couch. As we drank our wine in silence, I glanced over at him and couldn't help but make a comparison to Milo. While Milo had big, brown bedroom eyes, shaggy hair that needed a cut, and often sported a five o'clock shadow, Brady was the polar opposite. His blond hair was always neatly trimmed, his skin always smooth and clean-shaven, and his blue eyes were bright and attentive. The only thing the two men had in common was their beautiful, full lips. But it's not that Brady wasn't handsome. He was—very much so—just in a different way than Milo. With his buttoned-up, neat appearance and cropped hair, Brady had a Ken-doll quality about him. Milo looked more like he'd walked out of the Scooby-Doo Mystery Machine.

"How was your trip?" Brady interrupted my thoughts.

Wonderful.

Amazing.

Life changing.

Those were the first words that came to mind.

Yet, I shrugged. "It was good."

"What did you do?"

This exact question was one of the primary reasons I couldn't fall asleep last night. I'd gone round and round in my head about what I would say when Brady inevitably asked it. Did I tell him the truth? That I took a road trip with a complete stranger? Or did I lie? Seeing as I never had come to a conclusion, I told the truth... Well, sort of.

"I learned to ski, took some photos, and explored a bit."

After all, that wasn't a lie.

Brady frowned. "I was looking forward to teaching you to ski. Did you at least have a good instructor?"

I gulped some wine. "Yeah. The instructor was great."

God, why did I feel so much guilt? Brady was the one who broke my heart and called off our engagement. I had every right to be with another man—not that Milo and I had been *together* in that way. But still...the guilt was overwhelming. I needed to change the subject.

"How's your mother doing?" I asked. Brady's mom had been diagnosed with Lyme disease right before we

175

split up. She'd had a lot of joint pain and suffered from constant fatigue.

"She's doing good. The last round of antibiotics really seemed to help."

I nodded. "I'm glad."

Silence again filled the air. Eventually, Brady set his wine glass down on the table and exhaled a deep breath.

"Listen, Hazel." He reached out and took my hand. "I don't know how to start this conversation, so I'm just going to jump right in." He looked down, shaking his head. "I fucked up. I royally fucked up. I should never have called off our wedding. I still love you. I love you so freaking much it hurts, and I don't know how to make things right."

My heart began to race. While two-and-a-half months ago I would have given anything to hear those words, things had changed. *I'd changed.*

"I...I...I don't know what to say."

He squeezed my hand. "Saying you still love me might help me breathe a little. Right now I feel like I'm gulping air through a pinhole."

I stared down at our joined hands. Did I still love him? I definitely had feelings for him. But were they different now than they'd been before? Could feelings just go away? I wasn't sure how I felt.

And then there was Milo.

I definitely had feelings for him. In fact, in the two weeks I'd been back home, he'd been pretty much all I could think about. But were my feelings for him borne out of the excitement of our adventure and my need to feel wanted again? I didn't think so. But honestly, I wasn't sure about anything at the moment.

"Hazel..."

My eyes jumped to meet Brady's. I shook my head. "I care about you. How could I not? We spent three years together, and you were always very good to me. Honestly, I was devastated when you called off the wedding. But a lot of time has passed now, and I can accept that what you did was not meant to be hurtful. I can't imagine it was an easy thing to do. You had doubts, and you did what you felt was right. Now that time has gone by, I can even appreciate that you did what you did rather than take the easy way out."

I looked away for a long moment. When my eyes returned to meet his, Brady looked as nervous as I'd felt when he rang the doorbell. "I've discovered a lot about myself over the last few months," I said slowly. "I'm not even sure what I want anymore."

"What do you mean?"

I sighed. "I've been doing a lot of thinking, and I've realized that what happened between us wasn't *only* your fault. I'm not the same woman you met at that concert years ago. I've become someone very different, and I'm not sure I like her that much. So how could I expect you to?"

"I don't understand."

"The woman you met was passionate. She loved to travel and experience life. Over the years, I seemed to have lost that part of me."

"No, you didn't. You're still the same woman I fell in love with."

It had taken a lot of time and soul searching to discover that wasn't true, so I couldn't expect Brady to understand it right away. Plus, he meant well.

I forced a smile. "I'm not. But that's okay. Now that I recognize what I've lost within me, I can start to try to find it again."

Brady stepped closer. "I already recognize what I lost, and I want her back in the worst way."

I shook my head. "I need time. I'm confused about so much. Honestly, I didn't know if you were coming here today to ask for a coat you left in the closet, to say a final goodbye, or to say what you just said. It's a lot to take in, and my emotions are all over the place."

Brady nodded. "Sure. Of course. That makes sense. I don't want to push you. Where we are is entirely my fault, and I need to win you back. I need to put in the work and regain your trust."

"That's not what I meant, Brady."

"Just please tell me you'll give me a chance to show you what we can have together again. We can start slow—like we did at the beginning. Friends, even?"

"Friends?"

"Yeah. I'm desperate, sweetheart. I'll take whatever you're willing to give me. I know we're meant to be together, and in time you can get back to feeling it, too. Maybe we could have lunch once or twice a week, or have drinks or see a movie? I promise I won't pressure you."

"I don't know..."

Brady moved closer and caught my gaze. "Please? Just spend a little time with me each week. That's all I'm asking."

I needed to think things through. "Can I think about it?"

He forced a smile, but pretty much failed at it. "Sure. Of course."

Over the next couple of weeks, I realized for sure that Brady wasn't kidding when he'd said he wanted to start by being friends again. He was pulling out all of the stops, doing things I only remembered him doing in the early days of our relationship. He'd sent flowers to me at the studio. He'd come by and surprised me with my favorite takeout after work. He stayed to eat with me, but didn't seem to expect anything else. Which was a good thing, because we weren't *together* at the moment—although it was clear he was working toward making that happen.

As safe as Brady made me feel, I still felt like the trip had changed me. My time with Milo had me doubting whether the path I'd been on before I met him was the right one. I needed to be sure what was right for me long term before I made any decisions about where things stood with Brady. And as much as a part of me still loved him, I didn't know whether I could ever fully trust him again. He'd broken my heart when he canceled the wedding—not to mention the embarrassment that goes along with that, having to tell friends and family what happened. At least he'd had the decency not to stand me up at the altar, like Big did to Carrie in *Sex and the City*. Then again, Carrie ended up forgiving Big.

Was I really justifying forgiving Brady because a fictional character who had great taste in shoes did the same?

A part of me knew if I hadn't had the experience with Milo, I would be much more open to the idea of letting Brady back into my heart. But a part of my heart was with someone else now—a man I knew virtually nothing about in "real life."

I decided to pay a visit to my friend Felicity, who was still home recovering after her car accident. She had no clue about what an adventure my trip had turned out to be.

On the drive to her house, I gave Brady's mother a call. I hadn't spoken to her in a while, and given everything she was going through with the Lyme-disease diagnosis, it was time I checked in. After all, it wasn't her fault her son screwed up. She had been like a mother to me—more so than my own, who continued to travel the world with my dad.

I put my phone on speaker mode and dialed her.

She picked up. "Hazel!"

"Hey, Terry."

She cleared her throat. "It's so good to hear from you. How was your trip?"

"I'm sorry it's taken me so long to call. The trip was great. It was...necessary. Soul-cleansing, really. Thank you for asking."

"I'm so glad to hear."

"But more importantly, how are you feeling?"

"Better. Not a hundred percent. But better. You know, they say stress can exacerbate symptoms of chronic diseases. I have to admit that my foolish son doing what he did to you put me in a very bad place. I think that's what led to my symptoms."

I frowned. "Oh, I hope not."

"Well, you know you're like a daughter to me. I was very sad when Brady canceled the wedding."

"Oh, Terry. Please don't be. Everything happens for a reason. I feel like I understand that a little more now."

She let out a breath into the phone. "Please don't give up on him, Hazel. As much as he might deserve that, you have to remember that Brady was very hurt when his father and I divorced. It took him many years to get over it. I think he has a huge fear of history repeating itself."

That had definitely crossed my mind—that Brady had his reasons, ones that may not have been about me. But it was hard not to take everything personally.

I sighed. "I get that."

"He and I have had some time to chat while he's been looking in on me. Now, I know I shouldn't be violating my son's trust, but fuck it, he lost the right to my full protection when he did you wrong. I can tell you with absolute certainty that his decision was completely fear-based. He's afraid to bring a child into this world only to have a marriage end in divorce. He feels like he needs to be absolutely sure."

"Well, I agree with needing to be sure. And I think he made the right decision to not go through with marrying me if he wasn't sure."

"But here's the thing, darling. He *is* sure now. I don't agree with how he handled things to get to that point, but I can tell you he's never regretted anything more in his life than the decision to let you go."

Mixed emotions started to bubble inside of me.

I pulled up to Felicity's. "I'd better let you get some rest. I just got to my friend's house, in any case."

"Okay, have fun. Please keep in touch."

"I don't want you getting overly stressed about this. Okay, Terry? Take care of yourself and know that Brady and I are taking things slow again. We're focusing on rebuilding the friendship we had when our relationship started. If we're meant to be together, I'm sure fate will find a way to fix us."

"I sure hope so, honey. Because he'll never find anyone else like you."

After spending the better part of an hour telling Felicity about Milo and all of the places we visited, she was still sitting there with her mouth hanging open. I helped fold some of her laundry while we talked.

"I can't believe the entire time you were away, I was feeling sorry for you, thinking you were in Vail, wallowing over the fact that the wedding never happened. Never in a million years would I have imagined you were gallivanting around with a sexy stranger."

"Well, it certainly wasn't what I expected to come out of that trip, either," I said as I matched her socks.

She sat up straighter on bed. "Will you ever see this guy again?"

"That's the thing. He booked us a room at the hotel where we stayed in New Orleans for three months after the time we were there."

"Whoa. So, like, you're supposed to show up and see if he does the same?"

"Yeah, unless something changes—unless he doesn't want to see me for some reason or vice versa."

"That's exciting. Like something out of a movie."

"Exciting unless one of us doesn't show."

"So, the whole time you guys called each other by your fake names?"

"Yep."

"You never got his real name?"

I shook my head. "That was part of the fun. I'm sure if we end up reuniting, I'll tell him my name. It was just too much fun being Maddie Hooker—much more fun than Hazel Appleton."

"Hooker! What a name." She laughed. "But what if this guy had been dangerous? You really took a chance."

I carried the basket of folded clothes over to the corner of the room. "Never once did I worry about that. I had an innate sense that I was safe with Milo. He never even tried anything. Honestly, aside from that amazing kiss at the very end, he was the perfect gentleman." I chuckled, thinking about some of my own behavior. "I was by far the more aggressive one at times. It was hard to hide my attraction to him."

"I still have chills about what you told me—when the psychic brought his old girlfriend through."

That reminded me. "Oh. One part I forgot to tell you. Zoe, the dead girlfriend, apparently mentioned hazelnuts to try to give the psychic a clue about something. Pretty sure she was referring to me—Hazel. But even then, I didn't tell him my name."

Her jaw dropped. "So amazing. Wow."

"The whole experience was amazing." I plopped down on the corner of the bed and sighed. "But now, being home is...strange. I almost feel like I belonged out there on the road with Milo. I'm like a fish out of water on my own turf, even though things have actually been better than ever here—on the surface, at least."

"How so?"

I bit my bottom lip. "Well, that's the other thing I haven't mentioned yet. On top of everything that happened, Brady has been trying to get me to forgive him."

Her eyes widened. "Whoa. What?"

"Yeah. He wants to get back together, says he really regrets canceling the wedding."

She leaned in. "What did you say?"

"I've agreed to spend time with him, but made no promises. I'm open to seeing where things go, but if I'm being honest, a part of me is still with Milo. I feel like only half of me is here. That half of me has some feelings for Brady, but it's just so complicated."

"You're not considering giving up what you and Brady had for some guy you don't even know?"

Her reaction surprised me. *She's defending Brady?*

"Brady left me. Are you forgetting that?"

"Yeah, but he's come around. He came to his senses. I have no doubt Brady loves you. He takes the covenant of marriage seriously. If only all men were like that. Better to express doubt before getting married than after. Ultimately he's decided he can't live without you. It's not necessarily a bad thing that he fully thought through the idea of marriage first."

I sighed. "I know he never meant to hurt me. But he's going to have a long road to travel before I trust him again."

"That's understandable." She paused. "But you *will* take him back, right?"

My eyes narrowed. "I thought you were all gung-ho about my three-month meet-up with Milo a little while ago."

"That was before I knew Brady wanted to fix things." She paused to really look at me. "Hazel, Brady is a great guy. He loves you. Don't fuck things up with him over some drifter you had a fun time with."

Drifter?

Wow. I was actually offended on Milo's behalf. She hadn't heard anything I'd said about him over the past hour.

I raised my voice. "Milo is no more a drifter than I am."

"Okay, but you don't even know this guy's name. If you continue to obsess over him, eventually you're going to have to tell Brady—and then what? You'll lose him."

"Brady threw me away, Felicity. If he can't accept something that happened in the aftermath of his dumping me, that's his problem. Are you forgetting he left *me*?"

"Yeah, well, he's trying to rectify that. Give him a chance. Don't make a mistake you'll regret for the rest of your life."

Felicity's one-sided attitude aggravated me. I crossed my arms. "I have to say, I'm a bit surprised you're so supportive of Brady. You were the first to curse his name when he broke things off."

"Yeah, well, I was mad. But now that I see how he's handling things, I have to be honest with you. I think you'd be making a mistake in not taking him back. This guy you met doesn't sound like he has his shit together. I know you have an adventurous spirit, but when it comes down to it, stability is what you need. I mean, don't you want to have kids someday?"

I stared off. I wasn't sure what I wanted anymore. But though I may not have agreed with her advice, she'd certainly given me a lot to think about.

Chapter 16

Hazel

Brady had asked if I wanted to meet him at a bar in the city Friday night. He had business downtown, so he was already in the area. I'd have to take the train in after my shoot.

It had been a while since I'd ventured out of Connecticut, so I figured it would do me some good. After all, any time I could hang out with Brady without having to be alone with him was a good thing. Even though he'd been great about not making any moves on me physically, I always worried about how I would handle things if we were alone and he tried something. That was bound to happen at some point if we continued hanging out as "friends."

I'd given him no indication as to whether I would be taking him back. It would have been irresponsible to lead him on, since I was still figuring out what *I* wanted. I'd remembered how much there was to experience in the world, and I wasn't ready to close the door on a more adventurous future than currently lay before me.

Like a future with Milo. It wouldn't be risk-free, but it would certainly bring an excitement I didn't have now.

And despite Felicity's feelings on the matter, I was still torn about whether I could forgive Brady. If I ended up choosing to be with him, I'd likely never see Milo again. That was a hard pill to swallow.

I'd have to stand Milo up in New Orleans. The thought of that broke my heart. I couldn't imagine Milo showing up and not finding me there. Obviously, if I were considering taking Brady back one second and feeling horrible about potentially hurting Milo the next, I was still very confused.

The bar Brady had chosen in downtown Manhattan was a small but trendy place. It was dark and crowded, but he had already texted me that he'd secured a spot at the back right side of the bar, so I knew where to look. I managed to find him sitting at a four-top table in the corner.

When he spotted me, he raised his glass. He looked really good tonight, dressed in a black, tailored suit. He must have been trying to impress a new client today.

"Hey!" I said, a bit out of breath.

"You made it." Brady stood and leaned in to kiss my cheek. It was the most contact he'd aimed for since our first meeting after my return.

I had to admit, the feel of his lips on my skin sent a chill down my spine.

"How was your day?" he asked.

That was another thing. "New Brady" was more considerate. "Old Brady" would have immediately started going on about *his* day.

"The shoot in New Haven went well. I'll have a ton of edits to do this weekend."

"Good. What's on tap next week?"

"I have a couple of private assignments and then a retake shoot at the high school in Darien."

"Nice."

"How was your day?" I asked.

"The usual brownnosing that comes with wooing a new client. But I'm pretty sure I nabbed them. I'll probably hear next week."

"Well, early congrats then. We should celebrate."

"Definitely." He flagged down a waitress. "I hope you don't mind, I told Dunc to meet us here. He just got into town tonight."

Duncan was Brady's best friend from college back in Vail. He was supposed to be the best man at our wedding. That was going to be my first time meeting him, but of course the wedding never happened. I'd heard about him for years, but according to Brady, he'd been through a tough period and had apparently pulled back from everyone. I tried to fight the bitterness creeping in. The mere thought of Duncan reminded me of the canceled wedding and Brady's abandonment. I already had a negative association with the poor guy and hadn't even laid eyes on him.

Forcing a smile, I said, "It'll be nice to finally meet him."

"Yeah. He's coming here straight from the airport, but who knows what kind of traffic he'll hit at this hour."

"Oh, that's true."

The waitress finally came around to take my order. I opted for a Cosmo. Brady also ordered a medley of olives, cheese, and crackers.

"If you're hungry, once Duncan gets here, we can get out of this place and find a proper dinner."

"No, that's not necessary. This place is great. I can nosh on appetizer kind of stuff all night."

He placed his hand on my back. "Okay. Just let me know if you get more of an appetite."

The contact of his hand caused me to shift in my seat.

His eyes lingered on mine, to the point that it actually made me blush. "You look fucking amazing tonight, Hazel."

"Thank you."

"I want to kiss you so badly, but I don't know how you'd feel if I did." He groaned. "I wanna do a lot more than just kiss you, actually."

I couldn't remember the last time Brady had said something like that—expressed a need for me in such a way. It was definitely a turn-on to be wanted. I knew he wasn't lying; I could tell from the look in his eyes. It was interesting how much more attractive I seemed to be now that I was somewhat unavailable.

I decided to continue on the path I knew to be better for me.

"I think it's best if you don't...kiss me."

He looked a little defeated. "I figured." Then he smiled. "But I understand. I'll be patient."

The waitress brought the cheese and olive plate, and I began snacking while enjoying my drink, which was thankfully pretty strong.

My eyes wandered over to the door. And that's when my heart dropped.

I blinked.

Holy shit. I must be hallucinating.

I blinked some more.

There was a man at the door who looked just like... Milo.

My heart raced with every second that passed, and it felt like everything I'd just eaten was coming back up. I then remembered Milo had had plans to visit a friend in New York a few days after he left Atlanta. He'd never actually said how long he was staying.

Could it be him?

With eight million people in New York, there was no way we both happened to be in this same tiny bar at the same time. It just couldn't be. What were the odds?

I squinted.

Panic set in.

Oh my God.

The longer I looked over there, the more I was sure. It *was* him.

It was Milo.

Milo was in this bar!

Holy shit.

Holy shit.

Holy shit.

I froze.

Do I sneak into the bathroom?

Do I stay in this corner and hope he doesn't notice me?

Do I grow some balls and go up to him?

What do I tell Brady?

I couldn't put Milo in the situation of having to meet Brady, either.

I wanted to cry.

How could this be happening?

As I struggled to catch my breath, Brady turned to look at me. "Hazel, are you okay? Your face is, like, turning white."

"I'm fine." I panted.

"You don't look fine."

Things only got worse from there as Milo started walking in our direction. It felt like the room was spinning.

Then his eyes landed on mine, and it felt like the world had *stopped* spinning.

Milo looked straight at me.

His mouth dropped open, and he began walking faster, like he couldn't get to me fast enough as he weaved through the crowd.

I knew I had no choice but to deal with this situation head on.

Except I had no clue what I was in for.

Because when Brady turned around to face him, the last thing I ever expected occurred.

He raised his hand, waving Milo over. "Dunc! There you are."

What the hell is happening?

What. Is. Happening?

Duncan is Milo?

Milo is Duncan...Brady's best friend?

As soon as Milo got to our table, he hugged Brady and let his bag drop to the floor. He took one look in my eyes and pretended not to know me. What choice did he have? Before Brady could introduce us, Milo excused himself to the bathroom, saying he had to go badly after his flight. But I knew better. I suspected he needed to get his bearings. He had looked just as shocked as I felt in this moment.

I sat, still trying to make sense of this.

"He must have really had to go," Brady said, clueless to my turmoil.

All of the sounds of the bar became muffled compared to the pounding inside my head.

When I spotted Milo walking back to our table, my heart rate, which had already been racing, moved to sprinting.

He took a seat next to Brady. "Sorry about that."

"Hey." Brady shrugged. "When you gotta go, you gotta go, right?"

Milo's eyes landed on mine. If one look could ask a thousand questions, his certainly did. He looked so confused...hurt...angry.

"Dunc, now that you've properly taken a leak, I can finally formally introduce you to Hazel. I can't believe you two are only now meeting."

"Yeah. Only now. Amazing." Milo reached his hand out to me." Nice to meet you, *Hazel*."

He squeezed my hand. And in his touch, there again were the silent questions emanating from him. I wanted to cry. But I had to keep my composure.

"It's nice to meet you, too...Duncan."

He let go of my hand and explained, "Old friends from college call me Duncan or Dunc. Duncan is actually my last name." He looked into my eyes. "My name is Matteo."

Matteo.

Milo's name is Matteo.

Even though Brady was right there, it felt like we were in our own world as Milo—Matteo—and I introduced our true selves to each other for the first time. It was surreal.

"And I'm...Hazel."

"He already knows your name, babe," Brady interrupted.

I ignored Brady's comment, still staring deeply into his friend's eyes.

Matteo couldn't take his eyes off me, either. "Hazel...like hazelnuts..."

I nodded. "Matteo. Like Matthew."

Brady looked between us. "Okay, this conversation is like an episode of *Sesame Street*." He laughed.

Neither of us joined him.

I got chills. To think I'd called my father to check on him after that psychic mentioned the name Matthew, when it was in reference to *Matteo* all along. He was the one she'd warned me about, and now it all made sense.

The waitress came over and took Milo's... Duncan's...*Matteo's* drink order.

Matteo.

What a beautiful name. A beautiful name for a beautiful man—one who looked more tormented than I'd ever seen him.

His eyes still seared into mine. "So...what's going on with you two? Last I heard, the wedding was off. I'm surprised to see you here, Hazel."

Unable to form words, I looked over at Brady.

"Hazel and I are taking things slowly again. I haven't had a chance to talk to you since the wedding was called off."

"Yeah." He swallowed. "You definitely never mentioned anything."

"I'm sorry you'd already booked your ticket to Vail," Brady said. "But I'm glad you got to visit your family anyway, so it wasn't a waste of a trip."

"Well, yeah, it was about time I visited the old turf anyway."

"So, what have you been up to?" Brady asked. "You took some time off from your teaching gig, right?"

"Yeah. Still in the midst of my sabbatical. I ended up staying in Vail for a little while..." He looked at me. "Then randomly ended up taking a road trip from Colorado through the South. Stayed in Atlanta for a while longer than I'd planned, and then decided to go home to Seattle for a week before coming here."

Brady was still processing. "Wait...you took a road trip alone?"

"No, actually. I met someone in Vail. She and I ended up traveling together."

"Really." Brady smirked. "Was she cute?"

Matteo glanced at me. "Very."

"Where is she now?"

He paused, closing his eyes and looking frustrated, as if he wanted to answer *Right fucking here.*

"We went our separate ways," he finally said.

Brady smacked his hand on the table. "This is why I love this guy. Only Dunc could get some random chick to go on a road trip with him. He has balls. While the rest of us sit around working our nine-to-fives, my man here does the things everyone dreams about."

"Believe me, it's not as fun as you might think being me."

That hurt.

"Whatever happened to her—this girl? What's her name?"

I cringed.

The waitress set a beer in front of him. Matteo took a long swig and slammed the bottle on the table. "Maddie. Her name was Maddie."

"So, any plans to meet up with her again? Or was it just a one-time deal?"

His eyes darted toward mine. "Pretty sure now that our trip was the end of the line."

That message reached me loud and clear. My heart was breaking. There was an undertone of anger in his voice that was unfamiliar to me. I hoped he wasn't mad at me. How could I have known this was going to happen? This was like some kind of nightmare.

While it now made sense why he'd been in Vail—for my wedding that never happened—I still had so many questions.

Did he ever suspect who I was?

If not, how did he not put two and two together after I told him I'd been dumped by my fiancé? It never occurred to him that I could have been Brady's ex? Something was missing.

Then again, we never did exchange names.

Matteo.

Matteo Duncan.

I had to get used to that name.

What killed me about this whole experience was that I could tell Matteo was really hurting, and I couldn't comfort him. His body was rigid. His fists were closed. That told me he never saw this coming and very likely had no inkling who I was.

We were both the apparent victims of bad luck.

Very back luck.

He downed the rest of his beer in one long drink and shoved his chair back before standing up. "I'm gonna let you guys have a romantic evening. I'm pretty tired anyway. Gonna go check into my hotel and call it a night."

Brady's forehead wrinkled. He was definitely confused by his friend's behavior. "I thought you were staying with me?"

"Yeah...that was the original plan, but I decided to get a hotel at the last minute."

"Are you sure?"

"Positive, yeah." He lifted his bag off the ground and threw it over his shoulder.

"Maybe we can hang tomorrow night?" Brady said.

"Yeah. Sure." Matteo looked over at me. "Hazel, it was a pleasure." He reached out his hand, and when I took it this time, he squeezed even harder than before.

Then he turned around and never looked back as he disappeared out the door.

I stared blankly at the exit for what seemed like minutes on end, and Brady finally turned to me.

"Duncan seemed a little off. Something must be up with him."

My heart still reeling, I exhaled. "Yeah..."

"He's fun as all hell, but he's been through his share of shit. His girlfriend died a few years back in a skiing accident. Not sure I ever mentioned that when you and I met. It happened before you. Anyway, I wonder if seeing us together again reminded him of her or something."

I shut my eyes tightly.

"He's never really been the same since that happened. Duncan was so full of life before Zoe died. He used to sing—perform at clubs. You can imagine he had no problem getting women." He chuckled. "But once he met her, it was like he'd met his match. They started performing together. It seemed he'd found his soulmate, until the accident."

I swallowed. "That's so sad."

Brady stared off. "I should've been a better friend to him all these years. We lost touch a bit. He fell into his own world, and I should've made more of an effort

196

to be there for him. It's hard to do that from across the country, but I didn't try hard enough. Despite the fact that we'd grown apart, when it came down to choosing a best man, he was still the first person who came to mind." Brady took my hand. "Maybe he'll still have a chance to stand up for me if I'm lucky enough to marry you."

I wanted to vomit—not only because of this conversation, but because someone I cared about very much was out there hurting, and I had no idea how to get to him. I didn't have to even imagine how he was feeling. Because I was feeling every bit of it, too.

Brady looked around the room. "I think our waitress got lost. I'm going to go up to the bar and grab another beer. You want another drink, babe?"

I nodded. The lump in my throat made it difficult to push words out. "I'm going to go to the restroom while you do that."

After Brady disappeared into the crowd, I sat at the table alone for a minute, feeling completely shell shocked.

What the hell was I going to do?

I needed to talk to Milo in the worst way.

But we had never even exchanged phone numbers.

Taking out my phone, I Googled *Matteo Duncan*, hoping by some miracle a phone number would pop up. Of course, luck was again not on my side.

I really needed a few more minutes alone, so I decided to go to the bathroom before Brady got back. As I stood, I looked down and noticed Brady had left his cell phone on the table.

My pulse sped up.

Milo's number.

He *must* have Milo's number in there.

It wouldn't be so strange if I took it to the ladies' room? It would be sort of irresponsible to leave a thousand-dollar phone unattended on the table of a crowded bar.

Not allowing myself to overanalyze it, I glanced around the bar for any sign of Brady. Finding the coast clear, I swiped the phone off the table and practically ran to the ladies' room.

My heart pounded in my chest as I locked myself in a stall. With my hands shaking, I prayed Brady hadn't changed his passcode as I typed it in.

0-5-1-4

Bingo.

The phone unlocked, and I exhaled a loud stream of air.

Calling up the contacts, I typed in Milo and nothing appeared. Realizing Brady would certainly not have his friend listed by our fake Hooker names, I tried *Matteo.* But still nothing came up. So I typed Duncan, praying he was in there.

Thankfully, that was it. I took a deep breath and hit *Call.*

My entire body was tense as the phone just kept ringing.

Pick up.

Pick up.

Pick up.

But in the end, there was no answer. No voicemail, either. It just kept ringing and ringing. So were my ears. Leaning my head against the door of the stall, everything hit me at once. Tears fell down my cheeks, and I wondered how long it would be before Brady figured out there was something very wrong.

Chapter 17

Matteo

It had been two days, and I still felt like shit.

Though, some of this morning's pain might have to do with the amount of liquor I'd consumed last night in the hotel bar and not just the kick in the stomach my buddy and my girl had hit me with.

My girl.

Fuck. That really was how I thought of her. Or had thought. Or still do think. I don't know anymore. I wasn't sure about anything to do with Maddie at this point.

Or *Hazel.*

Her damn name was Hazel.

The fact that we'd never exchanged our real names had seemed almost romantic to me. But after the revelation two nights ago, I realized I'd been nothing but a romantic *fool.* Our fake names only clarified what our relationship had been from the start: *a fraud.*

Her fiancé dumped her two months before the wedding? *Yeah, right.* Funny how when my buddy had called to tell me the wedding was off, he'd told me *his fiancée* had been the one to back out. I'd believed every word Maddie had said to me, without questioning any of it. Even today, after forty-eight hours of letting things sink in, a part of me *still* wanted to believe her. Which was nuts, because why the hell would I take the word of a woman I'd known for such a short time—a woman who'd obviously lied to me about at least one important element of her breakup—over the buddy I'd had for nearly ten years.

An ache in my chest urged me to think about why. But I refused to go there.

I just couldn't.

What difference did it make what feelings I had for her, anyway?

She was my buddy's girl.

She wasn't mine anymore.

Or rather, she never had been.

For forty-eight hours, all I'd done was think about every interaction we'd had. Had I been seeing things that weren't really there? Was I so desperate to connect with someone that I accepted her injured-soul story even though—if I were to look more closely—there had been signs she was full of shit?

There had to be.

You can't spend night and day with a person for nearly two weeks and not see some crack in the façade they're wearing. I had to have been seeing what I wanted to see.

But for the life of me, no matter how often I looked back for those tiny fissures, all I could see was my Maddie.

My Maddie.

I couldn't see who she really was—Hazel who made up stories about being dumped when she'd really taken off on her loving fiancé. Not even in hindsight.

Which was fucked up. Because two nights ago, the truth had slapped me right across the damn face.

Forcing myself out of bed at almost eleven in the morning, I took a quick shower and guzzled a bottle of water, along with a few Tylenol. When I'd checked into the hotel, I'd only booked two nights. So if I didn't extend my stay, housekeeping would be walking in to clean the vacated room soon. I had to push myself to get dressed, hoping my pounding hangover would subside soon, and I headed downstairs to the lobby.

"Hi. I'm in room 1522. I'm supposed to check out today. Would it be possible to extend my stay?"

The hotel clerk typed into his computer. "Sure. Do you want just one more night?"

I had no idea what I wanted. "Yeah, I think so."

A few minutes later, I had a place to rest my aching head for another night, and I was standing outside on a busy Manhattan street corner. I didn't feel like sightseeing, yet I needed some fresh air. So I turned right and started to walk, with no destination in mind. It was the week after Thanksgiving, but unseasonably warm, so at least the weather was cooperating. I walked for about an hour and a half, still unsure where I was heading and not feeling much better than when I left.

When my stomach started to growl, I took out my phone to check the time just as it started ringing in my hand.

Brady flashed on the screen.

Shit.

He'd called me four or five times over the last few days, and I'd ignored every one of his calls. I knew I needed to talk to him. After all, I'd flown three-thousand miles across the country to visit him, and he had no clue what the hell was going on. At least I assumed he didn't. Though for all I knew, Maddie had told him everything, and he was trying to get a hold of me so he could find out where to come kick my ass.

My cell rang a third time, and I was just about to stick it back in my pocket when I decided at the very last second to bite the bullet. I couldn't put it off forever.

"Hello?"

"Dunc? What the hell? You disappeared off the grid. I've been trying to get a hold of you for two days. I was starting to worry."

"Sorry. I…I just…I've been at my hotel."

"What, are you sick?"

I dragged a hand through my hair, wishing I hadn't picked up. "Yeah. I haven't felt like myself."

Just then, a woman ran out of a small grocery store to my right. She wielded a broom in her hand, bristle side up, while chasing a teenage kid and swearing in Spanish. The kid, who was probably about fifteen, had on a backpack, and both his fists were full of candy. He laughed as he looked back over his shoulder at the upset woman.

Brady must've heard the commotion. "Where the hell are you?"

I looked up as I passed the store and read the street signs. "I'm at Fifty-First Street and Ninth Avenue. I just went for a walk."

"Well, you're not too far from my office. Let's grab some lunch."

"I, uh… I'm not sure I'm feeling up to it."

"Well, get up to it. Because I'm not taking no for an answer. You've blown me off for two days, and I'm worried about you, man. Walk down Ninth until you get to Forty-Sixth Street. There's a restaurant I like there called Becco. It's between Eighth and Ninth. I'll meet you there in twenty minutes."

"I really don't—"

Brady cut me off. "Twenty minutes, buddy. Or I'll hunt you down and find your ass."

Before I could say anything else, the phone went silent.

"Hello?"

Nothing.

Fuck.

He'd hung up on me.

Brady was already seated at a table when I finally walked in a half hour later.

He stood and did the one-arm shoulder hug. "There you are. I just ordered a drink without you. I figured you were standing me up. What took you so long? You were ten minutes away, tops."

I dragged a hand through my hair. I hadn't planned on coming until five minutes ago. I'd actually turned around and started walking the opposite direction. Then I realized I'd never get a good night sleep without knowing what the hell was going on, so I'd doubled back against my better judgment.

"Sorry. Got lost."

Brady chuckled. "Sit down, you damn out-of-towner."

The waitress came right over and handed me a menu. "Can I get you something to drink while you take a look at the menu?"

"I'll take a water, please."

My friend plucked the menu from my hand. "Change his water to a bottle of cab, the one you usually have from South Africa, and we'll take the frutti di mare for two."

He handed the waitress back the menus, and she looked to me for approval. Food was the last thing I had the energy to fight over. Plus, it sounded pretty fucking good.

I shrugged. "What he said."

After the waitress disappeared, Brady didn't waste any time diving in. He grabbed a breadstick from the center of the table and bit off a piece. "Talk to me. What's going on with you? Something's up."

"I'm fine."

He made a face that said he wasn't buying it. "I know I've been a shitty friend the last few years. But we dormed together for four years of college. I think I can still tell when you're full of shit."

I let out a deep rush of air. "Give me a bit, okay? I just walked in the door. At least let me get some wine in me before you start making me wake the skeletons in my closet."

Brady nodded. "Yeah, okay. I get it."

Feeling impatient and wanting the spotlight off of me, I turned the tables. "So what's going on with you? I didn't expect to see you with your ex-fiancée when I walked into the bar the other night."

"Yeah. We're working on things."

My heart sank. "So she wants you back after she called off the wedding? Change of heart?"

Brady frowned. "She wasn't exactly the one who called off the wedding." He looked me straight in the eyes. "It was me who ended things."

Ever have a moment in time where you're really down and something gives you a morsel of hope? Yeah? Well, that wasn't me at the moment. Instead of being elated that Maddie hadn't lied, I felt...angry. *Really fucking angry.* My nostrils flared, and I felt my face begin to redden.

Luckily the waitress brought our wine. I immediately drank half the glass back and spoke through gritted teeth.

"What the fuck did you lie to me for?"

Brady at least had the decency to look ashamed. He rubbed the back of his neck and shook his head. "I'd already told my mother and a few other people the truth and got my ass handed to me. I couldn't take any more lectures. Everyone loves Hazel. We'd each agreed to contact our own friends and family to let them know the wedding was off, and by the time I got five people into my hundred-person list, I was tired of staying on the phone for an hour. I didn't have an acceptable reason for doing what I'd done, and everyone thought I was a piece of shit."

"So you lied to the other ninety-five guests and made *her* look like the piece of shit?"

Brady's eyes widened. "Jesus, man. Relax. I lied to take the easy way out and get off the phone quick. I didn't kill anyone. You look like you're about to pop me."

He wasn't wrong. When I looked down at my hands on the table, they were balled tight. I had to make a conscious effort to unfurl my fists.

"Look," he said. "I'm sorry if I misrepresented the facts. But let's not let that get in the way of your visit." He reached out and put his hand on my shoulder. "I miss you, brother."

I needed to pull my shit together. Brady wasn't going to buy that I was pissed off because of what he'd done. Plus, I wanted more information. Like what the fuck happened between them? So I reined myself in.

"Yeah. Okay." I blew out a deep breath. "So...why did you do it? Call off the engagement?"

Brady sipped his wine. "I don't know. I'd met this woman at work." He shook his head. "Athena...Greek...a real bombshell. I started to think about only ever being with one woman for the rest of my life. That's a long-ass time."

I squeezed the wine glass so hard I thought it might break. "So you dumped Maddie because you wanted to screw some other woman?"

Brady's eyebrows furrowed. "Maddie? Who's Maddie? Wait...isn't that the woman you met on your road trip?"

Fuck. "Yeah, sorry. Hazel, I meant Hazel."

"Anyway, Athena and I... We—"

The waitress interrupted our conversation to deliver a giant platter. It smelled delicious, though I had no appetite anymore. She set the giant tray of pasta and seafood down in the middle of the table and used tongs to serve us two heaping plates.

"Would you like some fresh pepper?" She held up an oversized grinder.

"That would be great," Brady said. "Thanks."

When she was done, she turned to me. I shook my hand back and forth, even though I'd normally put pepper on anything. "No, thanks."

After she walked away, I waited for Brady to finish his sentence, to tell me if he'd cheated on Maddie. But instead, he shoveled a huge forkful of spaghetti into his mouth and spoke with it full while pointing at my plate. "Dig in. This stuff is fantastic."

I tried to not come off as overly interested, but I needed to know. Picking up my fork, I twirled it into the pasta. "So, continue your story. You were talking about this woman, Athena?"

Brady waved me off. "It's not important. What matters is I've come to my senses, and I'm getting my girl back."

I had no idea how I was going to swallow this forkful of pasta. "She wants to get back together?"

Brady shrugged and plucked a little-neck clam from his plate. He forked the meat off the shell and shoved it into his mouth. "She's getting there. She wants to make me work for it, though, of course."

He looked over at my plate and pointed again. "What's the matter? You don't like it? I figured it would be right up your alley. Remember that little shack we used to go to off Route 70 for all-you-can-eat fried clams? You always took home a doggy bag *and* a waitress. Well, that was before you met Z..." He frowned and caught my eye. "Sorry."

I looked away. "It's fine. I can talk about her now."

Brady nodded and offered a sad smile. "I'm glad, buddy. Really glad. Now tell me what's going on with you. I know something is off, so don't try to bullshit me again."

I tried to come up with an explanation he'd buy, but I couldn't. My mind was too fucked up to formulate a lie. So I went with the truth—a version of it, anyway. "It's no big deal. I met this girl back in Vail."

Brady popped a shrimp into his mouth. "Maddie? The one you went on the road trip with."

"Yeah. I, uh... I guess I fell kinda hard. I thought maybe it could go somewhere, but it turned out she's unavailable."

"Unavailable? So, what, she's married?"

I shook my head. "No. But...she's sort of seeing someone. I guess it's been off and on."

Brady smirked. "So steal her away, Romeo. I'm sure women still fall at your feet. I mean, I think you're ugly as sin, but the ladies always found something about you appealing."

Steal her away.

"I wish it were that simple," I said.

He picked up his wine glass and tilted it toward me. "Are you in love with her?"

My heart started to race. I'd asked myself that very question a few hundred times over the weeks since Maddie had walked out the door in Atlanta. And not until this moment did I truly know the answer. *Great fucking timing to have an epiphany.*

My shoulders slumped. "Yeah, I think I am."

He knocked back the rest of his wine. "Then let me give you a piece of advice—from one guy who almost lost his girl to another. Don't be a chickenshit and let her slip through your hands. I don't give a crap if she has a boyfriend or not. If you're in love with her, go for it. You don't always get a second chance."

I doubted more fucked-up advice had ever come from the man who has the girl to the dude who wants to steal her. I felt like total shit.

Not knowing how to respond, I simply said, "Thanks."

One torturous hour later, I felt like I'd run an Ironman as we walked out onto the street after lunch.

I was emotionally spent, and the abuse I'd done to my body last night had taken a physical toll. I needed to go lie down.

Brady patted my back. "So how long are you in town?"

I shook my head. "I'm not sure."

"What do you say we play cards like the old days? Some poker? Remember Trevor Winston? He was a year behind us at CU. When he drank too much, he'd repeat everything twice. '*Anyone want another beer while I'm up? Anyone want another beer while I'm up?*'"

I laughed for the first time in two days. I did remember Trevor, now that he'd described him that way. Nodding, I said, "We called him Trevor Two Times."

"That's him. He lives a few blocks away from me. Every once in a while, we pull together a card game. I'll see if I can organize one for Sunday, so we can watch football while we play. It'll be just like the frat-house days, except my apartment doesn't have sludge on the floor, and the beer won't be whatever is the cheapest on the shelf at the store that takes fake IDs."

The only thing I felt like doing was getting the hell out of here. Yet I figured playing cards with a few of the guys was getting off easy.

"Yeah, okay."

"Great. And tomorrow night, we're going out. I know a great little place that has amazing food and even better live music. You'll love it."

I shrugged, because Brady sounded so pumped, I figured he would fight me if I said no. But I had no intention of going. "Maybe."

"What hotel are you staying at?"

"The Executive. Downtown."

"Good. I'll be at your hotel at seven thirty tomorrow. I get that you're down. But we're brothers. Let me try to cheer you up a bit."

Brothers. That was the cherry on top of the shit cake.

I forced a smile. "I appreciate what you're trying to do. But how about I text you tomorrow and let you know?"

"Sure." He smiled. "Text me. Though, like I said, I'll be at your hotel to get you at seven thirty, either way."

I shook my head. I'd have to deal with this one later. Holding out my hand to shake, I said, "Thanks for lunch."

Brady used my hand to pull me in for a bear hug. He slapped my back. "I really missed you, man. I'll see you tomorrow night."

Chapter 18

Hazel

"Hey, babe."

The rare, recent smile I'd had on my face turned south when I heard Brady's voice on the other end of my cell—not because he hadn't been amazing lately, but because every time my phone rang, I got my hopes up that somehow it was Matteo. I'd snuck in and used Brady's phone to call him three times over the last few days. Each time, I'd left my cell number on his voicemail, hoping he'd return my call. No such luck.

I motioned to my photography assistant to finish unpacking the equipment we'd just carried into the school auditorium and stepped into the hall with my phone.

"Hey. What's going on?" I asked.

"Not much. Just wanted to hear your beautiful voice to start my day."

Brady was *really* trying. "Well, I can only talk for a minute. We're setting up to start kindergarten portraits over at an elementary school in Millville."

211

"Kindergarten? That's your favorite grade to shoot, isn't it?"

"Yeah. The experience is new and everything is exciting to them, so they usually have the best, most genuine smiles. By the time they get to sixth grade, they're already masters at posed selfies, so not much is genuine anymore."

"It's great how much you love your job."

While Brady meant well, his comment was a reminder of how little he actually paid attention. Ninety percent of the time, my job bored the hell out of me. I found myself thinking, *Milo would know*, and that made my head hurt. Especially when I realized I'd just thought of him as *Milo* and not Matteo.

Ultimately, I had to remember it was my responsibility to find happiness for myself—whether that meant a career change or somehow finding my way to the right decision about my life partner. *Ugh.*

"Listen, I know you're busy," Brady said. "I just wanted to check in with you and say good morning, and see if you had plans for tonight. I was thinking we could go to that dinner place with live music in the West Village that you like so much."

"Finn's?"

"Yeah, that's the one. It would be a double date."

"A double date? Who's the other couple?"

"My buddy Matteo."

It felt like the needle on a record had screeched to a halt, along with my heart. "Matteo has a...date?"

Brady chuckled. "He doesn't know it yet. I thought I'd ask my sister to set him up with one of her friends. We had lunch yesterday, and he's really down over some woman. Figured it would help cheer him up."

My eyes widened. "A woman?"

"Yeah. The one he'd mentioned that he met on his road trip. Sounds like she's jerking him around. He could definitely use a fun night out. And music is his thing. The poor guy is walking around like someone ran over his dog."

Heaviness settled into my chest. "So Matteo's... sad?"

"Yeah, he is. So whadda you say? Double date tomorrow night?"

There were so many reasons to decline. First, the thought of Matteo on a date with another woman made me feel sick, much less a date I'd have to watch up close and personal. Second, Matteo and I still hadn't spoken, so I had no idea how we were supposed to handle things. Though obviously, he'd followed my lead and was still pretending we didn't know each other. A double date with Matteo and Brady would very likely be a colossal disaster. Yet...I couldn't get him to return my calls, and I had no idea where he was staying to go knock on his door. So, as much as I knew more things could go wrong than right, I found myself feeling desperate.

"Okay. Yes, I'll go."

I heard the smile in Brady's voice. "Thanks, babe. You're the best."

Since Brady was already in the city, the plan was for me to meet him and Matteo at Finn's.

I'd taken the train in and arrived early. Unfortunately, Brady's sister's friend, Kimber—Matteo's apparent date—had also arrived early and was already sitting at our reserved table. To my dismay, Kimber had supermodel looks—long, blond hair and long legs to match—and that made sense because she was—surprise, surprise—a model.

I was stuck making small talk with her until the men arrived.

"So, where are you working, Kimber?"

"Right now I'm waitressing in between modeling jobs."

"That's exciting...being a model."

She shrugged. "Everyone always told me I should be a model, so I figured I might as well."

Looking around the room, I muttered, "Yeah."

I had zero to say to her. Then again, my jealousy over the fact that she was here to meet Matteo might have skewed my opinion of the whole situation just a tad. Let's face it, she didn't stand a chance with me tonight. I was going to hate her no matter what.

For a while, there was nothing but dead air between us as we sipped our drinks. My eyes kept wandering over to the door, hoping Brady and Matteo would walk in.

Kimber excused herself to visit the bathroom, and I let out a sigh of relief to not have to stare at her face for a few minutes.

I immediately picked up my phone, calling Brady to find out where he was.

He answered, "Hey, babe. Got out of work a bit late. Just headed over to Dunc's hotel now. We should be there within a half hour."

I let out an exasperated breath. "Great. I was hoping you'd say you were right around the corner. I've been sitting here with your sister's friend."

"How is she?"

"She seems young and shallow."

"Sort of like my sister..." He laughed. "No wonder they're friends."

"So, you don't care that you're setting Duncan up with someone like that?"

He chuckled. "I don't think Dunc is going to care. She's attractive and will hopefully get him out of the funk he's in."

"Do you really think setting him up with someone who can't offer him more than a pretty face is helpful?"

"Trust me, what he needs right now is a good lay. I told you, he's hung up on that chick he went on a road trip with—the one who went back to her boyfriend. He needs a distraction. He doesn't need to be getting involved with someone right now while he's traveling. He just needs someone to get his mind off things. From my understanding, based on what Leah told me, Kimber's perfect for that."

I was so frustrated. And the fact that Matteo had discussed me cryptically with Brady made me uneasy.

"Okay, well...try to get here as fast as you can."

"I'll do my best."

I was just about to hang up when he said, "Hazel?"

"Yeah?"

"I can't wait to see you."

I sighed. "You, too."

Brady was still being so sweet and considerate. But I couldn't appreciate it tonight. I felt sick to my stomach as I tried to remind myself why I was here. It was my opportunity to see Matteo, to read him, and to make sure he was okay.

After Kimber returned from the bathroom, the two of us made more small talk. She showed me some modeling photos of herself on her phone. It was the first time we actually had anything to talk about since the photos led to me mentioning my photography business, and the conversation evolved somewhat from there.

When I spotted Brady and Matteo walking into the restaurant, my heart began to pitter-patter.

I waved to let them know where we were seated, even though the hostess was clearly already leading them in our direction.

"Holy shit. That's him? With the longish hair?" Kimber licked her lips.

Down, bitch.

I swallowed. "Yes."

Her jaw dropped as she took in Matteo, and that made me more nauseous.

"He's even hotter than Leah said."

Wearing a black wool coat and dark jeans, Matteo did look handsome. My heart clenched as I longed to be back on our road trip, when things were so much simpler. If only I could have snapped my fingers and made that happen, erasing this whole complicated mess we'd gotten into. The fact that I was admiring Matteo with Brady right there also made me feel a little guilty.

Brady kissed me on the cheek. "Sorry to make you wait." He then looked to Matteo. "Duncan, this is my sister's good friend, Kimber."

Kimber made googly eyes at him. "Really nice to meet you."

"You, as well." He didn't look at me as he sat down next to her.

It took a while before his eyes finally landed on mine.

I got up the nerve to say, "It's nice to see you again, Matteo."

He nodded and forced a smile.

Kimber immediately struck up a conversation with him, leaning in and twirling her hair. She definitely seemed to want him. And why wouldn't she? I couldn't say I blamed her. But I was burning up with jealousy watching it all go down.

Matteo seemed to perk up a little more with each minute that passed as he listened to her go on and on about her recent night out to see *Hamilton* on Broadway. That morphed into a conversation about music, and it seemed like they were actually getting along pretty well.

Then Brady chimed in, "What Duncan is neglecting to tell you, Kimber, is that he's a pretty damn good musician in his own right."

Her eyes widened. "Gorgeous and talented? Wow, you're just the whole package, aren't you? What do you play?"

My eyes were glued to her hand on his arm. I wanted to scream, *"Don't touch him."*

"Guitar, and I do some singing," Matteo answered humbly.

"*Some* singing?" Brady laughed. "His voice is incredible. You should hear him."

Kimber squeezed Matteo's arm. "I'd love to."

As impressive as it all seemed, this girl had no idea just how much of a catch Matteo was. She didn't know him like I did. Because not only was he gorgeous and talented on the surface, he was respectful and giving. He was just as beautiful on the inside.

Every second that passed while they were talking and seeming to get along really well was pure torture. I wanted to wiggle my nose and disappear like the chick from *Bewitched.*

Brady placed his hand on my knee under the table, and it made me fidget. I smiled over at him from time to time, but for the most part we were quiet, listening in on Matteo and Kimber's conversation. I knew, in Brady's mind, the purpose of tonight was to get his friend laid. I could tell by the look on his face as he watched them that he assumed his mission had been accomplished.

I was also starting to believe that scenario was a real possibility, which worried the hell out of me. Sure, Kimber was attractive. But I also wondered if Matteo felt the need to also take her back to his hotel just to spite me, to punish me for spending time with Brady. Or worse, what if he wrongly assumed I'd somehow known who he was all this time and hated me because he thought I'd deceived him?

Overcome with emotion, I needed a breather.

"I'll be back. Heading to the restroom," I said as I got up.

Nearly knocking into two people as I walked across the restaurant, I finally found my way to the bathroom. Once in the safety of that private space, I stared at myself in the mirror. I looked flushed. That came as no surprise, considering I'd been white-knuckling my way through this evening.

I didn't feel like going back to the table, so I took my time, checking my makeup, washing my hands carefully.

When I finally forced myself out of the bathroom, the last thing I expected was to see Matteo exiting the men's room at the same time.

He froze, and we stood facing each other in the small hallway between the restrooms. Had he come here hoping to find me? Or did he just have to go to the bathroom?

I finally said, "How come you didn't answer my calls?"

He glanced out toward the dining area before his eyes returned to mine. "Because I didn't know what to say to you, Maddie. I still don't." He looked down at his feet and muttered, "Fuck, I mean Hazel."

"Are you taking her back to your hotel?" I blurted. I couldn't help it. I needed to know.

He looked up at me. "No."

I let out a sigh of relief that was probably a bit too obvious. "I know I have no right to admit how damn jealous I am right now, but I can't help it. This whole situation is a nightmare."

Matteo gritted his teeth. "*Nightmare* is a good word to describe what it felt like when I discovered who you are."

"I know." I exhaled. "I can't imagine what that must have been like. I only know what it was like for me. Pure shock...and then sadness." I felt tears forming. "I'm so sorry, Matteo."

His expression softened a bit. "It feels so weird to hear you say my name. But it sounds fucking beautiful, too."

My heart clenched. The words that had been at the tip of my tongue all night but unable to be unleashed finally escaped.

"I miss you," I whispered.

He let out breath of frustration. "Do you realize how messed up this is, Hazel?" He shook his head. "So messed up."

"We need to talk."

It nearly broke my heart when he said, "Is there anything left to say?"

"Maybe it's not right, but yes, I have so many things I need to say to you, things I need to *ask* you."

He glanced out to the dining room again before he lowered his voice. "You think I want that girl out there? I feel like I haven't been able to breathe since I left you in Atlanta. And now I'm just...*choking*. I want to be with *you* tonight, and that's so fucked up, because you're my best friend's woman."

I wanted to take him into my arms and hold him, but I refrained. His words left me speechless.

Fishing in my purse, I took out a pen and found a gum wrapper to write on. I jotted down my number.

"We can't do this right now. But please call or text when you can. Don't go back to Seattle until we've had a chance to talk," I begged. "Please."

He took the wrapper and placed it in his pocket before heading back to the table ahead of me.

We didn't say anything to each other for the rest of the dinner, and he barely looked at me.

And once the live music started, everyone's attention turned to the band. That was a good buffer in the midst of a tense night. But as the four of us supposedly watched the performance, Kimber was gazing at Matteo. And I was watching both of them. Matteo and Brady seemed to be the only ones truly paying attention to the music.

While I was sure Kimber would try to weasel her way back to his hotel room, I trusted Matteo's word when he said he wasn't going to entertain that. He didn't owe me anything, but I somehow knew he wouldn't do anything to hurt me.

During a break in the performance, Matteo left the table. At first I thought he was headed for the bathroom.

But then he went up to the lead singer and started talking to him.

The next thing I knew, the guy handed him a guitar. My heart beat faster as it hit me that he was about to perform.

Matteo took a seat on a stool and adjusted the microphone in front of him. "These guys were nice enough to let me entertain you during their intermission. Just don't throw stuff at me, okay?"

The audience laughed.

"This is a song called 'Almost Lover' by A Fine Frenzy."

Almost Lover.

When he started to sing, everything else in the room faded into the background.

I closed my eyes, listening to his gravelly yet soothing voice and took in every word of the song he'd chosen. It was about saying goodbye to an unrequited love. It was haunting and beautiful all at once, and I was one-hundred-percent sure he was singing it to me.

Chapter 19

Matteo

It had been a couple of days since I saw Hazel, and I still hadn't called her. I'd also been avoiding Brady, which was ridiculous considering the purpose of this trip was to visit him. Brady had no clue that the song I performed at Finn's was meant for his girlfriend. There was no end to how screwed up that was. And yet I couldn't help trying to get that message to Hazel, wanting her to know that I cherished what we'd had, but nothing could likely ever come of it now.

I struggled with whether I was in the wrong for continuing to want her, despite knowing the truth. And what Brady had confided in me about her had made the situation even more confusing. He'd called off the wedding because he had the hots for some Greek chick and that made him have second thoughts? *What the fuck?* And now he'd come to his senses? He seemed to really care about Hazel, but I wondered how she would feel if she knew the full story. And was I bastard for wishing she did? Would that even change anything? If she left him, we still couldn't be together. As much as Brady was in the wrong for how he'd handled things. He was my friend and deserved my loyalty. At least that's the way it's supposed to work.

Sitting on a bench in the middle of Central Park, I'd become so wrapped up in my own head that I didn't notice an old man sitting to my right until he said something.

"Boy, you must have gotten yourself into some serious shit."

I turned to him. "Why do you say that?"

The guy had bushy eyebrows and was holding on to a cane. He gestured to a woman sitting across from us on another bench.

"That looker over there has been eyeing you for a full ten minutes, and you haven't noticed her once. You must be preoccupied."

I sighed. "Yeah, I guess you could say that."

"It must be a lady. Only a woman you're hung up on could keep you from noticing that one over there."

Nodding, I chuckled. "You're right."

"Feel like unloading on an old geezer?" He leaned in. "Maybe I can help?"

While I doubted the guy could offer me any solid advice, I took the opportunity to vent to a stranger who couldn't judge me. I proceeded to tell him everything over the next twenty minutes.

It turned out his name was Sherman. He'd lived in Manhattan all his life and had never been married. He shared a story with me about the one who got away—a woman who'd been traveling through the city some forty years ago. They'd had a whirlwind romance for two weeks before she left to go back to Norway. In those days, there was no Internet or any easy way to keep in touch. So he lost track of her and always regretted not fighting harder to make things work.

He had a lot to say about my situation. "By the time you come to your senses, sometimes it's too late. Now, I'm not telling you to do wrong by your friend. But it doesn't sound to me like this guy knows exactly what *he* wants, either. I get you not wanting to betray him. It's not my place to tell you what to do one way or the other. But in the end, you fell for this woman without realizing who she was, not even knowing her name. You can't help that you fell, and you didn't do anything wrong. But the most important thing here is not what you or he wants. The question is...what does *she* want? Do you know?"

If only it were possible to figure out what Hazel was really thinking.

"I thought I had the answer to that before I came here. I would've bet all my money that she would have met me in New Orleans. So, seeing her with him really shocked me. And now I can honestly say I don't know what she wants."

He pointed with his cane. "Here's the thing. If you want to be with her, and she wants to be with you—well, that's two out of three. I get that your friend would be hurt, but it wouldn't be fair to him if the woman he claims to care about really wants to be with his friend, either. People can't change how they feel. I think you need to figure out what *she* wants and take it from there."

It was simple advice, but it made sense. If Hazel intended to stay with Brady, he'd never have to know anything. If she wanted to be with me, then and only then would I have a decision to make. Concluding that it all came down to what Hazel wanted seemed to clarify the situation.

"You know what? You've been really helpful." I hopped up.

He laughed, seeming amused by my sudden realization and need to flee.

"You take care of yourself, Sherman. Thanks for the talk."

I pulled out my phone as I rushed away and texted the number Hazel had given me.

Matteo: Where are you?

The three dots moved around as she typed.

Hazel: Hey. Just finishing up a shoot.

Matteo: Can we meet?

Hazel: Yeah. Of course.

Matteo: I can come to you.

Hazel: That would be great.

Matteo: I need to be sure Brady won't see us. Where is he?

Hazel: He's working late tonight. He told me he has a business dinner. So, if you come to Connecticut, we should be good. You can meet me here at the studio.

Matteo: Text me the address. I'll hop a train now.

Hazel's studio was on Main Street in a quiet suburb. Surrounded by local boutiques and restaurants, it was definitely in a prime location.

She opened the door before I even made it to the steps. She'd been watching for me.

Without saying anything, she pulled me into her arms. It surprised me, but it felt so damn good to hug her again. The feel of her soft breasts pressed against my chest further ignited the turmoil inside of me. I wished so badly that we were back in Atlanta, taking up where we'd left off before reality hit us like a ton of bricks.

Letting a long breath out against her neck, I took a moment to enjoy the feel of her in my arms without guilt.

"I've been dying to see you," she said. "I'm so sorry about everything, Matteo."

"Stop apologizing." I moved back to look at her face. "You didn't do anything wrong, Hazel. I need you to know that."

"I was afraid you thought I'd somehow known who you were."

"Of course not." I sighed. After several seconds of silence, I took her back into my arms and whispered into her skin. "I just want you to be happy, okay? You have to follow your heart. If being with Brady is what makes you happy, then—"

"I haven't been able to think about anything but you." She pushed back to look me in the eyes.

Her admission stopped me in my tracks. Now I was speechless.

"I know it might look like I'd been planning to take Brady back, but the truth is, I hadn't made any decisions. We've just been spending time together and—

"You don't owe me an explanation. We're not a couple. We're two people who had a great time together. We had plans to maybe meet up again, but nothing was set in stone. It was always supposed to be about what felt right. You need to do what *feels* right. If you want to be with Brady, then— "

"When I came back, everything that happened between us almost felt like a dream, Matteo. Then when Brady told me he regretted canceling the wedding, it was like a reality check. I thought I owed it to myself to give him a chance, but at the same time, I owe it to myself to figure out who I really am and what I want. Either way, through it all, I haven't been able to get you out of my mind." She reached for me. "Then to find out who you really are... It's just been too much."

I squeezed her hands. "I've been a wreck."

We stared at each other until she finally said, "I have to ask you something."

"Ask me anything."

"How did it not occur to you even once that I could have been Brady's ex?"

This was the one question I'd feared her asking. Because in order to tell her the truth, I'd have to betray Brady's trust and admit that he'd lied to me.

How could I admit what Brady had told me? I couldn't. I had to come up with a generic answer that would buy me some time.

"I can honestly tell you it didn't occur to me even once." That was technically a truthful statement.

"I figured you couldn't have known... It's just so hard to believe this happened." She blew out a long breath. "Tell me what you did after I left Atlanta."

"I was in a funk. I missed you...badly. Originally, I was gonna go straight to New York, but I just felt like being home for a little bit first. So I went back to Seattle, spent Thanksgiving with a friend, and also checked in on my apartment and Bach."

Her mouth curved into a smile. "Bach is your cat's name?"

"Yeah." I smiled. "He's been staying with a friend of mine. She's one of the other teachers and offered to take him in."

"So you checked in on Bach and then came to New York. What were your plans for after this trip?"

I needed her to know.

"You want the truth?"

"Yeah..."

"These next few months were going to be about biding my time until I got to see you again. I feel like now I may have to hold my breath forever." I cupped her cheek. "I don't know where your mind is, Hazel. I can tell you that without a doubt, my plan was to meet you in New Orleans and not to let you go again. But at this point in time, I have no plans. I can't see beyond today."

She shut her eyes tightly, looking tormented. "How long are you staying in New York?"

"I keep changing my plans. I've extended my hotel a few times and rebooked my flights. Right now I'm supposed to check out tomorrow and fly home."

A look of panic crossed her face. "What time is your flight?

"Around eight at night."

"Can you please change it again? Will you stay a little longer?"

I had no idea how to answer that. "As it is, Brady knows something is up with me," I told her. "He won't stop talking about how I ditched Kimber the other night. He knows I'm hung up on someone. He just doesn't know it's *you*. I don't know how much longer I can keep pretending to be okay when I'm not, Hazel."

"We need a bit more time to figure this out," she begged. "Please..."

I nodded. "Maybe I could tell Brady I've decided to explore the city some more."

She breathed a sigh of relief. "Please do that."

Hazel took my hand and led me over to the white backdrop she had set up for portraits.

"What are you doing?"

She smiled. "Humor me for a minute, please?"

After situating me on a stool in the middle of the backdrop and brushing a few wayward pieces of hair out of my eyes, she grabbed a camera from her desk. Raising it to her face, she said, "Smile pretty for the camera."

"That's not an easy request these days."

She lowered the camera, and her playful smile wilted. "I know. But give me whatever you can, please. I want to show you something."

I stared at her, realizing that even now there wasn't much I wouldn't do for this woman. Pretty sure if she told me to get up and hop around like a frog, I'd be busy ribbiting on the floor. So I guess forcing a smile wasn't so bad.

Giving in, I flashed my best pretend smile, and Hazel snapped a bunch of pictures. When she was done, she looked back through the digital shots in the viewfinder and printed one out on an enormous printer in the corner that looked more like a copy machine. Walking back toward her desk, she unzipped a leather carrying case on the floor, took something out of a folder, and came back to where I still sat on the stool.

She held up the picture she'd just taken with one hand, and I frowned. *Jesus Christ. Do I really look like that?* The best I could describe my expression is that it looked like someone had just told me they'd run over my dog and then forced me at gunpoint to smile. I was about to comment on the photo when she raised the one in her other hand.

The second photo wasn't of my face, but I was certain it was me. Not because I'd spent countless hours studying my mouth and knew intimately what my teeth looked like, but because one glance at the smile on my face and I knew *exactly* what I'd been thinking in that moment. My mind had envisioned me lying flat on my back with her sitting on my face. Her pussy was practically smothering me, while my cock was down her throat. Yeah...I *definitely* remembered that smile. Swallowing, I looked up at her.

"*This*..." She shook the hand with photo sixty-nine back and forth. "I miss *this*, Matteo. This beautiful smile and the man who gave it to me so easily and often. You can't leave..." She held up the other photo. "You can't leave like this."

We stared at each other for a long time. Eventually, I nodded. I was confused about a lot of things—how life could have thrown this curve ball our way, if I could ever be *that guy* to Brady. You know the one. We all have one in our circle of friends. He's kind of on the outside perimeter, but nevertheless still part of the group. We're all friends with him, yet we wouldn't leave our girlfriend who's had a little too much to drink alone with him either.

Yeah, that guy.

I wasn't sure if I could be that guy. Though I also wasn't sure how I could walk away and never look back at this woman again. So I was totally turned inside out right about now. But I knew I didn't want to leave yet. Hazel and I might not wind up with a happily ever after. In fact, I was pretty certain that wouldn't be the case. Still, I couldn't end this story right here.

Not yet.

Not like this.

"So...can we spend some time together?" she asked hesitantly.

I raked my hand through my hair and blew out a deep breath. "Yeah. We need to be careful, though. I don't want Brady to find out and screw things up for you, if..." I just couldn't bring myself to finish the damn sentence.

Hazel smiled sadly. "You're even thinking of me first when it comes to this." She reached out and touched my cheek. "It takes a special heart to be able to do that. I hope you know that."

Here she was telling me what a good heart I had, and just her simple touch on my cheek made me want to press her up against the wall and kiss the living shit out of her.

"Trust me." I nuzzled into her cheek. "My heart isn't thinking about my friend at this moment."

The spark that had always been there between us began to burn inside of me again. Looking into Hazel's eyes, I saw the change in her, too. Which meant I needed to get the hell out of here. My head wasn't clear, and I didn't want to fuck things up if I was going to stick around for a while.

I took her hand from my cheek and held it in mine. Squeezing, I said, "I should go."

She nodded. "When can I see you again?"

"Tomorrow afternoon I'm supposed to be playing cards with Brady and a friend we went to college with while we watch the Giants game."

"Could I see you after that, maybe? Monday I have a photo shoot that's going to go all day, and then I have a private maternity shoot in the evening. I don't want to wait until Tuesday. I could come to your hotel after you get back?"

I shook my head. "I don't think that's a good idea. It's a New York hotel room. The room is basically a bed."

"Does it have a lobby bar? Maybe we could have drinks? Or if not, go somewhere nearby?"

"I don't want you traveling into the city at night."

"I do it all the time."

"Maybe. But not because of me. I'll come to Connecticut."

"How about my house? I could show you my wall of smiles."

As long as we kept things confined to the living room, I figured that would be okay. Plus, I didn't want to be walking around where we could run into any people she and Brady might know. "I'd like that."

I tilted my head toward the door. "I'll text you tomorrow when I leave the city."

We looked at each other awkwardly. The last time we'd said goodbye in private, we'd mauled each other.

But there was nothing wrong with a hug. Friends hug. So I took a step forward and brought her into an embrace. Hazel wrapped her arms around me and squeezed hard, not letting go.

I finally forced the separation. Pulling back, I nodded one last time. "Have a good night, Ma..." I corrected myself. "Hazel."

She smiled sadly. "You, too, Mi...Matteo."

Chapter 20

Matteo

I felt like a damn traitor.

"What the hell are you doing? Memorizing the things? Do you want a card or not?"

I blinked a few times and found Brady staring at me. "Huh?"

He chuckled and shook his head. "You're lucky I'm a good friend, or you'd be walking out of here with only the lint in your pockets. You usually kick my ass at poker. What the hell is up with you today?"

Trevor stood from the card table. He pointed to Brady. "You want a beer?" He pivoted and pointed his finger in my direction. "You want a beer?"

That made me smile. *Trevor Two Times.* "I guess you caught a buzz, huh? I guess you caught a buzz?"

Brady smirked. "He drank, like, eight already. He drank, like, eight already."

Trevor flipped the table the bird. "*Dicks.* I'm only getting myself a beer."

Eddie, Brady's neighbor and the fourth in our card game this afternoon, stood. "I have to run downstairs and put whatever gross concoction my wife made into the oven so she can burn it when she comes home. I'll be back in five minutes."

Brady stretched his arms over his head. We'd been playing a few hours, since the first game started at one. "So what did you wind up doing last night?" he asked.

Ugh. I was going to have to start writing down my lies so I could remember them all. "I just walked down to a bar near my hotel and had a few drinks."

He sipped his half-empty beer. "Out cruising? You could've taken Kimber home with you the other night if you were looking for a hookup."

I shrugged. "Wasn't feeling it."

"Yeah. She's a gorgeous model who was into you, doesn't want a commitment, and lives halfway across the country. I can see why she wouldn't be the perfect candidate for a hookup," he said sarcastically. "Have you talked to that girl you're hung up on yet?"

Shit. "Uh, yeah. Just for a few minutes."

"She still jerking you around?"

I shook my head, feeling defensive of Hazel. "She's not jerking me around. She just came out of something, and she's not sure if it's over."

Brady finished off his beer and set it on the table. "Oh, that's over."

My brows furrowed. "What makes you say that?"

"Well, even if she doesn't wind up with you, if she's out there falling for another guy, whatever she had with the first guy wasn't going to last anyway."

If he only knew...

Brady had never been philosophical, but he did have a point. If you're truly in love with someone, your heart should be full, and there wouldn't be room to let another person in. "I guess..."

"Did you fool around with this girl?"

I couldn't believe I was having this conversation. "No. It wasn't like that."

"So it's not about great sex then?"

I shook my head. I definitely needed to extricate myself from this somehow—change the subject. Then it dawned on me, I could turn the tables. My own morbid curiosity wanted to know what had gone down with the Greek woman who caused Brady to call off his wedding, and this was the perfect opportunity to toss out a question and get the heat off of me at the same time.

"What about you?" I asked. "You just said if you're in love with someone and you're out there falling for another person, the first relationship is doomed. Didn't you tell me about some woman—Athena, I think you said her name was? Doesn't that mean you and Hazel are doomed?"

He smiled. "That's different."

"How? Because we're talking about you now and not me?"

"No. Because I never *fell* for Athena. It was just a physical thing between us. If you saw what she looks like, you'd understand."

Trevor came back from the kitchen. He passed us each a beer, even though he'd said he wasn't getting us any, and twisted the cap off his. "What who looks like?"

Brady responded. "A Greek goddess from my office."

Trevor took a swig of his beer. "Oh yeah? Set me up." He wiggled his brows. "Greek is my favorite thing to eat."

"She's not your type," Brady said.

Trevor looked offended. "Why not?"

236

He smirked. "Because she's into tall, clean cut, physically fit, successful dudes, that's why."

Trevor was short, scrawny, and had a long, hipster beard. He looked at me and thumbed in my direction. "So I guess he's not her type either? Dunc needs a haircut."

Brady laughed. "Didn't you go to college with us? Dunc is *every* chick's type. I only hung around him for the leftovers."

Eddie came back into the apartment, and I knew our discussion was about to go off track. I gave it one last-ditch effort. Picking up my beer, I twisted off the cap, tossed it into the middle of the table, and pointed the bottle at Brady. "So set me up with Athena then. Maybe I'll like her better than Kimber."

Brady grabbed the cards from the table and started shuffling. "I would. But you have that rule. At least you did in college."

"What rule?"

"You don't dip your pen where your fraternity brothers have inked before."

It was almost nine by the time the conductor on my train announced Maddie's station was next. I'd spent the last hour and a half beating myself up over where I was going after where I'd just come from. What kind of a guy spends the day with one of his best buddies from college, a guy whose wedding he was supposed to be in, and then sneaks off to his fiancée's house at night? Or his ex-fiancée anyway.

An asshole—that's who pulls that kind of crap. I knew a few guys who'd done shit like this over the years, and I'd always kept my distance, looking down my nose at them for breaking bro code. Yet while I beat myself up over it, I also could have gotten my ass off the train at a dozen different stops along the way and gone back home.

Instead, I'd found a way to justify my actions.

Brady had cheated on her. He'd come clean on that fact tonight.

So he didn't *deserve* Hazel.

He was the real piece of shit in this equation.

What I'd done, I'd done innocently.

In fact, it was totally *his* fault. If he hadn't called off his damn wedding because he couldn't keep his dick in his pants, I wouldn't have had to take a trip to Vail, and I would have met Hazel when she was his wife.

Goddamn Brady. He was the real cause of the mess we were all in.

Not me.

That was the truth.

Now…if only I could *believe* the shit I'd been telling myself the last hour and a half, I might feel a little better.

I sighed as the train slowed and pulled into the station. I'd texted Hazel when I'd first gotten on to let her know I was on my way. She'd offered to pick me up, but I told her I'd grab a cab and asked for her address, which she'd texted. So I was surprised when the doors slid open, and I stepped off the train, and the first thing I saw was Hazel standing in front of a car parked smack in my line of view.

My mom used to read romance novels and leave them laying around the house open to whatever page she'd stopped at. When I was a teenager, I'd pick them up and read aloud as she cooked dinner—poking fun at what I interpreted as over-the-top, bullshit women's fantasies that didn't exist in real life. But apparently that *crap*—the sweaty palms and swollen hearts skipping a beat when you see the person you love—might not have been so unrealistic after all.

Wiping my hands on my pants as I walked over to Hazel, I heard my blood pumping through my ears. She smiled, and I swear to freaking Christ, I couldn't see anything else but her for a minute. I had complete tunnel vision. I'd known how I felt about her before, but damn... I had it *really* damn bad.

"Hey." I smiled as I reached the car.

She wasted no time wrapping her arms around me and engulfing me in a big hug. "I've been so on edge all day thinking you were going to back out."

I squeezed her as hard as she was squeezing me. "I almost did a dozen times on that train. But I just couldn't."

Hazel pulled back and looked into my eyes. "I'm glad."

I brushed a piece of hair from her face. "Yeah, me, too."

She took a deep breath. "Come on. I have something in the oven, and when I left I couldn't find Abbott to put her in her cage. She likes to hide sometimes."

I smiled. "That's right. I get to meet Abbott the Rabbit."

"You do. And if you're lucky, I'll let you hold the leash when we take her for a walk. It's just about the time I take her for her evening stroll before she goes to bed."

The ride to Hazel's house was only about ten minutes. I'd expected it to be awkward like the other day in her studio, but we'd spent half of the time we'd known each other in a car, and somehow sitting next to her just felt right again. I almost didn't want to get out when we pulled up in front of her house.

"This is me." She pointed to a small, white, Cape-style house on a street with a shitload of tall trees. The neighborhood was quiet and well kept and reminded me a lot of where I lived, actually.

"This looks like the suburbs of Seattle."

"Does it?"

I nodded. "Yeah. I live in an apartment, but the houses and streets are similar."

"It's tiny. But we never had more than two bedrooms growing up, so I think I'd feel lost in a big house."

I loved that she didn't need a lot of flash. And as we walked up the driveway toward her front door, it made me think about how different she was than Brady. Brady's family had some money, and if you were friends with him, you knew that. He didn't come right out and say it in a pompous way, but you could see it in the things he'd waste money on—a hundred bucks for a wool hat just because it had some logo on it or how he always had the most recent iPhone, even though there was nothing wrong with his old one. I hadn't been surprised that his apartment was in a building with a doorman, either. The whole scene was just *him*—guy in a suit opening the door as he approached, sleek-looking stainless steel in the kitchen, and marble in the bathroom. I couldn't see Brady living in something understated like this.

Inside Hazel's house, I looked around. The first room we walked into was the living room, and it led to the kitchen behind it. Hazel made a beeline to the stove, and I followed her into the kitchen.

"Mmm... It smells great in here. Is that brownies?"

"Yup."

My eyes went wide as I stepped into the kitchen. The counters were lined with goodies. There was a plate of what looked like chocolate chip cookies, a plate of Rice Krispies treats, cupcakes frosted in vanilla, and a whole cake frosted in chocolate—not to mention the pan of hot brownies Hazel was currently removing from the oven. "Did you make all of this?"

Hazel set the glass baking dish on top of the stove and bit her bottom lip. "Yeah. I...I'm not good at sitting still when I'm nervous, so I figured I'd make you a snack or two for when you got here." She looked around. "I sort of got carried away."

I smiled. Glancing around, I noticed her kitchen was pretty simple—basic white appliances and store brands, nothing over the top like Brady's place.

"Where were you going to live after..." I couldn't bring myself to finish the question.

"I was going to move to the City, into Brady's apartment."

I didn't see any hint of disappointment about that not happening in her face. "Is that where you want to live? In the City?"

She shrugged. "I'm not really a city girl. It's funny. I love an adventure, but I want my home to be my calm place. I guess I don't find the City that never sleeps very soothing."

I tilted my head. "So why would you have agreed to move there if you didn't really want to live in Manhattan?"

She tugged off the oven mitts and sighed. "I don't know. Compromise, I guess."

My lip twitched. "You do know a compromise is one person giving a little and the other person giving a little, right?"

Squinting at me, she reached over and picked up the plate with the cake. She balanced it in one hand. "Hmmm... I feel like hitting you in the face with this cake. Should we compromise on that? Maybe you'd prefer a cupcake, *wiseass*."

I put my hands up like I was surrendering, and she laughed and set the cake back down. But the minute it was on the table, I scooped out a huge chunk and held it up like I was going to smear it on her face.

Her eyes sparkled.

"You want to start a cake fight, huh?" I took a step closer as little pieces crumbled to the ground from my hand. "I'm ready now."

She took a step back as she laughed. "You wouldn't."

I raised a brow and took another step. "You sure about that?"

Hazel stepped back again, this time bumping into the counter behind her. She had nowhere to retreat. "I made you all of these delicious snacks, and this is how you're going to repay me? Cake in the face?"

I closed the gap between us and put one hand on the stove behind her. Blocking her in on three sides, I brought the cake to within a few inches of her face. "You started it."

"Alright! Alright!" She laughed. "I won't throw cake in your face, and you won't throw that mess in your hand in mine."

I grinned. "Well, whaddya know? The woman knows how to compromise suddenly." I lifted the cake to my mouth and bit off a big chunk. "Mmmm... It's pretty good. Are you sure you don't want some in your face?"

I was teasing, but the cake was actually delicious. I licked my lips to swipe the last morsels off, and when I looked up, I found Hazel's eyes zoned in on my mouth, watching intently. It looked like she was hungry, but not for cake. I became mesmerized, watching her watch me—the way her pupils dilated and the blue of her irises darkened right before my eyes. Eventually, she looked up, and our gazes caught.

The moment was so damn perfect to take her in my arms and kiss her. And I wanted to so damn badly. But I'd just walked in the door. We were alone. And although I'd only passed through the living room and into her kitchen, I could already count fifty different surfaces I wanted to have her on. So I wasn't about to even attempt a kiss. Though, apparently Hazel had other ideas.

I stopped breathing when she pushed up on her toes and moved toward me. Her face was so close that I could feel her warm breath tickling my lips. My heart beat out of control when her eyes closed, assuming she was readying to make the first move. But then suddenly, just before our noses touched, she veered to the right, bringing her mouth to the large clump of cake in my hand. She opened her luscious lips wide and sucked all four of my fingers into her mouth.

Oh shit.

Hazel had the most devilish glint in her eyes as she looked up at me from under her thick lashes. Confirming she had my complete attention, she sucked my fingers in deeper, reaching all the way to my knuckles before pulling back to slowly lick off all of the cake.

Fuck me.

It was the most erotic thing I'd seen in a long-ass time. My jeans grew snug as she finished cleaning me up, releasing my fingers with a loud pop.

Seeing my face, she smirked like the devil she was at the moment. "That was a good compromise, wasn't it?" She tilted her head coyly.

I shut my eyes and shook my head with a groan. "Remind me never to negotiate anything with you. Where's your bathroom? I need a minute."

I wasn't kidding. I needed a bathroom, because the situation in my pants was not going away on its own.

She laughed. "Down the hall on the right."

"Be right back," I said.

She smiled, seeming to know why I needed to rush away. "Okay. I'm going to find Abbott."

My growing erection and I made our way to the bathroom, still thinking about how it had felt when my fingers were in her mouth. *That was too much.* She'd made it way too easy to imagine how that mouth wrapped around my cock would feel.

In fact, it would only take about two seconds to relieve myself. Although I didn't think anything would really do the trick to calm me down tonight. My sexual attraction to Hazel was off the charts, totally out of control. Not sure how I'd thought it was a good idea to come here when I apparently couldn't control my dick, and couldn't trust myself. And she couldn't be trusted either—that finger licking damn near killed me.

Locking the door behind me, I walked over to the sink and splashed some cold water on my face.

Then something came out of nowhere, landing right on the top of the sink.

What the fuck?

I jumped back.

Scared. The. Living. Shit. Out of me.

With long, floppy ears, the little creature looked up at me. The next thing I knew, its two beady eyes were scrutinizing me...judging me for the bulge in my pants.

Abbott the Rabbit.

This is not the opportune time to meet you.

"Holy shit. You scared the crap out of me, little one."

I took a few deep breaths and proceeded to wash my hands, all the while noticing her watching me.

Yeah. I was glad I hadn't decided on a quickie jerk-off session or I'd have had an audience.

"Let's just forget what was going on in here, okay?"

Out of nowhere, she made a noise like a growl. I didn't even know rabbits growled like that.

Reaching out, I carefully lifted her into my arms. She made the same noise again but seemed to be tolerating the contact.

When I emerged from the bathroom, Hazel caught sight of me holding her.

"Oh my heart." She rushed toward us. "You found Abbott! I'd been looking everywhere for her."

"Yeah, everywhere but the bathroom. Little bugger scared the snot out of me—hopped up from inside the bathtub to the top of the sink."

"She has a habit of doing stuff like that. I find her in the weirdest places."

The rabbit purred, seeming to have acclimated to being in my arms.

"She likes you." Hazel smiled. "Her mom likes you, too." Her cheeks turned red as she looked up at me.

Oh, Hazel. All the things I would do to you tonight if I could. I wanted to devour her mouth so badly right now. My eyes lowered to her neck, and I wished I could bite it.

Maybe it was a good idea if we got the hell out of here for a bit.

"Didn't you say you needed to take her out for a walk?"

"Yeah. It's that time of evening. Let me get my leash."

I laughed to myself as she walked away. This was going to be interesting.

After she returned, I bent down, setting the rabbit free and watching as Hazel adjusted the leash around her. We grabbed our coats and headed out for a brisk walk around Hazel's neighborhood.

It was dark aside from the light coming from people's houses. Abbott scurried a few inches in front of us.

"So, no one ever questions why you're walking a rabbit?"

"Oh, I get looks, believe me. I just don't care."

"I love that you don't care. Fuck people if they have a problem with it."

Hazel slowed her pace and arched her neck to look inside one of the houses.

"What's so interesting over there?" I asked.

"Oh, nothing. One of my favorite things to do is walk at night and look inside people's homes," she said. "When it's dark and people have their lights on, you can really see inside. There's something so interesting about catching people in the midst of their daily lives without them knowing, whether it's a man reading a book in the

246

corner of his living room, or a family sitting down to dinner. It's real, unfiltered life, you know?"

"I believe there's a name for that."

"Yeah?"

I knocked my shoulder playfully into hers. "It's called voyeurism."

"Very funny." She laughed.

"So, this...spying inside people's houses while walking Abbott on a leash is basically your nightly routine?"

"Yeah. Abbott likes fresh air, and I find it calming for me, too. Well, except for that one time a dog tried to attack her. Have you ever heard a rabbit scream?"

"Can't say I have."

"They don't do it often, but it sounded like a screaming child. It was a shock to hear that noise come from her. They say rabbits scream when they're feeling truly threatened."

I could relate to that. As soon as she said those words—*feeling threatened*—they reminded me how I felt about losing Hazel to Brady. Maybe I'd feel better if I screamed out into the night like a scared rabbit to let out my frustrations.

I breathed in some of the cold night air. This walk was good for us. The less time alone in her house together, the better.

As Hazel and I continued our stroll, it seemed her habit had rubbed off on me. I was now checking out the insides of people's houses. We caught one couple having a pretty heated argument and watched about two minutes of the news on someone's television.

"Thank you again for agreeing to stay in town a little longer," Hazel said.

I looked down at my shoes hitting the pavement. "Leaving so soon didn't exactly feel right, although I'm not sure I'll be going back with any more closure than if I'd left when I was originally supposed to. This feels like...an impossible situation. And right now, time doesn't seem to be fixing it."

That was more than I should've shared on what was supposed to be a casual walk. Without knowing how she truly felt about Brady, the future was a blur to me. I didn't know what would happen with us, or with my friendship with him, for that matter. I didn't even know if I'd see her again after I went back home. I had to trust that I'd gotten into this situation for a reason, and what was meant to happen would.

I backtracked. "You know what? I shouldn't have gone there. Let's just enjoy each other's company tonight."

She reached for me, looping her fingers with mine, and we walked the rest of the way hand in hand.

Chapter 21

Hazel

O nce we returned to the house, the mood brightened as Matteo and I hung out in the kitchen, demolishing some of the sweets I'd baked. A part of me wanted to dip his fingers in the frosting so I could suck on them again. But I refrained. This more relaxed vibe as we noshed was almost reminiscent of our Milo and Maddie Hooker days.

A feeling of nostalgia came over me. How much simpler things had been back then, only a matter of weeks ago. Catching myself getting emotional, I shook that thought from my head.

"I never really gave you a proper tour of the house." I got up. "Come on, I'll show you around."

He seemed hesitant but got up anyway. I knew why—because I knew Matteo. We'd always worked so damn hard to not be in a bedroom alone together. It was almost comical how diligent we'd been about that. But you know what? I took a lot of pride in my house and wanted him to see every room.

We started with the wall that displayed my sixty-eight smile portraits.

"Wow." He stopped in front of it and grinned, marveling at the black and white photos. "The famous smile wall."

"Yeah."

I watched his expression as he took it all in.

He pointed to one of them. "Who was this?"

"That was a man watching his girlfriend approach him at the airport. He was very happy to see her, as you can see."

He moved to another photo as I followed close behind him.

"And this?"

"That was a grandmother watching her granddaughter roller skate at the park."

"They're all genuine smiles."

"Yup. That's key. You saw the difference when I showed you your own smiles."

"It's surreal to be standing here, seeing this in person. When you described it to me, I had a vision in my mind, but never imagined I'd actually get to see it."

"That's wild, huh? That you're here."

He gazed up at the wall, and after a long moment said, "I don't regret it, Hazel." He turned to me. "Even with everything we know. I don't regret a minute of it."

"It sounds crazy to say, but neither do I."

"No matter what happens, I will always be a better person for having met you and for having gotten to spend time with you."

Why did his words sound kind of final?

With an uneasy feeling in my chest, I wrapped my hands around his face and reached up, placing a gentle kiss on his forehead.

After several seconds of gazing into each other's eyes, he turned his attention back to the photos on the wall.

He moved closer. "This is the one, isn't it? The one you said was your favorite. The little girl."

"Yep. That's it."

His eyes seared into mine again. "You get so much joy from the happiness of others." He moved closer and cupped my face. "Are you happy, Hazel? That's all I need to know. And you don't have to answer now. Just think about the answer to that question and tell me when you know. Because if you're happy with Brady, that's all I need to hear. But if you're not, you shouldn't settle for anything less than total happiness."

I was happier than I'd ever been when I was on the road with him; that I knew for sure. And I needed to find a way to keep that self present in my life. But if I admitted that right now, would it make me seem insensitive to Brady? Matteo's words sparked a series of questions that were now bombarding my mind. I'd thought I loved Brady. But his canceling the wedding really left me with trust issues. I also thought I cared deeply for Matteo. But how much did I know about him, about what life would be like with him?

Brady was safe. Brady loved me—or so he claimed. But could Matteo love me now that we had this dark cloud hanging over us? And could I ever hurt Brady in such a profound way by leaving him for his friend? Would Matteo betray Brady like that, just to be with me? There were so many unknowns that wouldn't be resolved before Matteo had to leave.

"There's so much I'm unsure of right now, Matteo. But how I feel when I'm with you isn't one of those things."

He lifted his index finger and traced my lips. It lit my insides on fire. I closed my eyes, relishing his touch to the point that I found it hard to breathe. I could feel his quickened breaths on my cheeks. I wanted him. There was no denying that. My nipples hardened. I knew now that I would forego showing him my bedroom because I truly couldn't trust myself.

He apparently knew exactly where my mind was.

"Got any face mask cream?" he asked.

The next morning, I could still smell Matteo's cologne in my house. It was apparently all over the couch from when he sat there last night. I hadn't wanted him to leave, but eventually we'd both agreed it was best if he hopped a late train. What choice did we have? We both knew the chances of us slipping were high if he spent the night. And now it felt like a clock was ticking, because the flight he'd rescheduled would be leaving New York in a few days. His leave of absence from work was almost over, and he had to get back to his teaching job after Christmas break.

I had no clue how I was supposed to say goodbye to Matteo or how I was going to deal with the Brady situation. But once Matteo went back to Seattle, I needed to make some real decisions about how I wanted my future to look.

That afternoon, I paid Felicity a long-overdue visit. I hadn't seen her since before Matteo came to town, so she knew nothing about his connection to Brady. The thought of explaining everything to her had been daunting, which is why I'd put it off.

She was finally recovering well from her accident and was now up and about, cleaning the kitchen as I sat at her table with my feet up on a chair.

Even though I knew she was completely biased—Team Brady—I needed to confide in someone about this situation. And I knew I could trust Felicity.

She looked me up and down. "You look like you've lost weight."

"Yeah...I've been under a lot of stress the past several days."

"What is it? Did something happen with Brady?"

"Indirectly, yes."

I told her the whole story about Milo being Duncan. She had to stop what she was doing and take a seat across from me.

"Are you kidding me? Tell me you're kidding."

"I'm not, unfortunately."

She sat there silently pondering for a long time. "It kind of makes sense, if you think about it—him being in Vail at the time. Pretty crazy that he didn't figure out it was you."

"Well, remember, we never told each other our names..."

"That's right. But still." She shook her head. "Are you going to tell Brady at some point?"

"I honestly don't know what's best. I know you're rooting for me to get back with him, but I'm just not sure anymore."

Next I told her about my time with Matteo last night and how connected I felt to him.

She smirked skeptically. "Nothing happened?"

"No. We took Abbott for a walk. Then he came back to my place, and we just hung out. We ended up putting on the funniest movie we could find and watching it from opposite ends of the couch—quite intentionally."

I didn't need to tell her about our couple of close calls or the fact that I'd sucked Matteo's fingers. I was pretty sure Felicity already looked at this whole thing as a betrayal to Brady. But I didn't. Both Matteo and I were victims of bad luck and timing, which had put us in this situation.

"Poor Brady. If he finds out about this... God, I just can't imagine."

I sat up, placing my head in my hands. "No one meant to hurt anyone."

"The more I think about it, the more I feel like you shouldn't tell Brady. He'll never look at you the same, and it can only hurt him."

"I haven't worked that out yet. A lot of it depends on how Matteo feels. Their friendship is on the line, too, and no matter what, this is going to have to be a decision Matteo and I make together."

"You sound like you're a couple or something. Don't get ahead of yourself here. This is your road trip fling. You need to do what *you* feel is best for you and for Brady without anyone else guiding your decisions."

Once again, I found myself regretting opening up to her. She'd never see both sides.

"Do you have a picture of this guy?" she asked.

I searched through my phone and scrolled down to a photo of Milo and Maddie Hooker taken on Bourbon Street. To be honest, I was surprised she hadn't asked to see a photo sooner.

"Okay. I can see why you're smitten. He looks like something out of a movie. Love the mop of hair, too. Wow. And those lips."

"He's so much more than that, though, Felicity. You have no idea. I know you fully support me getting back with Brady but—"

"He's a fantasy, sure," she interrupted. "But I would be willing to bet if you spent even a week with him back in—is it Seattle?"

"Yeah. Seattle."

"I bet you'd find things to be a lot different in the real world."

"Maybe. But we did spend an awful lot of time together on our trip. I feel like I know him enough to trust him."

"Doesn't matter. You were on vacation. You know how it is. Everyone is carefree on vacation. You weren't worrying about finances or your job or anything else. You were just living in the moment. But that kind of thing can't last forever."

Despite her trying to convince me what I had with Matteo wasn't real, I refused to believe it.

"Here's the problem, Felicity. I can't stop thinking about him. Say what you will about what seems wrong or right, but from the moment I met him, I've thought of little else—both before and after I found out who he really was."

She sighed. "Well, the issue is... You would be taking a very big risk in assuming things would work out. You've never spent a single day with him when you weren't either on vacation or hiding something from your fiancé."

"Ex-fiancé."

"Okay, but how can you possibly know what it's really like to be with Matteo?"

I thought about that. She had a point.

"You're right. I don't know what the day to day would look like for us. Heck, I don't even know where we would live. He's in Seattle. My life is here. None of it makes sense, and yet..." My words trailed off.

"Yet you still can't stop thinking about him."

"No. I can't. And it's not fair to Brady. So, I have some real thinking to do after Matteo goes back."

"When does he leave?"

"In a few days. He took some time off from his teaching job, but he's supposed to be returning to work after the holidays. So he needs to get back."

"Well, maybe once he's gone, you'll start to forget, little by little. You can focus on Brady and hopefully come to your senses."

I didn't want to forget Matteo. Every piece of advice Felicity gave me made me want the opposite scenario. She was slowly and unintentionally showing me what my heart was screaming for.

And that scared me. Because no matter how this all ended, someone was going to get hurt.

Two nights later, I was starting to freak out because I hadn't seen Matteo since the night he came to my house. Between work and Brady being around, coordinating a meet-up just hasn't worked out.

And tonight, it was Brady's birthday, so I had no choice but to spend it with him.

When a text from Matteo came in, my heart sped up a bit.

Matteo: Hey, Brady wants me to join you guys for his birthday dinner tonight, but I told him I came down with the flu. I just wanted to make sure you knew I wasn't sick. Didn't want you to worry. I just...can't.

That broke my heart.

Hazel: I get it. Totally.

Matteo: The pretending thing is too hard. I can't look him in the eyes anymore.

Hazel: It's getting harder and harder for me, too.

Matteo: I'm gonna miss you, Hazel.

Panic set in. Did he mean forever? Or was he referring to the fact that he was leaving soon?

Hazel: Your flight leaves tomorrow night. When will I see you?

Matteo: Can you come to the city during the day? I'm afraid if I go to you, I won't make it back in time for my flight.

Hazel: Yes. I was planning to but wanted to make sure you wanted me there.

Matteo: Of course I do.

Hazel: Okay. I guess I'll see you tomorrow then? Am I meeting you at your hotel?

Matteo: Yes. Just text me when you arrive. I'll come down.

Hazel: Okay.

Matteo: Have fun tonight.

Chapter 22

Hazel

"Hey." Brady smiled and leaned in to kiss my cheek. "You look gorgeous."

It was a good thing the way I felt on the inside wasn't on display, because then he would have said, *You look like a complete and total wreck.*

"Thank you," I said.

"Is that a new dress?"

I nodded and looked down. "I actually bought it for our honeymoon."

Brady frowned. "Come inside."

My train had been delayed getting into the city, and I knew our reservation at the restaurant was for seven thirty. "Shouldn't we get going? I'm a little late."

Brady opened the door wide and stepped aside. "You're not late at all. Chez Oppenheimer is ready whenever you are."

I peered into the apartment from the hall. The lights were dimmed, and the dining room table had been set for two. Candles flickered in the center of the

259

table, and a huge bouquet of flowers sat atop the plate at the chair I normally sat in.

"I thought we were going out?"

"Change of plans. I hired a chef to come in and make your favorite dinner instead. You said you'd had a long day today, so I figured you'd like that better than going out."

At one point I would have. But right now the thought of a romantic dinner alone with Brady didn't sit right in my stomach. I would have given anything for him to make such a romantic gesture *before*. And yet at this moment, I didn't much want to set foot inside his apartment.

Brady sensed my hesitation, but luckily mistook it as surprise. He smiled and took my hand. "I know. It's out of character for me. But you said we could go anywhere I wanted for my birthday. And honestly, the only place I want to be is right here with you." He squeezed my hand. "I don't want to share you with anyone else."

He gave my hand a soft tug, and I had no choice but to walk inside. When the front door clicked shut, a horrible, ominous feeling washed over me. As screwed up as it was, it felt wrong to be here in such a romantic setting with Brady. I knew in my heart that Matteo would be devastated if he found out. I didn't want to hurt either of these men.

Brady went behind me and helped take off my coat.

"Thank you."

After he hung it up, he pulled out a chair at the dining room table. "Come. Sit. We have three courses."

I took a seat while Brady went to the kitchen. Even though I could see him working the corkscrew into a bottle of wine, I still jumped when the loud pop came. That cork had nothing on how tightly I was wound this evening.

Brady poured us each a glass of chardonnay and brought out a tray of appetizers. It was a huge antipasto assortment with all of my favorites.

"Are you sure it's not *my* birthday?" I laughed nervously. "You're the one serving me, and this is my favorite food, not yours."

He smiled and sat down across from me. "Whatever makes you smile is my favorite food."

Where had this Brady been the last few years? "That's very sweet."

We dug into the appetizer, and I guzzled my wine pretty fast. My nerves were frazzled.

"So..." Brady set down his fork and wiped his mouth. "I've been thinking about this apartment."

"Oh? What about it?"

"Well, my lease is up in two months, and I don't think I'm going to renew."

"Really? I'm surprised. You love it here. Do you want to be closer to the office or something?"

Brady reached over and took my hand. "I want to be closer to you."

"Brady, I..."

He squeezed my hand. "Let me finish. I know you aren't ready to move in with me...yet. And we'd planned to live here after our wedding. But your work is in Connecticut. You have to lug equipment and stuff around with you, which isn't easy on trains. It would make more sense for me to be the one to commute."

Wow. He was *really* trying.

"Plus, I'd like to be able to see you more than just on the weekends. So if I live closer to you, we can spend more time together." He winked. "Might even speed up the process of me winning you back."

I didn't want him to uproot his life for me, since every day it became clearer that things might not pan out for us. "Where would you live?"

"I'm sure I could get an apartment somewhere near you." He flashed a sheepish smile. "Unless you wanted a roomie, maybe."

Seeing the look on my face, Brady chuckled. "Okay, so not ready to be roomies yet. I get it. I can start looking for my own place—unless you don't even want me in the same state as you."

I shook my head. "It's not that. It's just a lot. It's a big change. Can you give me some time to think about it?"

He nodded and tried to pretend I hadn't hurt his feelings, though it was clear I had. "Sure."

We made it through dinner without any more major bumps in the road. But the pressure I felt was enormous. Brady wanted to change his life for me. It wasn't fair to let him do that if things were coming to an end. So while we made conversation and even laughed a few times, our situation really weighed on my shoulders.

After a delicious meal, we cleaned up together. Brady washed the dishes, and I dried. It might've been the first time I'd ever seen him use a sponge. At one point, I was standing in the dining room, wiping down the counter that separated the dining and kitchen areas, and Brady was on the other side, wrapping a tray of food in foil.

I found myself staring. *Could I be with him again?*
Did I love him still?
If I didn't, had I ever?

Can you just fall out of love in a few months?

I remembered the day I met him. I'd been taking photos at a Coldplay concert. One of my duties was to snap pictures of the audience. Usually I'd find some girl on a guy's shoulders with her arms in the air, or a group of guys thrashing around in a mosh pit—something that captured the essence of the show. But that day, when I was scanning through the audience with my lens, I landed on a cute guy staring right back at me. He smiled and waved. I snapped a few pictures just because he was so easy on the eyes and smiled back. But the concert was coming to an end, so a few minutes later I went backstage. I'd forgotten all about the cute guy by the time I finished for the night. After the concert, I stuck around to hang out with the band and take some candid photos while they celebrated. The parking lot was long empty by the time I walked out at nearly two AM.

Except for Brady. There he was, standing right at the front door, waiting.

We wound up going to a nearby diner and talking until the sun came up that morning. When I'd asked him how he knew I was still there, since he'd waited for so many hours, he'd shrugged and said he didn't. But he was willing to put in the time on the off chance he'd get to see me again.

Lost in my own little world reminiscing, I didn't even realize I was still staring until Brady smiled. "What are you thinking about over there?"

"Nothing."

"Come on. I know you better than that. You were somewhere else."

I shook my head. "I was just thinking about the night we met."

Brady smiled and tossed the dishtowel on the kitchen counter. "Best night of my life."

"You waited for me for a really long time."

He turned off the kitchen light and came around to the dining room side of the counter. The candles were the only light now. Brady cupped my cheeks in his hands. "You're worth waiting for, Hazel."

My heart swelled. Brady was a really sweet guy. "Thank you for a nice dinner."

He leaned in, dipping his head, as if he was about to kiss me.

I flattened my hands on his chest, stopping him. "Brady, no."

"Oh come on, babe. Just one kiss. For my birthday."

I didn't want to be a jerk, but I also didn't feel right about kissing him. So when he leaned in again— this time ignoring my shove at his chest—and his lips covered mine, I turned my head.

"Brady, I said no."

"What's the big deal? It's just a kiss, for Christ's sake. I've done it a million times."

"I don't... I don't want to lead you on."

He cupped my cheeks tighter. "You won't. I get it. Just a kiss. I won't try to cop a feel or get in your pants. I promise." He lowered his head yet again and pressed his lips to mine.

"Brady, stop!" I pushed him hard this time.

He stumbled back and raised his hands in the air, showing me his palms. "What the fuck, Hazel?"

"I told you not to kiss me."

His face twisted in anger. "Well then stop sending me mixed fucking signals. You're staring at me and thinking of the day we met, but I can't kiss my girlfriend of four years on my damn birthday?"

"I'm not your girlfriend."

"Whatever you want me to call you. How about friends without benefits? Does that work? Or should I be more specific? Woman I wine and dine but don't get to sixty-nine?"

I looked down. "I should go."

Brady stepped in front of me. "No, tell me. I want to know. What are we, Hazel? Because I'm really not understanding what we're doing. You somehow think we can just be friends. But you know what? We were never friends. I've been in love with you since the first time I saw you, and I don't know how to be anything else."

I took a deep breath. "I think we need a real break, Brady."

He laughed maniacally. "A break? Isn't that what we're on now? You mean there's something even less than not being able to kiss you?"

I shook my head. "We need a clean break, Brady. One where we don't see each other for a while. Don't have any contact."

"Great. So you want me to fuck other people?"

It felt like someone sliced into my heart. "If that's what you need to do."

Brady rubbed the back of his neck and shook his head. "It was just a kiss. Just a damn birthday kiss."

"I'm sorry, Brady."

"Whatever." He shrugged, sounding defeated. "Go, if that's what you really want."

While I hated to leave on such a sour note, I knew it was time to get out of here. I'd never been nervous around Brady, but for a split second there, when he didn't heed my nudge, it made me realize how much bigger and stronger he was. And I didn't like that feeling *at all*. He was upset. I knew that. But it was time to go.

Brady stood and watched while I went to the closet and grabbed my coat. Thinking it was best to not drag things out, I walked to the front door without trying to talk to him further. I never looked back as I opened the door and walked out. Whatever the future was for Brady and me, it was not in the past, and that's where we seemed to be stuck. It was time I gave myself permission to let go, decide what I wanted for myself, and see where life took me.

I walked for over an hour.

It was cold out, but somehow I didn't feel it. Once I stepped out of Brady's building, I turned right and just walked and walked and walked. After a while I didn't have even a vague idea where I was. But I wasn't in Brady's apartment anymore, and at the moment, that felt right.

Maybe I *had* been giving Brady mixed signals. I couldn't be sure. Every time I played back what had transpired tonight in my head, the only thing crystal clear was the memory of my heart racing as I shoved Brady off of me. Everything else was a blur. So rather than continue to focus on what had happened, I decided to concentrate on what would come next.

Before, even though I might not have been dating Brady anymore, that felt more like a technicality. Somehow I'd still been tethered to him in a way that spending time with anyone else made me feel disloyal. But now, that tether had been severed. It was truly the first time in four years that I was free.

Of course, that didn't mean my feelings for Brady disappeared, because they didn't. Nor did it mean I wanted to jump into something else. Besides, whatever was going on between Matteo and me, I knew it couldn't happen while I was running away from Brady. Matteo was a man who deserved to have a woman running toward him because she wanted to—not because she needed to get away from something else.

That being said, Felicity had also been right. I needed to spend some time with Matteo. Not on an adventure, but just living our ordinary lives, to see if that changed the way I thought I felt about him. And now that the shackles were off, maybe I could do that. I'd never really been with him without Brady being at the forefront of my mind.

I turned right at some corner, and my cell phone buzzed from my purse. Taking it out, I saw a New York City number, but one I didn't recognize. I swiped to answer anyway.

"Hello?"

"Are you okay?"

"Matteo?"

"Yeah. I'm calling from the front desk at the hotel. I didn't want my cell phone number to flash on your phone and Brady to see it. But it's late. You'd said you'd probably be leaving by about ten, and I was getting worried about you."

I shook my head. "I'm sorry. I should have called. I'm fine. I just went for a walk."

"A walk? By yourself?"

"Yeah." I sighed. "I needed to clear my head."

I stopped walking for the first time and looked around. But nothing looked familiar, and I couldn't make out the street sign up ahead from this far away. "I'm not sure where I am."

"I did that the other day. I walked out of my hotel and just kept going. I had no idea where I was, and I didn't really care. But it's getting late now. So I'm not sure if it's such a good idea for you to be walking around the city aimlessly while in a fog thinking."

"What time is it?"

"It's almost eleven thirty."

Wow. I'd gotten to Brady's apartment at seven thirty. Dinner couldn't have been more than two hours. I would've guessed I'd been walking for about a half hour, but apparently it was more like two.

"I'm sorry. I didn't mean to make you worry."

"Are you okay, Hazel? Did something happen that made you take the long walk?"

"No. Well, yes. No... I mean, I'm fine. Don't worry about me."

"Where are you? I'll come to wherever you are, and we can talk about what's on your mind."

"It's okay. I can just grab an Uber to you. At least if I call for a car it will know where I am."

"You sure?"

"Yeah. But do you think we could talk in your room? I know you were trying to avoid that, but I really just want to take off my shoes and sit with you for a while."

"Yeah. Sure. Of course."

"Okay. I'm going to call a car now. I'll see you in a little while. What room are you in?"

"713."

"Okay. See you soon."

Chapter 23

Matteo

Hazel arrived just as room service was leaving. Her nose and cheeks were bright red from the cold, and she looked a little lost.

"Hey."

She practically ran into my arms. It felt so good to hold her. I hadn't realized how tense I'd been all day until I felt the equivalent of a giant sigh roll through my body. Hazel's hair smelled so good, and she just fit so perfectly under my chin. We stayed glued to each other for a solid five minutes. I stroked her hair with one hand and held her close with the other while she clung to me. But the desperation in her touch had me concerned, and I needed to see her face to know she was really okay.

Pulling back, I cupped her cold cheeks in my hands. Her teeth were chattering. "Are you okay? What's going on?"

She smiled sadly. "I'm fine. Freezing suddenly, but okay. It's funny, I walked for a long time and didn't feel the cold at all. But now it seems to have caught up to me."

"I figured you might need to thaw out, so I ordered a carafe of hot chocolate. Let me pour you some."

Hazel had on a dress and high heels. Her legs were bare, and she'd said on the phone that she wanted to take off her shoes. So I poured her a steaming mug of hot chocolate and lifted my chin toward her feet. "Do you want a pair of socks or something?"

She sipped the hot cocoa. "I'd love that. Actually, do you have a pair of sweatpants and a T-shirt I could borrow, too, maybe?

I loved the thought of her wearing my clothes. "Yeah, of course."

Digging into my luggage, I searched for something clean. I'd gone through most of my stuff by now, but I still had a fresh pair of socks and an unworn pair of sweats. I was out of clean T-shirts, but I held up one I'd only worn for a few hours the other day.

"This is all I have left. I wore it, but just for a few hours. It wasn't to the gym or anything."

Hazel smiled and took the clothes from my hands. "Pretty sure I'd wear your smelly gym clothes if it meant I got to change into something comfortable and sit down and enjoy this hot chocolate."

While she went into the bathroom to get changed, I poured myself a cup of hot cocoa and clicked off the TV. Hazel emerged a few minutes later, looking freaking adorable. The first smile I'd had in days spread across my cheeks. "You look really cute."

She glanced down. My sweatpants were rolled at the bottom and top. The T-shirt was so big that she didn't even really need the pants to cover herself. It hung down to her knees.

"You're sweet. But I think I could've worn this with my mud mask as a deterrent."

I grinned. "Trust me. You wearing my clothes is the exact opposite of a deterrent."

She smiled.

I looked around the room. It was nothing but bed and a lone chair stuck in the corner. And the chair held my luggage, because otherwise there wasn't even enough space for me to walk to the window.

"Do you want me to move my luggage so you can sit on the chair?"

She shook her head. "Can we just sit on the bed together? Maybe I can put my feet under the covers? They're still freezing."

"Yeah, of course. Let's get you into bed and warmed up."

Hazel climbed up onto the bed and sat with her back against the headboard. She snuggled under the covers and patted the bed next to her. "Come sit."

I took a seat, but toward the foot end of the bed, and I lifted the blanket from the bottom. "Give me your dogs. I'll warm them up."

Taking one of her little feet in my hand, I could feel the cold radiating through the socks. So I rubbed like I was trying to start a fire with a stick through friction.

"How's that?"

"That really works!"

After a while, I put down the first foot and picked up the other. "So talk to me. Did something happen between you and Brady tonight?"

Hazel sipped her hot chocolate and nodded.

"Do you want to tell me about it?"

"Not really. He just..." She looked down at her hands. "I don't think I was doing either of us a favor by spending time with him. He apparently thought my head was in a different place than it was and... Well, I told him I couldn't see him anymore. Not until I figured some things out."

It was like I'd been carrying around a boulder on my shoulders and someone had lifted it for the first time. She wasn't saying she'd ended things *for good*, but at least I didn't have to sit around wondering what the hell the two of them were doing anymore. That had been tearing me up inside, particularly today. Though I couldn't imagine Brady took that news well, especially on his birthday. It hit me for the first time that Hazel would never have gone over there on Brady's birthday to break things off, so something big had to have gone down between them.

She was still avoiding my eyes, so I leaned forward, put two fingers under her chin, and gently lifted. "What did he do?"

Hazel frowned. "How do you know he did something?"

"Because I know *you*. You weren't going to hand him his walking papers on his birthday unless he fucked up royally." The muscle in my jaw flexed. "Did he...hurt you in any way?"

She looked down again. "No, I'm fine."

We sat there quiet for a few long moments. A hundred different things spun through my head. He *had* to have done something pretty shitty. The longer she kept quiet, the worse the shit I imagined became. If he laid one hand on her...

Hazel reached over and covered my hands. I looked down to find them in fists. I watched as she gently unfurled my fingers and laced her hand with mine.

"Matteo?"

I looked up.

She smiled, looking into my eyes. "Could I come home with you?"

"Home with me? You mean to Seattle?"

She nodded.

"I'd love that. When?"

Her smile was sheepish. "I'm free tomorrow night. If that's not being too forward."

"What about your work?"

"I only have one more shoot tomorrow. Then things are always dead for me until after the holidays. That's the way the schedule runs in my business. Since I do mostly school photography, I'm really busy at certain times, like the beginning of the year and the spring. Then I get a lot of downtime when the schools go on break."

"You really want to come to Seattle?"

"I do. I can stay for a few days and leave before Christmas. I want to see where you live. I want to see the places you go to spend your free time, meet some of your friends, see where you work... I even want to meet Bach."

I smiled. "You want to meet my cat?"

Her face lit up. "I do! You've met Abbott. I think it's only fair."

I'd gone from wanting to beat the shit out of someone, to feeling like I just won the lottery in the span of five minutes.

"Come here." I opened my arms, and she crawled over into my lap. I pushed a lock of hair behind her ear. "I would love to take you home with me."

"Then let's do it!"

I felt like the luckiest man alive. My girl was free and coming home with me. The only problem was: How the hell was I ever going to let her leave once she did? And would I ever be able to look my friend in the eye again?

Being at the airport with Hazel the next day felt downright nostalgic. It was as if the past couple of weeks had never happened, and we could just be Milo and Maddie Hooker again—in spirit, at least.

Hazel had booked the last available seat on my flight. Luck was on our side, and I could only hope that continued once we landed out west.

Last night, we'd fallen asleep in each other's arms, the shitty and exhausting experience she'd had over at Brady's thwarting any potential of something happening in that hotel room. Which was for the best. Even though she was on an alleged break from Brady, I needed to proceed with caution. It ain't over till it's over.

As we stood in line to board, I still couldn't believe she was coming home with me. It felt like a dream. Although, the fact that Brady kept calling her phone was the reality check and reminder that we were never really in La La Land anymore.

She kept letting his calls go to voicemail.

"What are you going to tell him?"

"You mean about where I'm traveling?"

"Yeah."

She blew out a breath. "Right now, I'm avoiding having to lie to him. I'll probably text him later, letting him know that I went away to think. There's no good way to lie to anyone, but I told him I needed a break, so I'm not sure why he's continuing to call."

"Well, he probably regrets letting you walk away like that."

A little pang of guilt hit me all of a sudden. That seemed to happen in waves. But then I'd remember what I knew about Brady cheating on her, and that would help curb the guilt. I still struggled with whether to tell her what I'd discovered. But ultimately, I knew why I hadn't. I needed to make sure she made the decision she truly wanted in her heart without my influencing it. If she chose me only because of Brady's infidelity, how would I ever know I was the one? The uncertainty would kill me.

If she ended up choosing him, I'd probably figure out a way to tell her, though—because once a cheater, always a cheater. I'd deal with that when the time came.

We were still standing in line when Hazel turned to me.

"So, what's their story?"

I looked around at the swarms of people, remembering the game we used to play at airports. "Who's our target today?"

She gripped my shirt and pulled me close. "These people. *Us*. What's their deal?"

I paused. "Oh, these two crazy people? They're running away for a while."

"Why?" she asked.

"Because their reality is crazier than any fantasy. But they handle life better when they're together. And they missed that feeling."

She smiled.

"He just hopes she doesn't want to turn around and head back home when she realizes how small his apartment is."

"I thought you were going to finish that sentence a different way." Hazel laughed.

When it hit me what she was referring to, I smiled. "Oh no. My apartment is the only thing you'll find too small. I can assure you of that."

Chapter 24

Hazel

Despite his warning, Matteo's studio apartment was definitely smaller than I'd imagined. But because it had three windows, it didn't feel so claustrophobic.

I looked around as he wheeled our suitcases to a corner.

"This place is cute."

He raised his forehead. "Code word for tiny and stifling?"

To the left was a small kitchenette. To the right was the living area. A guitar stood upright against the wall, and a shelf housed dozens of vinyl records.

"It's small...but it's you."

"Please don't associate the word *small* with anything having to do with me." He winked.

"Sorry." I laughed. "What I meant is, it has your personality."

"It's what I can afford if I want to be in the middle of the action downtown. Most one-bedroom apartments in this area go for about triple the rent, so I figured I'd make due with a studio. It's really only cramped when I have people over, which I rarely do."

I peeked out his window at the city. "I'm really looking forward to seeing Seattle."

"Tomorrow we can see whatever you want. Everything is within walking distance."

I turned to him. "It's also perfectly fine if we don't sightsee, by the way. I can imagine you have a lot to catch up on after being away for so long. I can help with anything you need around here. We should go food shopping and stuff."

"Yeah, I have absolutely nothing in the fridge. We can do that, but I'm not gonna put you to work, Hazel. This is supposed to be a vacation for you."

"Actually, it's not, Matteo, remember? I want to experience life with you as it is. So, yes, while I'd love to see Seattle at least one day, the rest of the time, just do what you normally would do without me here. That likely doesn't include sightseeing. I'll just go along for the ride."

"So, you want me to sit around scratching my stomach like Al Bundy from *Married with Children* while eating pork rinds and watching TV?"

"If that's what you do, sure." I shrugged.

His tone turned serious. "This trip is a test in a sense, isn't it? To see if there's something about my life that turns you off?"

I hated that he thought that. "That's not it at all. Please don't feel that way."

"Well, it *is* a competition, isn't it?"

His change in mood surprised me. But I guess it was stupid of me to expect him to display no frustration, given this messed-up situation.

"Matteo, at this moment, no, there is no competition. I'm just so happy to be here."

His expression softened.

A knock on the door prevented us from continuing the conversation.

"Are you expecting someone?" I asked.

"Not at this hour," he said as he walked over to answer it.

When he opened the door, I was surprised to see an attractive girl standing there. She looked to be in her mid-twenties and was holding a large, orange-haired cat.

Bach.

He started to meow at the sight of Matteo.

"Hey!" Matteo said. "I wasn't expecting you to bring him back tonight."

"Yeah. I know we said tomorrow. But I figured you missed him."

Matteo rubbed the cat's ears. "I did."

Her eyes met mine, and she seemed surprised to see Matteo had a guest.

Yeah, sure. You came to his apartment this late at night because of the cat.

"Hazel, this is Carina," Matteo said. "Carina, this is Hazel."

Carina had dark brown hair, big brown eyes, and full lips. And there was absolutely zero doubt in my mind that she'd slept with Matteo.

"Nice to meet you," I said, feeling a bit unbalanced.

"Same to you." She tilted her head and asked, "How do you two know each other?"

Matteo answered before I had a chance to say anything. "Hazel is someone I met while traveling. She's from Connecticut."

"Oh...okay. Interesting." She looked between him and me. "Well, welcome to Seattle."

Surely she really didn't mean that. "Thank you."

Carina finally set the cat down, and it purred, weaving in and out of Matteo's legs.

"So, nothing crazy to report as far as Bach goes?" he asked her.

"Nope. I actually had a tough time getting him into the car. I think he finally got used to being at my place and didn't want to leave."

"Yeah. He's probably gonna hate me now that he's seen how the other half lives. You have so much more space."

"Well, he's welcome to come visit whenever he misses it."

"Thanks again for taking care of him."

"My pleasure. Anytime." She looked over at me. "Well, I better get going. Hazel, it was nice meeting you."

I swallowed. "You, as well."

As she turned to go, she asked Matteo, "You're returning to work after the holidays, right?"

"Yup. I'll be there right after Christmas break."

"I know everyone's looking forward to having you back."

"I'm sure once I get there, I'll be happy to be back," he said. "The idea of returning is a little daunting. But I'll get into the swing of things fast. I do miss my kids."

"They definitely miss you." She sighed. "Alright. Well, you guys have a good night."

"Thank you," I muttered. The door closed, followed by a few seconds of awkward silence. "She seemed... nice. So, you work with her?"

"Yeah. She teaches English at the high school."

"Ah. I know you said it was a friend watching your cat, but I hadn't imagined she was so..." I shook my head to stop from making a total fool of myself. I was coming off as really jealous.

"Alright, Hazel, ask what you really want to ask."

"It's none of my business."

"I don't hide anything. There's nothing going on with Carina now—although we used to date. But it was a long time ago."

That admission stung, though I'd known something had happened between them even before I asked.

"There's nothing lingering between you two?"

"Not on my end."

"But she still likes you."

"I don't know. Maybe? It doesn't matter to me."

"Why did you stop dating her?"

"She wasn't the one. I told her I didn't want anything serious. She's a friend now—one who happens to like cats and is one of the few people Bach seems to tolerate."

"Oh, well, I know she still likes much more than your cat. It's eleven thirty at night, and she came by with Bach when you told her to bring him by tomorrow? There's only one reason someone goes to a guy's house at this time of night. And it's not to deliver an animal. She wasn't expecting me. And she's clearly not done with you."

Well, if it wasn't obvious before, my jealousy was definitely out in the open now.

"I honestly couldn't tell you what her intentions were. But she saw that I'm with you."

I had to know one more thing. It was eating away at me. "When you came back for that brief stay here between our trip and New York, you said you wanted to check on Bach. Nothing happened with her?"

His tone grew insistent. "No. Nothing happened, Hazel. It's been over between Carina and me for a while. And I was way too hung up on you to even think about someone else. If you think I could've switched gears that easily, you don't know me." His eyes looked pained. "Although, *you* seemed to switch gears pretty fast when you got home."

Those words hurt, but I knew they were true. Or at least they'd seemed to be on the surface.

He backtracked. "I'm sorry. That was uncalled for."

"I never forgot you for a second, Matteo. I was just confused when I got back."

His eyes seared into mine. "And you still are... right?"

I couldn't blame him for questioning my intentions. Here I was telling him I needed to test the waters. I'd given him no guarantees. And quite frankly, he deserved better.

"I see things much more clearly now," I said. "And my reasons for being here are pure and show where my heart is. My intentions are in the right place, Matteo. I'm not out to hurt you."

He closed his eyes and shook his head, seeming to come out of his momentary funk. "Come here. I'm sorry."

As he pulled me into a hug, I spoke against his chest. "No, I'm the sorry one."

"These have just been some of the toughest weeks of my life," he admitted.

Something he'd said earlier was still weighing on my mind.

I moved back, out of his arms. "Can I ask you something?"

"Yeah."

"You said you told Carina you didn't want anything serious with anyone. But that's not truly how you feel?"

"I didn't want anything serious with *her*. But I'm not wasting your time, Hazel. I wouldn't do that."

"I'm sorry for all the questions. I'm trying to be mature about this. I was caught off guard by her showing up within the first minutes of my being here."

His mouth curved into a smile. "You were jealous."

"Yeah. And it's not pretty."

"Do you have any idea how happy that makes me— not to be the only one jealous as fuck lately?"

"You're seeing a very tired, vulnerable, jetlagged side of me right now."

"Well, how about we rest?"

Matteo walked over to the couch and fluffed the pillows. "Come lie down. I'll make you some tea. It's about all I have in the house until we shop tomorrow. We'll just chill before bed."

Noticing the very obvious fact that there *was* no bed in sight, I asked, "Where exactly *is* the bed?"

"This couch folds out into a very comfy one. And it's gonna be all yours tonight."

I sat down on the sofa. "Where are you gonna sleep?"

"We always work it out, don't we?" He walked over to the closet. "Anyway, check this out." He took out an air mattress. "This thing blows up in seconds. It's where I crash whenever I have a visitor—although my parents swore they'd never spend the night here again after the last time. They prefer a little more space. So they're staying at a hotel when they come in a couple of days. They're coming for Christmas, but they fly in early to avoid the busy times at the airports."

That took a few seconds to register. "Wait, your parents are coming...to Seattle in a couple of days?"

"Yeah, I was going to mention that."

I'm going to meet his parents? "How come you didn't tell me?"

"Well, I'm telling you now. When you said you wanted to come home with me, I didn't want that to be a downer or deter you. I'd hoped you wouldn't mind meeting them."

"It's not that I mind. I just wasn't expecting it, although I should've figured you'd be spending the holidays with your family. Not sure why that hadn't occurred to me. Probably because my family dynamic is so different than most people's."

"Most of the time I go to Vail, but they decided to come here this year since I was just there. They spend some holidays with me, some with my brother and his family up in Boston, and other times everyone goes to Vail. Every year is different. Do you ever see your parents over the holidays?"

"My parents are always traveling. Occasionally, I meet up with them wherever they happen to be. But I'd already told them I wanted to do my own thing this year. I'm actually going to Felicity's. I figured she could use help cooking with her injuries. Of course I never imagined I'd end up in Seattle about to meet your parents right before that. Oh my gosh."

"Well, you said you wanted a feel for what my life was like, right? So might as well meet my folks. I know it's not ideal timing, but it's not like I thought in a million years that you'd be here with me right now."

"I really am happy to be here, Matteo. Let's start over, okay? I feel my insecurity tonight got us off to a bad start."

"You shouldn't have to apologize for jealousy. I certainly haven't apologized for mine."

He took me into his arms, but then the whistling of the tea kettle interrupted our moment. He stood up and walked over to the counter to pour me a cup.

As he ripped open the teabag, he said, "I could technically afford a slightly bigger place than this. But after Zoe died, I became sort of a minimalist. I never felt like I needed much more than a small space. It's less to clean. Obviously, if I lived with someone, I'd have to move."

"I'm sure the location more than makes up for the size."

"Yeah, well, I had to get rid of fifty percent of the stuff I owned to live here. And if I buy something, I have to throw something out. But on the upside, I can clean my entire place in fifteen minutes."

The cat had been following Matteo around the entire time he was talking to me. After he handed me my tea, Matteo picked him up.

"Bach had to adjust to the space. He was kind of depressed when we first moved here. The only reason it works is because of the windows. Looking outside gives him plenty to do all day."

He carried the cat over to the couch and sat next to me.

When I reached over to pet Bach, he hissed at me.

I quickly retreated. "Does he always do that to strangers?"

"Well, I could lie and say yes, but..."

"Ouch."

"Maybe he senses how much I like you and considers you a threat."

"Well, that was a good save on your part, I suppose."

Bach eventually took off to a cat bed in the corner of the room.

Matteo and I stayed up talking for a little while before he opened up the couch bed for me. I fell asleep very quickly once my head hit the pillow.

The next thing I knew, we were awoken by a knock at the door. Light filled the apartment. I reached for my phone and saw it was nearly 11 AM.

Matteo scratched his head as he dragged himself up from the air mattress.

He looked through the peephole. "Okay, don't freak out."

I straightened on the bed, running my hands through my matted hair. "What?"

He cringed. "I don't know why they're three days early, but it's my parents."

Chapter 25

Matteo

I opened the door to the sight of my parents' smiling faces. They were holding grocery bags.

"Surprise!"

"Mom, Dad...what are you doing here? You're not supposed to be here yet."

"Well, you told us you were arriving last night, so we figured we'd surprise you a few days early. We were bored back in Vail, quite frankly."

Poor Hazel looked like she'd seen a ghost. I would never have chosen to put her through this ambush. She'd fallen asleep last night in her clothes, which were now all rumpled. This was a rude awakening, to say the least.

My mother's eyes widened when she saw Hazel. "Oh...you must be Carina?"

Fuck.

Shit.

You could've heard a record scratch. I knew my mother's assumption must have pissed Hazel off. But the only female I'd mentioned to Mom since Zoe was Carina. And that was mainly so they knew who was watching Bach in case something happened to me.

"No, Mom. This is Hazel. Obviously I didn't know you guys were coming. I'd planned to give you a heads up that I wasn't alone. Hazel is a very dear friend I met during my travels. She decided to come to Seattle for a visit before Christmas."

Groggy-eyed, Hazel walked over to greet them.

"It's a pleasure to meet you, Mr. and Mrs. Duncan."

"As it is you." My father smiled.

Dad was a much easier sell than my mother. In Mom's eyes, no one was good enough for her son. It had taken her a long time to warm up to Zoe. Other than that relationship, I'd rarely brought women to meet my parents.

"Well, we certainly didn't expect to be interrupting your time with your guest. I'd planned to cook you a nice brunch. But I suppose this might be an unwelcome surprise. Should we go?"

My stomach growled at the mere mention of food. "Pretty sure the brunch plans can stand. I'm starving."

My father laughed. "If Hazel doesn't mind two old geezers joining you, then?"

"Not at all. I would love that." She smiled.

I had to give her credit for even smiling. This couldn't have been easy to wake up to.

My parents started taking out the groceries they'd bought. Within minutes, the smell of coffee filled the air. Shortly thereafter, the sound of bacon sizzling was music to my ears. Things were getting better by the minute.

Hazel had wanted real. You couldn't get more real than my parents showing up at the door on day one.

Once brunch was served, the four of us crammed around my tiny kitchen table, although I did at least have four seats.

"So, Hazel, what do you do?" my mother asked.

"I'm a photographer back in Connecticut."

"You have an established business there?"

"Yes."

"So, you likely wouldn't be moving out this direction?"

"I haven't really thought too deeply about that."

"I could never see Matteo settling in Connecticut. He's always needed to be where the action is—if he's even in one place for long at all."

"Stop scaring her, Mom," I said, shoveling bacon into my mouth.

"I didn't mean to. It's just rare that I get to meet anyone you're spending time with." She took a sip of her coffee. "I noticed the two separate beds, though."

"Marianne..." my father scolded.

"It's okay," Hazel said.

It is? Because it doesn't seem fucking okay to me.

Mom's brow lifted. "I'm now wondering if you really are a dear friend—as he said—and nothing more? I'm sorry to pry, I'm just genuinely curious, and my son tells me nothing."

"We're taking things slowly," she said.

"Well, I find that very impressive in this day and age."

"Mom, Hazel's being a good sport and answering shit because she's polite, but I'm about to not be if you don't stop. My sex life is none of your business."

Everyone went quiet for a moment. It was Hazel who finally broke the ice.

"Or lack thereof," she mumbled.

My brows pulled together. At first I had no idea what the heck she was talking about. Then I started to laugh, and Hazel did, too. Maybe we'd needed the levity, or maybe we'd both just finally lost it, but once we started, we couldn't stop. We fell into a fit of laughter.

At one point, when we were finally starting to slow down, Hazel snorted, and that just cracked us up all over again. Tears streamed down our faces. My father seemed amused, but my mom definitely didn't look too pleased.

When I was finally able to speak, I reached over and patted my mother's hand. "Hazel makes me happy, Mom. That's all you need to know."

A little while later, we agreed to meet my parents for dinner at a restaurant they loved nearby, and they left to see if they could check into their hotel early. Hazel and I were finally alone. I washed the dishes while she dried, and after, she said she needed to check her work email, so I took a quick shower before turning the bathroom over to her.

When she emerged wearing the T-shirt I'd left on the hook on the door with her hair wrapped in a towel, I couldn't stop staring at her. She looked gorgeous.

"What?" She rubbed her cheek. "Did I miss some moisturizer on my face or something?

I shook my head. "I just like to look at you."

Her face softened, and she walked over and took a seat on my lap. Wrapping both arms around my neck, she rubbed her nose to mine.

"I'm so glad I'm here with you, Matteo."

"Even with my meddling mom asking you if we're sleeping together?"

She smiled. "Especially with her here. I get to know even more about you than I expected."

I cupped her cheeks in my hands. "Thank you for handling the surprise drop-in so well. And for the record, what I said to my mom was the absolute truth. You make me happy. And right now, I think that's all any of us needs to know. We have a lot of background noise, but let's try to focus on us while you're here."

She smiled and nodded. "I like the sound of that."

I knew it was a slippery slope being with her in my little apartment. But when her eyes dropped to my lips, I couldn't help myself. "Come closer," I said.

Hazel's lips parted, and she moved within an inch or two of my face. Her voice was breathy. "Here?"

I slid my hand around to her neck and pulled her to me, planting my lips over hers. Neither of us wasted any time as our tongues eagerly collided. Hazel had been sitting sideways on my lap, and she shifted to straddle me. Her breasts pushed against my chest, and it felt like we couldn't get close enough. I tilted my head and deepened the kiss, grabbing her ass with two hands and tugging her even closer. Hazel moaned into my mouth when she landed right on top of my raging hard on. Not unlike its owner, my dick had revved from zero to ninety in the span of thirty seconds from touching this woman.

I wanted nothing more than to be inside her, but I wasn't sure where her head was. As much as I wanted it, she needed to be sure of her decision. Though, when she threaded her hands into my hair, yanked, and ground down onto my cock, I got the feeling she was telling me exactly what she was in the mood for.

Our kiss broke with a pant. "Fuck." I leaned my forehead against hers. "This isn't easy, Hazel."

She grinned. "No, it's most definitely *hard*."

I chuckled and dropped my head. "Tell me what you want? Is it okay that I kiss you?"

She groaned. "I want *you* so badly, Matteo." She scooted back on my lap and looked down. Biting her lip, she said, "I think I left a little evidence of that on your pants."

Fuck. Sure enough, when my eyes dropped, I found a big wet spot right over the bulge in my jeans. Hazel didn't have any pants on under my long T-shirt. I raked a hand through my hair. "That's the fucking hottest thing I've seen in a long time. Don't be surprised if I never wash these pants again. I'm not ashamed to say, I may even sniff them a time or two after you leave me."

Hazel giggled, and her cheeks turned pink.

The towel she had wrapped around her head had fallen off while we'd made out, and her wet hair had tumbled down all over the place. I pushed a lock of it behind her ear and kissed her lips gently once more. "Why don't we have this conversation when we aren't in the heat of the moment? That way we're more likely to be honest with ourselves about where we want to take things."

She smiled. "Okay."

"I'm going to go take a shower," I said.

"But you already took one."

"Apparently, I need to wash some parts again." I winked. "Hope you left your face cream in the bathroom."

Chapter 26

Matteo

That afternoon, I figured there was no rush going to the supermarket since we were meeting my parents for dinner. The Seattle sky was blue for a change, so it turned out to be the perfect day to show Hazel some of the local sights.

We went to the Space Needle, took a ride on the Seattle Center Monorail, and then on our way back, headed over to Pike Place Market. Hazel had brought her camera, and I wanted to show her the fish market where they threw the fish around before they wrapped them for customers. I figured it would make for a fun photo op.

While we both had a good time sightseeing, the highlight of my day was really just walking around freely, holding my girl's hand. Our road trip had been the trip of a lifetime, but we were Milo and Maddie back then. And in New York, we had to sneak around like we were doing something wrong. So being out and about, our fingers laced while I showed Hazel my city, getting to watch her smile as she saw things for the first time, was about the best afternoon I could've asked for.

Hazel loved the fish market and snapped at least a hundred pictures of the workers throwing gigantic mackerel and cod. When she was done, I grabbed us two large coffees and told her I knew the perfect spot to have the conversation we'd started this morning. I walked us a few blocks, around the perimeter of Pike Place Market and down a quiet alley to the backside of some of the fish stores. One store had at least fifty milk crates stacked up behind their door, and next to them was a pungent-smelling dumpster. I grabbed two of the stacked milk crates from the pile and set them facing each other on the side of the foul steel container.

I motioned for her to sit. "Here we go. This is the place. Have a seat."

Hazel's face wrinkled up. "You want to sit and have our coffee here?"

"I do. I can't think of a more perfect location."

She laughed. "But it stinks!"

I sat down on one of the crates. "My point exactly. We're about to have a conversation about sex. I figure if anything can keep our heads screwed on straight and our libidos in check, it's sitting next to this thing."

Hazel seemed unsure whether I was kidding or not, but when I crossed one leg over the other and settled onto my milk crate, sipping my coffee, her eyebrows perked. "Oh my God, you're not joking, are you?"

I shook my head. "I take my discussions about fucking you very seriously. Now take a seat, and let's get this over with before we both pass out from the fumes."

Hazel looked at me like I was nuts, but the smile never left her face. Eventually, she pulled the other crate closer to me and sat. Sipping her coffee, she said, "Okay, let's talk about sex, Mr. Duncan."

Seriously? I might've started to get hard just hearing her say the damn word *sex*. And I really liked her calling me Mr. Duncan. *Note to self, we need to play schoolteacher and student at some point.*

I shook my head. Who the hell knew sitting in an alley with the rancid smell of dead fish surrounding us wouldn't keep my horny dick in check?

Taking a deep breath, I closed my eyes and forced myself to focus. "Yes, let's talk about sex. I love it, and I'd like nothing more than to have it with you. Missionary, doggy style, you beneath me, riding me, reverse cowboy, spooning, against the wall, or snow angel. I'd like to have it all."

She laughed. "Snow angel? What's that?"

I wiggled my brows. "Maybe I'll show you after this conversation."

Her eyes went wide. "Oh my God!"

I looked behind me to my right and left, assuming she'd probably just seen a rat run by. "What? What's the matter?"

Hazel covered her mouth. "I'm actually getting turned on next to a dumpster full of dead fish."

I chuckled. "Oh, yeah. *That*. I know the feeling."

Hazel sighed. "But seriously, Matteo. I want you so much it hurts. My desire for you has never been the problem. I've been unable to stop thinking dirty thoughts about you since the first night we became the Hookers. And that was even before I knew what an amazing person you are on the inside, too."

I reached forward and took her hand. "I feel the exact same way. That's why yesterday, when you asked me if I slept with Carina while I was home before I went to New York, I thought you must not really understand how I feel about you. A gorgeous woman could've shown up at my door completely naked and thrown herself at me, saying all she wanted was a one-night stand, and still *nothing* would've happened. You know why?"

"Why?"

I squeezed her hand. "Because she's not you, babe."

Hazel smiled, but then she looked down at her hands for a moment. "The night of Brady's birthday, he kissed me."

My heart sank into my stomach. Seeing the look on my face, Hazel shook her head.

"Well, we didn't really kiss. It was more like he *tried* to kiss me. I pushed him off, but he tried again."

My jaw clenched so tight, I thought I might crack a molar. "Are you saying he forced himself on you? Because that's *not fucking okay*. I don't give a shit if you're mine or not, I'll rip his damn heart out."

Hazel took my other hand and squeezed both. "It wasn't like that. At least it didn't get that far. I told him to stop, and I left."

I got up and started to pace. "Why the hell didn't you tell me any of this when we were in New York?"

"Because there was no reason to upset you. I'd handled it, and Brady... Well, it was more my fault than his. I'd gone to his house on his birthday, and we were getting along well. He just read the situation wrong. After four years of being together, you grow a certain level of comfort at reading the signs, and it's not like you ask permission anymore. Even though we weren't together, he thought it was okay. And when I said no, I guess he thought I just needed a little convincing. I'll be honest, over the years there were a few times when I was tired or not in the mood, and he'd just pushed a little, and I'd changed my mind. So I think in his head, that's what was going on. Only my mind was somewhere else altogether."

I dragged a hand through my hair and kept walking back and forth. I wasn't normally a violent person, but the rage I felt inside as I pictured what had gone down between the two of them made me want to put my fist through the side of the steel dumpster.

Hazel stood and walked into my path, halting my pacing. "I didn't mean to upset you."

"Hazel, he had no right to touch you, especially not more than once. I don't give a shit how you justify it, that is *not* okay."

In my fury, I'd gotten up and started to lose my shit, but I hadn't stopped to really look at Hazel. Seeing her face now, my heart broke. Her eyes were rimmed with tears.

I cupped her cheeks in my hands. "Baby, please don't cry. I'm sorry. I didn't mean to make you upset."

She covered my hands with hers and shook her head, sniffling. "This came out all wrong. I didn't mean to bring up what happened with Brady to upset you. I told you because I was trying to explain that I couldn't kiss another man, not even a man I was once supposed to marry, even when it was his birthday, Matteo."

I pulled her into my chest and wrapped her in a hug. I'd been holding back on taking things any further partly out of some old allegiance to my friend—a friend who cheated on his fiancée, broke her heart when he dumped her, and then tried to force himself on her when he decided he was done fucking around with the other woman.

But you know what? This was the last straw. Regardless of my feelings for Hazel, Brady wasn't the type of guy I needed as a friend. And I was an idiot for not using the little time I had with the woman I loved to try to make her mine.

I looked into Hazel's eyes. "Listen, I'm going to make this conversation very simple. I want you. I want to walk around town holding your hand, whether that's in New Orleans or Seattle or New York City. I want your mud masks in our bathroom and your smiles all over our walls. I want you in my bed and underneath me—or on top if you want. I'm not holding back anymore. So when you're ready, just say the word."

We stared into each other's eyes for a long time. Eventually, Hazel nodded. "Okay."

"Okay?"

She smiled. "Except what's the word?"

My forehead wrinkled. "The word?"

"You said I just had to say *the word* when I'm ready. Well, what's the magic word?"

I kissed her forehead. "How about *hooker*? I think that's fitting, don't you?"

She laughed and wrapped her arms around me. "Thank you for being you, Matteo."

I chuckled. "No problem, considering I don't know how to be anyone else."

Hazel looked over at the dumpster. Her adorable nose wrinkled. "Do you think we can get out of here now?"

"So, how's your hotel?" I asked my father, who sat across from me.

We'd met my parents at Homer's, a restaurant I'd taken them to last year when they'd visited.

"Good. I'm happy because they get my sports stations. Your mother's happy because she found two things to complain about already."

My mother had been looking down at the menu. She took off her reading glasses. "The bottled water in the room was opened. Who knows what someone could have put in there. The world is a crazy place these days. And the blinds didn't close all the way. Your father makes me out to be some sort of complainer, but really I'm not. I'm just—"

My father spoke over her, finishing her sentence. "*Particular.* We know, Marianne. You're just *particular*, not a complainer."

I chuckled. My parents never changed.

Leaning over to Hazel, I asked, "What are you going to order?"

"I can't decide. So many things look good."

My eyes dropped to her lips. "I know what I want."

Her eyes sparkled, and she turned back to her menu to hide her smirk.

"What about you, Mrs. Duncan?" Hazel asked. "What are you going to get?"

My mother leaned forward and wrinkled her nose. "I was thinking of getting the fish, but there's a weird smell in here. It's faint, but I caught it while we were huddled in the corner waiting for our table. Smells like maybe the mackerel went bad."

I put down the menu and folded my hands. "Oh, no. That's just Hazel. She smells like dead fish."

Hazel's eyes widened. "What?"

I shrugged. "You don't smell it?"

"I smelled something earlier. A few times, actually. But I'd figured the smell was stuck in my nose. You think *I* smell?"

I leaned to her and sniffed twice. "Yep. Dead mackerel." I smiled at my mother. "Good guess, Mom."

My mother looked horrified, while I found the entire thing amusing as hell. Hazel was fun to screw with.

She quietly lifted her sweater and took a big whiff. Her eyes grew as wide as saucers as she realized the smell really *was* coming from her.

Completely freaked out, she tried to explain to my parents. "I...I don't usually smell like fish. We went to the fish market earlier today. This sweater is a synthetic blend, and I guess it picked up some of the smell when I was sitting next to the fish dumpster."

My mother's brows lifted. "You sat next to the fish dumpster?"

I could barely contain my smile. This shit was getting even funnier by the minute.

"Yes. I did," Hazel said. "Your son thought it would be a good place to have our coffee."

Deciding I should probably help Hazel out, I leaned across the table to my mom and nodded. "We were talking about sex."

My mother blinked a few times, pursed her lips, and picked the menu back up. I looked over at my dad, but he just chuckled and hid his face behind his menu.

Hazel, on the other hand, wasn't too amused. "Thank you for telling me I smelled."

I shrugged. "Doesn't bother me any."

"Well, it bothers me!"

I leaned close and lifted my head in the air showing her my neck. "How about me? Do I smell?"

She sniffed. "You smell fine."

I smiled. "Yeah, I thought it was just you."

Hazel glared at me, but eventually she gave in and started to laugh. "I'm going to kill you later," she whispered.

I winked. "I look forward to it."

After that, my mom and Hazel got into a long discussion about whether the expense of truffle oil was worth it or not, and then Hazel mentioned she had a pet rabbit, and my mother lit up like I'd never seen her before. Apparently Mom had had a pet rabbit when she was a little girl, something I'd never known. The two of them exchanged half a dozen stories, and my mother told my father she wanted to get a pet rabbit when she got home so she could walk it on a leash, too. All in all, by the time the check came, my mom had really taken a shine to my girl.

"How long are you in town for, sweetheart?" she asked Hazel.

"Just a few days."

"And then what?"

Hazel and I looked at each other, and our faces fell. Without knowing it, my mother had just asked the magic question. *And then what?*

"We haven't figured that out yet, Mrs. Duncan."

My mom reached across the table and patted Hazel's hand. "I have a good feeling about you and my son, Hazel, and please, call me Marianne."

"Thank you, Marianne."

Chapter 27

Hazel

I couldn't believe my final day in Seattle had arrived. The thought of leaving Matteo made me sick, but I needed to go home to Connecticut and face the music—whatever that even meant at this point. I'd been avoiding giving Brady any specifics as to my whereabouts. This obviously couldn't continue forever.

While spending the past few days together had only solidified my bond with Matteo, neither of us had broached the subject of how the hell we were going to handle Brady or what would happen in general after I returned to Connecticut. We didn't want to waste this precious time talking about the inevitable conflict looming.

For our last night, Matteo took me to an open mic event at a local coffee place. With its deep, worn-leather couches and gritty air, it was everything I'd ever imagined a Seattle coffeehouse to be. They also had the best, most robust espresso I'd ever tasted.

Matteo said he'd always wanted to perform here but had never had the guts in the years since Zoe's passing.

This was his third performance in the short time I'd known him, and it gave me so much pride to feel like I might have contributed to that. I was so proud of *him.*

The musicians were given a small area in the corner that was illuminated by white Christmas lights hung on the wall. The darkness of the rest of the room helped keep the focus on the stage.

When Matteo's turn came, he got up and performed his own version of "I'm Yours" by Jason Mraz. Of course, I clung to every word, analyzing the song choice. It may or may not have been about me, or about love, or just a testament to fate and surrendering to it. That was definitely something we were going to have to do moving forward—trust in fate.

When the song finished, the crowd went wild. I rushed up to the stage and wrapped my arms around him. Despite the loud cheers, it felt like we were the only two people on Earth. Holding Matteo under the white lights of the stage where he'd just killed it was the best way I could've imagined winding down this trip.

The mood, though, after we left the coffee shop, seemed to turn melancholy.

It was just after nine, and our plan was to grab a late dinner somewhere out in the city.

"Do you know what kind of food you're in the mood for?" he asked.

For these last hours together, I'd decided I didn't want to share him.

"I was thinking about it, and I'd really like to just hang out Chez Duncan tonight. Maybe we can grab a pizza and take it back to your place?"

"Sure." He grabbed my hand and squeezed it. "We can do that."

We stopped and picked up a pie, half pepperoni and half cheese, since I preferred mine without toppings.

Back at Matteo's place, we casually ate on the floor, the vibe still somber. Each of us had only one slice. I wasn't that hungry, and apparently he wasn't either.

When my phone rang, I knew right away who it was, even before I looked at it. Once I confirmed I was right, I hit ignore.

"Is that him?" Matteo asked, his tone bitter.

I answered hesitantly. "Yes."

"Why the fuck does he keep calling you when it's clear you don't want to talk to him?"

Of course I had no answer.

One thing I'd noticed during this trip was Matteo's growing lack of tolerance for Brady. Something had changed. In the beginning, he'd seemed to have had more sympathy for his friend. Now it was like the mere mention of Brady irked him. I could only assume that as Matteo's feelings for me grew, he'd come to see Brady as more of an adversary.

I sighed. "I'm sorry, Matteo. You deserve better than to have to deal with this situation."

He looked contemplative. "I don't think we should communicate after you leave here."

My heart sank. "What?"

He got up and reached into his side table drawer for a piece of paper. Then he returned to the spot next to me on the floor.

"I bought you a ticket to New Orleans for Valentine's Day. Here's all of the information for the reservation," he said, handing it to me.

"What does this have to do with not communicating?"

"I think you need to take the time when you get home to figure everything out, without any interference from me. You make me feel as though you want me, that you want this—us. But Brady is clearly still in the picture. I don't want you to make any decision you'll regret, one way or the other. You can see from being here in Seattle that a life with me would be different than what you're used to. I obviously can't give you the financial stability that someone like Brady could. I don't even know where we would live. Everything would be up in the air. But I will tell you one thing... I don't want to be with anyone who isn't absolutely sure she wants to be with me."

This trip had only made my feelings for Matteo stronger. So I was confused as to why he seemed more worried.

"Have I done something to give you the impression that I'm still confused? Because every second I've spent with you here has made me more sure that you're the one for me, Matteo."

He looked like he wanted to believe my words, but something was holding him back.

He shook his head. "You say that now. You're still with me here. But look what happened when you went back home the first time. Brady came crawling back, and you let him into your life."

There was no disputing that. I'd definitely been confused when I got home from our road trip. At the time, Matteo—Milo—had been new and scary. And Brady was old and familiar. Even though he'd abandoned me, Brady had still seemed like the safer option. And I'd somehow felt like I'd owed him a second chance. But safe or not, my soul didn't light up with Brady the way it did with Matteo. Over the past several weeks, I'd learned that my happiness was more important than stability.

"At this moment, there is no part of me that's not yours," I said. "But I know only time will show you where my heart is."

Matteo was quiet for a couple of minutes.

He finally turned to me. "I always assumed having someone I loved die was the most devastating thing that could happen. But losing someone I love, who's still alive, might be just as bad, if not worse."

It took me a few seconds to realize Matteo had just told me he *loved* me—hidden inside a painful statement. But nevertheless, he'd said it. This might have been the best opportunity to return the sentiment, but it felt like the wrong time. I didn't want him to think I was saying it only because he had.

He deserved to hear those words from me when I had nothing else tying me down. I wasn't with my ex anymore, but until Brady knew the truth, Matteo and I were living in the shadow of a lie with a huge weight on our shoulders.

Before I could figure out how to respond to Matteo, my phone rang again.

Shit.

Brady again.

Terrible timing.

I knew every time Brady called, it was like a knife to Matteo's heart. This time, rather than saying anything, he stood up and walked to the bathroom. When the door slammed shut, my body shook. But I couldn't blame him. The bathroom was really the only place to escape in a studio apartment.

A few minutes later, I heard the shower running. It was an odd time to have decided to shower, but I understood. Matteo probably knew he was about to say or do something he'd regret, so instead he'd opted to cool off.

I didn't want to leave on bad terms, especially since he didn't want to communicate until New Orleans. I knew he was angry at how life had tricked us, but I also knew every bit of that anger was because of how much he cared for me.

What felt like an invisible pull led me to pick myself off of the ground and head for the bathroom. I was only going to make sure he was okay—at least that's what I told myself.

But after I opened the door to the steam-filled room and took in the sight of his naked silhouette through the foggy glass door, I knew there was no turning back.

For a few minutes, I just watched him as he massaged soap through his hair.

But the longer I stood there, the more my need for him became unbearable.

He finally spoke to me. "What are you doing?"

Slipping my shirt over my head, I didn't answer. I stepped out of my pants before moving my panties down my legs. Then I slid the door open and stepped inside.

Our eyes locked as his breathing became heavy. His gaze moved down. The water rained over his gorgeous face as he took in my stark naked body for the very first time.

"Fuck. You trying to kill me tonight or something, Hazel?"

As I gawked at his beautiful, carved body, all I wanted to do was spend every last minute here in Seattle worshipping it.

I dropped to my knees and answered his question by taking him into my mouth.

He let out a loud groan that echoed through the bathroom as he bent his head back. I worked my mouth over his cock, letting it reach the back of my throat. I sucked harder with each second. Never had I done anything as bold as this.

He gripped my wet hair. "Fuck. Slow down, baby. This is too much." But he used his hand to guide my head over him, to push himself in deeper, proof that he didn't really want me to stop.

He thrust his hips hard one last time, nearly causing me to gag before he pulled out of my mouth.

"Stand up, Hazel."

I did as he said, and he backed me slowly against the wall. His tone was gruff...taunting. "You think you can just waltz in here naked, let me fuck your beautiful mouth, and make everything better?"

My breaths grew heavier. "I figured if you're going to be angry, you might as well take it out on me."

Matteo spoke over my lips. "That's what you want? To fuck the anger out of me?"

Turned on more with each dirty word, I turned around and placed my hands against the tile.

I felt his hot, throbbing cock against the crack of my ass. Then his mouth landed on my neck and he sucked my skin, slow and hard. My clit buzzed with an intense need. I leaned my ass into him, wanting him inside of me.

"What did I tell you, Hazel?"

Barely able to speak, I muttered, "Huh?"

I could feel his laughter on my skin. "What's the magic word?"

In my haze, I'd completely forgotten about our pact.

"Hooker," I breathed, barely audible.

"What's that?" He pressed his cock harder into the crook of my ass. "I can't hear you."

"Hooker!" I said louder.

He covered my back in firm, slow kisses before I felt the burn of him entering me. The friction hurt ever so slightly as he buried himself inside. With my hands still against the wall, I moved my hips to meet his thrusts, the feeling so incredible I knew it wouldn't last very long. Normally, I had the opposite problem.

His breaths were frantic, the calm and cocky demeanor of a few seconds ago, seemingly replaced by the same uncontrollable need I'd been experiencing from the moment I set foot in the shower.

He wrapped his arms around my waist to push himself even deeper.

"You're mine, Hazel," he whispered. "You're fucking mine."

His words sent a chill through my body. I liked possessive Matteo. If only I had more time to experience him.

Chapter 28

Matteo

Being inside of Hazel was better than I'd ever imagined. I loved the way her body reacted any time I spoke. She was so tight, and I felt like I was going to blow my load whenever she so much as moved. But somehow I was able to control myself.

When I finally did lose it, emptying my cum inside of her as I stared down at the smooth skin of her beautiful ass, it happened suddenly and unexpectedly.

"Shit," I muttered. I was disappointed until I realized she was coming, too.

The moan she let out made the last of my orgasm even more intense.

I held her there for several minutes, not wanting to pull out. Hazel had always felt like mine, but now she'd given her body to me, and that upped the ante. If I thought I'd felt possessive before, it was even worse now.

We were running out of time, and I knew I needed her several more times before I had to give her up again.

Maybe everything would turn out perfectly. She'd show up in New Orleans and declare I was the one. But what if she didn't? What if she got home and Brady brainwashed her? My gut told me her heart was with me, but if for any reason tonight was all there was, I was going to damn well make it matter.

I shut the faucet off and squeezed the water from her hair. It turned a different fiery color of red when wet.

"Come," I said as I led her out of the shower, grabbing a towel and wiping her down as my own body dripped beads of water onto the floor.

Once we were both fully dry, she squealed in surprise as I picked her up and carried her out of the bathroom, pausing in the living room to kiss her before I was forced to put her down in order to open up the couch.

I'd never worked faster to turn it into a bed. Bach looked pissed as he sat at the windowsill watching all this go down. He'd have me all to himself soon enough; he needed to suck it up.

Taking her hand, I led Hazel onto the bed. She lay on her back while I hovered over her on all fours. I was already hard as a rock again.

"It's surreal to finally have you naked under me like this."

"Is it strange that I want you again already?" She looked almost embarrassed to ask, which was fucking adorable.

"Can you not feel how hard I am again? I need the opposite of a Viagra pill right now—something to calm me the fuck down."

"Speaking of pills," she said. "In case you didn't know, I'm on birth control. So what we just did—"

"I know, Hazel. I saw them in your makeup bag during our trip, so I knew you were on them. But I'm not sure I could've resisted you tonight, even if you weren't." I planted a long kiss on her lips. "I don't know how I'm supposed to let you go after this."

She wrapped her hands around my neck. "Don't let me go until you have to. Let's make every minute of this night count."

On that note, I spread her legs and pushed myself inside of her again, enjoying the feel of her body in a different way now that we were skin to skin without the interference of the water. And I had to say, feeling the heat of her pussy without any barrier—it was even better than the first time.

Hazel squeezed my ass with her delicate hands as I rammed into her. She opened her legs wider, eager for me to fuck her harder. Realizing how uninhibited she was pleased me to no end.

I sure as hell wasn't thinking about Brady right now. Nothing mattered except getting to come inside of this amazing woman, getting to show her with my body how much I wanted and needed her.

"You're so freaking wet. It's a beautiful thing."

"It's all you. You're doing this to me."

"I've been waiting to do this forever," I groaned.

With every movement in and out of her, I was tempted to beg her to stay, to let me love her like this every day and forget the mess that waited for her back in Connecticut. But I knew I needed to set her free. If she went back to Brady, she wasn't the one for me anyway. But I hoped to God I was right about her. Right now, I had to trust my gut. And my gut told me Hazel had been mine from the moment we met.

I was able to hold off my orgasm until she began to quiver under me. We climaxed together. As I came this time, I imagined I was leaving a piece of myself with her. It was fucked up how much I wanted to claim her. It was also fucked up how little I cared about Brady in this moment. Maybe that made me a shitty person; but nothing else seemed to matter besides Hazel.

The next morning, Hazel was wrapped in my arms. I wasn't planning on moving from the bed until we absolutely had to get up. And of course, it was one of those rare mornings where some sun peeked into the window. Why wasn't it one of the usual cloudy, rainy days here in Seattle instead?

We were tired because we'd spent a good majority of the night making up for all the moments we'd ever held back. And now I wished we'd given in a lot sooner—like back in Vail on night one. Because we'd really missed out.

"I'm so sore in the best way." She smiled.

"I hope I wasn't too hard on you last night."

She shook her head. "It was the best sex I've ever had."

After we fell into a long kiss, I wanted to make sure she knew where I stood before she got on the plane.

I looped my fingers with hers. "Listen, Hazel. I need to say this..."

A look of concern crossed her face. "Okay..."

"I don't know what the next several weeks are going to hold for us. But I don't want you to think that my giving you space in any way means I'm not here for you if you really need me. I'm here, okay?"

"Thank you for clarifying that. I don't know if I can go without talking to you for that long."

"But I do think it's best if we try not to communicate."

When she looked down, I used my hand to lift her chin. " Listen, I want to be your ride or die, okay? So badly. But there's only one thing I want more than that. And that's for you to be happy, to live the life you truly want—whether that's with me or someone else. Don't let Brady manipulate you into thinking you owe him anything. Just be true to yourself and what you want. Listen to your heart." I took her hand and placed it on my chest. "But mine? It will continue to beat for you until New Orleans."

Chapter 29

Hazel

The flight home to Connecticut was long and painful. I just wanted to be back in Matteo's arms. Leaving him felt so unnatural and premature, like we'd been ripped apart.

When the Uber dropped me off in front of my house, I was shocked to see Brady's car parked outside. I had finally responded to his texts at the airport, letting him know I'd be home today. So he must have taken it upon himself to meet me here. I couldn't say this was a pleasant surprise.

I should have had him give me his key back when he ended things, but stupidly I hadn't thought to do that. His being in my house right now without me felt like a violation.

My heart pounded. I was unprepared to see him. I wondered if he'd be able to tell just by looking at me. I was covered in Matteo.

When I opened the door, I feigned a smile at the sight of him. "Hey. This is a surprise."

He took a few steps toward me. "Yeah, it must be."

"How come you didn't tell me you planned to stop by?"

When he didn't try to hug me, I knew something was off.

"Did you have a nice trip?" he asked coldly.

"Yeah."

With each second, I became more weirded out by his vibe.

I became especially alarmed when I entered my kitchen and noticed photos lined up in a row on my counter. Not just any photos—the photos I'd taken of Matteo.

I broke out in a cold sweat. "What...what is all this?"

Brady folded his arms across his chest. "I don't know. I was hoping *you* could tell *me* that. I came here to talk to you because you haven't been responding to any of my messages. I've felt awful ever since the night of my birthday, and I wanted to apologize in person. Your camera was on the living room table, so I thought I'd snap a few pictures of myself like we used to do with each other's phones. You remember how we used to do that, right, Hazel? I'd leave my phone out while I went to the bathroom for a minute, and the following day I'd find a nice surprise of fifteen different pictures of you smiling, sticking your tongue out, and making cross-eyes. You always looked so happy in those photos. But that's not what I got this time, is it?"

Brady seemed to be waiting for an actual answer, but I didn't have one. I must've looked like a deer caught in the headlights. After a minute of staring intensely at me, he walked over to one of the photos of Matteo and picked it up. It was a picture I'd taken of him playing on stage in New Orleans.

"I saw this one first. But I'm so goddamned naïve that I just assumed you must've taken it the night we went on a double date at that café in the Village, even though I didn't remember you having your camera. You know what I thought when I looked at this photo?" He waved the glossy print around in the air. When I didn't answer, he asked again, this time louder. "*I said*, do you know what I thought when I saw this photo?"

I shook my head and whispered, "No."

"I smiled and admired your work." Brady laughed maniacally. "I was so fucking clueless that I sat there thinking how talented you are."

Brady paused. The way his eyes flashed with anger made me really nervous. He looked down at the photo again, and with a pissed-off flick of his wrist, tossed it to the floor. Then he picked up a second photo—a close up of Matteo. He'd just finished playing a song and was looking at the camera with so much emotion in his eyes.

"You know what I thought of when I looked at this one?"

Again, he stared at me, waiting for an actual answer.

I shook my head and looked down, again whispering, *no*.

"I thought to myself, it's a good thing this guy's my best friend. Because damn, he's one good-looking son of a bitch. I remember how he used to play his guitar and sing up on stage in college. A few strums and some lyrics, and the women were lining up to offer him their pussy. But I don't have to worry about that. My girl is loyal, and my best friend? He always has my back."

He snapped his wrist again and whipped the second photo at the floor. Picking up another, he flung them one by one to the ground with each staccato word he spoke.

"Not." *Toss.*

"My." *Toss.*

"Girl." *Toss.*

"Or." *Toss*

"My." Toss.

"Best." *Toss.*

"Friend." *Toss.*

There were three photos left on the counter. He picked one up and waved it around.

"Then I got to this one. A photo of my best friend with a shit ton of *snow* in the background. It hasn't snowed more than a few flurries in New York this year, at least that I'm aware of. But again, I assumed I must be wrong. There had to be some big pile of snow in a parking lot somewhere that I'm not remembering." Brady flicked his wrist and added the image to the pile on the floor.

"Then I came to this one." He held up the second-to-last photo from the counter and showed it to me before staring down at it himself. "Here's my buddy wearing a T-shirt and shorts, and he's standing in front of what looks like some sort of southern mansion or something." Brady turned the photo to show it to me again. "This doesn't look like New York City, does it, Hazel?"

I shook my head.

Brady tossed it to the floor and picked up the last photo. "But even then, after a dozen pictures staring me straight in the face, I still refused to believe it. There had to be some logical explanation as to why my girl would have all of these pictures of my best friend in her camera from what seemed like places that are not New York. So I kept going, in oblivious denial, until I got to this one."

The photo was a selfie I'd taken of Matteo and me on the day before we left New Orleans. I was smiling broadly for the camera, and Matteo had his lips pressed to my cheek.

"Tell me, Hazel. How was I going to explain this one to myself?" He paused and laughed. "I'm seriously such a dumb fuck. A part of me was *still* holding on to hope that there was some reasonable explanation for all of this. It wasn't until I saw you walk in the front door with guilt written all over your face that I *actually knew*." Brady walked over to my suitcase and lifted the airline's luggage tag, which I hadn't thought to detach before wheeling it inside.

"SEA? If I'm not mistaken, that's the airport code for Seattle." His voice cracked as he continued, "How was your trip to fuck my best friend, Hazel?"

Tears streamed down my face. "Brady..." I shook my head. "I'm so sorry. I didn't mean for this to happen."

He tossed the last photo onto the floor, and his shoulders slumped. His anger seemed to dissipate into sadness, and that broke my heart. I took a few steps toward him and reached out, but Brady held his hands up and stepped back.

"Don't. Don't touch me."

I shook my head. "We didn't mean for this to happen, Brady."

"How long? How long have you been screwing my best friend?"

I looked down. "We met when I went to Vail."

He scoffed. "That's perfect. Did you fuck him in the honeymoon suite I'd booked us?"

I shook my head again. "That's not how it was. You have to believe me."

"Oh I do, do I? Why is that? Because you've been so honest with me lately? I spent time with the two of you together. You guys must've had a good laugh at my expense. *What a dope he is for not catching on.*"

"Brady, I swear, we randomly met in Vail at a hotel, and neither of us had a clue that we had a connection to each other. We had absolutely no idea until Matteo walked in the door at that bar you and I met at for a drink a few weeks ago."

"Yeah, that sounds believable. The two of you meet in Vail, where you were both supposed to be for our wedding, and with totally common names like Hazel and Matteo, and it never dawned on either of you."

"We...we weren't using our real names."

Brady's eyebrows jumped. "*Oh*! Right. Everything makes a lot of sense now. Thanks for filling me in. I understand completely how that could happen. It's crystal clear."

The fact that Matteo and I had used fake names for two full weeks, and we'd never figured out the reason we were both in Vail, were the same reasons it really *did* seem ludicrous right about now. The story sounded so far-fetched, it was almost unbelievable to me.

Brady and I stood in silence for a long time. He stared at the ground, at the pictures of Matteo spread all over the floor, and shook his head.

When he looked up, his eyes were rimmed with tears. "Do you love him?"

I wasn't sure if I should be honest or not, but I thought if Brady was ever going to believe any of the crazy story of how Matteo and I had met, I needed to start being truthful right now.

I nodded. "I do."

Brady shook his head. "Athena never meant anything to me. I was just dumb and scared. I might've cheated first, but it was just sex, Hazel. Cheating of the heart is much worse."

It felt like the wind had been knocked out of me. "Who...who's Athena?"

Brady scoffed. "Great. So this wasn't even you getting even with me? You had no clue I'd screwed up when you went and started fucking my best friend. You know, I always thought you and I were different, that you were too good for me. But it turns out, you're just as big a piece of shit as I am."

I shook my head, still not fully understanding. "Who's Athena? The woman you work with?"

Brady waved me off. "You know what? I'm done here. If you want the details of what happened between Athena and me, ask your boyfriend. He was such a trusted friend to me that I told him all about her."

Holy shit. Hot anger rushed through me as I realized how long I'd blamed *myself* for the end of our engagement. And *no one* had been telling me the truth.

He caught my eyes one more time, then turned around and walked out the front door.

Chapter 30

Matteo

"Come on...pick up." I paced back and forth in my apartment.

My mom frowned. "She's still not answering?"

I dragged a hand through my hair and shook my head. It had been three days since Brady had called, slurring his words, the night Hazel flew home. My cell phone had woken me at four in the morning East Coast time. No call that comes in at that hour is ever good, but when I grabbed my cell off the nightstand and saw the name flashing on the screen, I knew. *I knew.*

I'd been a coward over the last month, sneaking around behind my friend's back, so I'd answered, steadying myself to take my lumps. But Brady was barely comprehensible in his drunken state. I'd managed to make out that he'd been waiting at Hazel's house after she landed and found some photos of the two of us on her camera. After that, the rest of the conversation mostly consisted of him rambling and calling me a lowlife piece of shit. He was right. I couldn't argue with him about that. Every time he hung up on me and then called back fifteen minutes later to yell some more, the least I could do was answer the phone and let him get some of it out. My cell finally stopped ringing a little before six, his time.

I'd waited another hour to call Hazel, but she didn't answer. By late afternoon, I'd hit redial at least fifty times and was starting to think the worst. Desperate to know she was okay, I even tried Brady again. But he didn't pick up either. Entirely freaked out on the other side of the country, I was considering calling the police and having them check in on Hazel. But then I remembered she'd once used my phone to call her friend Felicity, so I searched my call history and dialed her instead.

After explaining who I was and giving her a quick rundown, I begged Felicity to go over and check on Hazel. The hour it took for her to call me back was sixty of the worst minutes of my life. The crazy shit running through my head was unimaginable. But Felicity eventually called, and she assured me Hazel was physically fine. While I was relieved, I didn't understand why she wouldn't have picked up the phone and told me that herself.

Granted, I was the one who'd suggested we have no contact when she went back home, but this was an emergency. It didn't make sense. I couldn't get Felicity to tell me much other than Brady had found out, and Hazel didn't want to talk to anyone right now.

It had killed me to not hear Hazel's voice myself, but I'd given it two days before trying to call her again. But six days had passed now since she flew back home, and I still couldn't get her to pick up. I'd texted, called, and even tried sending her messages on social media.

Last night, on Christmas Eve, I was certain it would be the day she'd finally pick up. When she didn't, I couldn't stop myself from calling Felicity a second time. While I couldn't get her to tell me much more than the first time I called, she did shed some light on why Hazel was ignoring me. *Fucking Brady* had told her about the woman he'd slept with, along with the fact that I'd known about it.

This morning, I'd thought about flying to Connecticut. But then my mother had knocked on my door without my father. She sat me down, asking what was going on and if I was alright. And I'd spilled my guts to her, telling her the entire crazy story—from how Hazel and I met, to our road trip, to the shock of walking into a bar in New York City expecting to see my old pal Brady, only to find out that *my* Maddie wasn't my Maddie at all. She was my buddy's Hazel.

My mom could be a busybody, but today she was there when I needed her. She'd even given me some good advice, had me looking at things from a woman's perspective. If it weren't for her talking me down, I'd probably be on a plane on my way to force Hazel to talk to me before she was ready.

I sat down at the table and blew out an audible breath.

"I know, sweetheart." My mother patted my hand. "She'll come around. You just need to give her a little bit of time. I saw the way she looked at you. It's not over. Right now, she's confused and feels betrayed by both you and Brady."

"I thought this was supposed to be a pep talk to make me feel better."

"It is. But that doesn't mean we ignore the part of the truth that isn't pretty. I understand that you were in a tough situation, and I understand your reasons for not wanting to tell Hazel about Brady. You wanted Hazel to pick you because she wants to be with you, not because she didn't want to be with Brady after she found out he'd cheated. I get it. I really do. But that doesn't change the fact that you kept something from her. From everything you've told me, she was honest with you right from the start—even when she told you she wasn't sure if things with her and Brady were over when she went home after your trip. That couldn't have been easy for her to tell you. She risked losing you by saying that. But she was honest with herself and with you."

I blew out a jagged breath. "Unlike me, who wasn't honest. Because I didn't trust her to make a decision to be with me for the right reasons."

My mom nodded. "I'm afraid so. Sometimes the best thing you can do for someone you love is give them the space they need. Although it's also the most difficult thing you can do."

I forced a smile. "Thanks, Mom."

My dad came over later in the day, and we managed to have a quiet, but nice Christmas. When my parents left, I thought a lot more about what my mother said. I'd been calling Hazel nonstop just so I could hear her voice, which was selfish and only going to make *me* feel better. So I decided to stop, to let her have the space she needed. Though before I did that, I wanted her to know that my lack of contact wouldn't mean I wasn't thinking about her. So I composed a text:

Hazel, I'm sorry you're hurting right now. I'm even more sorry that something I've done has contributed to that pain. I know you need some space, so I'm going to give that to you. But please know, not a moment of the day goes by when you're not in my thoughts. I'd hoped to tell you this in person, but if it's going to be the last thing I get to say to you for a while, I need to say it now. I love you, Hazel. I think I have since the first moment I laid eyes on you. When I look back, I'm not sure how I lived for so long without you in my life. But then I remember, I hadn't really been living until you made my heart beat again.

I was surprised when a few minutes later my phone buzzed. Seeing Hazel's name light up on the screen made me feel more hope than I had in days. But then I read her text:

Thank you. Take care of yourself, Matteo.

And whatever morsel of hope had bloomed inside of me instantly wilted. Her message sounded a hell of a lot more like goodbye than just needing a little space.

Chapter 31

Matteo – Seven weeks later

I arrived a day early.

The last seven weeks had felt more like seven years. Each day, I got out of bed and went through the motions, but it didn't really feel like I was living. Thank God my leave of absence was over, and I'd had to go back to work. Otherwise I'd have a Vitamin D deficiency from lack of sunlight. I really hated to compare anything to do with Zoe to my situation with Hazel, but the way this was hitting me might've been worse than what I went through after I lost Zoe. That sounds crazy, I know. And in a lot of ways it felt disrespectful to Zoe to even think that. But when she died, I had no choice but to accept that she was gone, and I had to move on. That didn't mean I wanted to find a new girlfriend or anything. Yet after the shock wore off, I accepted that she was gone from my life forever. What had happened was a cold, hard fact that I couldn't change.

I wasn't sure I'd ever be able to accept it was over with Hazel, knowing she and I were still breathing the same air.

But for the last seven weeks, every day that went by that I hadn't heard from her made me feel like the chances things would work out in the end were dwindling.

Sitting in my hotel room, the *same exact* room Hazel and I had shared only a few months ago, wondering if she would show up tomorrow, was making me stir crazy. So I decided to take a walk. Bourbon Street always had some action. I needed a distraction, even if just for a little while.

I walked past the little restaurant where Hazel and I had shared jambalaya. Every step I took away from it made my feet feel heavy. It was as if I was trudging along, wearing ten-pound weights on each foot. I passed a bar where we'd shared drinks, then the open mic place where I sang while looking at her beautiful face in the audience. This damn walk was supposed to help me clear my head, but it was doing anything but.

When I came upon a storefront I'd completely forgotten about, I stopped in my tracks. *Psychic and Chakra Balancing.* How the hell could I have not remembered this place? Zara had given me a message from Zoe. And she'd also told Hazel she saw a big conflict with a person whose name began with M. At the time, Hazel and I were Milo and Maddie and we'd had *no clue* about the big conflict we were about to be smacked in the face with.

I couldn't resist going in to see if Zara was around. The small, front reception room was empty. A dark purple, velvet curtain separated the adjoining room where I knew she did readings. So I stayed quiet, not wanting to interrupt if she was with someone else. After a minute or two of silence, a familiar voice spoke from the other room.

"It's about time you came back."

I assumed she was speaking to whoever was in the room with her, so I said nothing. But when I didn't respond, a minute later, the voice yelled, "Come on, what are you waiting for? I'm not getting any younger, you know."

My forehead wrinkled. "Uhhh... Are you talking to me?"

"Well, I'm not talking to myself. I'm a psychic, not a loony tune."

I pulled back the heavy curtain and found Zara sitting at her table alone. She waved at me impatiently. "Come on, come on. Let's get this show on the road. You didn't bring your little chickadee this time, huh?"

I sat down hesitantly, confused. "You remember me?"

"Mostly I get drunks who smell like day-old beer and girls who want to know if they're going to find Mr. Right flashing their tits on Bourbon Street. I don't get many coming in who look like you."

I smiled—a rarity these days. "Thank you. You did such a great job last time I was here, I guess I was kind of hoping you could help me out again."

Zara extended her hand, palm up. "Of course. That'll be forty bucks, please."

I dug into my pocket and pulled out my billfold. "Forty? Last time it was only twenty."

Zara shrugged. "I charge a premium now when I talk to dead celebrities."

After a moment I laughed. "You mean David Bowie? That actually wasn't Bowie, it was *Zoe*."

Zara shook her head. "Well, it's still gonna have to be forty, because apparently I need to buy a damn hearing aid for when I speak to people on the other side."

I peeled two twenties from my billfold and placed them in Zara's hand. Forty was actually a steal. Hell, I'd have emptied my bank account if she could tell me whether or not Hazel was going to show up tomorrow. It would be worth it to finally get a night of solid sleep.

Zara tucked the bills into her bra and shut her eyes, holding both hands out to me.

When I didn't immediately do anything, she peeked open one eye. "Give me your hands."

"Oh. Yeah, sure. Sorry."

I sat there watching her in silence for a solid five minutes. Her closed eyes went through a series of different expressions. At one point, her brows and mouth pinched tight, and she looked annoyed. Then a minute later, a smile spread across her face. Eventually, she opened her eyes and let go of my hands.

I was anxious. "Did you see something stressful?"

She waved me off. "Nah. I just wanted to hold your hand a little bit. It's been a long time since a man who looks like you did that." She twisted in her seat and pulled out a deck of cards from a storage box on a chair next to her. I recognized them as the tarot cards she'd used last time.

Zara pushed her dreadlocks from her face and flipped over three cards. Studying them, she pointed down to the first two. "We already spoke about your past, so I assume you're here today to learn about your present and future."

I nodded. "Yeah, that would be great."

She picked up the middle card and held it to her forehead with her eyes closed for a minute. "You're lonely," she said.

I frowned but nodded.

Zara leaned forward and lowered her voice. "I can send you to a little place on the other side of town. Tell them Zara sent you, and for fifty bucks you won't be lonely anymore."

I chuckled. "That's okay. I think I'm good."

She set down the middle card and picked up the next one, again holding it to her forehead for a moment. "Your pussy doesn't want a new friend."

My brows drew together. "Excuse me?"

"You do have a cat, right?"

"Yes."

"Well, he is not going to like his new friend."

"Who's his new friend?"

"How should I know? I'm just telling you what's coming to me."

"Okay, okay." Might that mean Hazel is coming? My cat didn't exactly love her the first time they met. Maybe that's a positive sign?

"And the apple you'll be looking for? It's in the trunk of the car."

"The apple? That's what you see? I'm going to misplace a piece of fruit?"

"Hey," Zara snapped. "Don't get pissy with the messenger."

I dragged a hand through my hair. "Yeah, you're right, sorry. I'm just anxious."

"You're anxious about the girl you were here with last time? The redhead?"

My pulse started to race. "Yeah. What do you see about her?"

Zara closed her eyes tightly for moment, and then opened them. "Nothing. Sorry. I'm not seeing her at all."

My heart sank into my stomach.

"But I do see something else," Zara said. "Are you into astrology, by any chance?"

I shook my head.

"Is your birthday in May, or maybe a woman in your life has a birthday in May?"

I shook my head again.

"I'm seeing a bull. But not just any bull. It's the kind they use in those astrology charts to represent people born under the Taurus sign."

I racked my brain for any kind of a connection to the month of May or astrology, but came up empty.

Seeing my face, Zara frowned. "Look, kid. Normally I'd make up some bullshit like you're going to meet your future wife next Wednesday, or tell you I see a breakup in your future when nothing exciting is coming to me. But you don't strike me as someone who wants to hear that crap."

I smiled sadly. "I'm not. I appreciate you trying, Zara."

"No problem, sweetheart." She reached over into the storage box where she'd pulled out her tarot cards and took out something else. Extending what looked like a business card to me, she said, "This is a half-off coupon for the place I mentioned earlier that could help you get rid of your loneliness. Just in case you change your mind."

I shook my head and stood. "Hold onto that for me, Zara. I may be back to take it tomorrow night."

Chapter 32

Matteo

Wandering the French Quarter in the morning as the sun came up was an interesting experience, like a surreal calm after a storm. Pretty sure some of the people passing by me hadn't even gone to sleep yet; some still seemed drunk.

Then you had the older couples slowly strolling along, looking for a place to eat breakfast as the sound of a street performer's clarinet played somewhere in the distance. The cleaning trucks were out, attempting to wash away the sins of the night before. And early-morning commuters rode by on their bikes. The city was waking up, and I longed for Hazel to be here with me, so we could wander these streets together.

To anyone else here, it was like any other morning in New Orleans. But for me? It was the start of a day that would dictate the rest of my life—a day that would inevitably mean the difference between a hopeful future or an irreparable broken heart.

I stopped at a café and ordered two powdered beignets and some coffee. As delicious as they were, my stomach felt unsettled, so I wasn't able to eat them. I couldn't stop thinking about tonight.

Given that Hazel hadn't reached out to me in a month and a half, if I were a betting man, I'd say she wasn't coming. But wild horses still couldn't have kept me away on the off-chance she did show.

The longer Hazel and I were apart, the more I missed what we had. But she'd lost a certain amount of trust in me that I might never be able to earn back. I just had to hope that whatever was meant to happen would.

I'd spent the day trying my best to pass the time before the flight I'd booked for Hazel was set to arrive. Nothing could stop the preoccupation in my mind, though.

As it got closer to late afternoon, my nerves were going haywire.

Around 4PM, I went back to the hotel room and did my best to occupy myself: taking a shower, watching HBO, eating mindlessly out of the mini bar. There was only so much I could do. I didn't want to leave the room. I couldn't risk something happening that would delay my getting back by the time she was supposed to show.

I shut off the television at about 5:45 and started to pace.

When the clock finally struck six, I decided to log onto the airport's website and check the status of the flight.

LANDED.

My heart raced as I stared at that word.

LANDED.

This was it; she was either here or she wasn't. There was no turning back now.

The minutes after that crawled. I estimated it would take her at least an hour to get her luggage and get from the airport to the hotel.

So when seven o'clock rolled around, my forehead started to sweat. I stood at the window, as if being closer to the outside world was going to somehow make her magically appear.

When seven thirty hit, my heart sank.

And the half-hour until eight was probably the most excruciating, because eight o'clock was the time I'd internally decided to give up on any chance of her showing. I'd told the registration desk to expect her, instructing them to give her a key so she could come right up to the room. I toyed with the idea of calling downstairs to make sure there wasn't a mix-up, that she wasn't waiting for me down there. But who was I kidding? If she were here and unable to check in, someone would've called me. *She* would've called me. So, no. Calling the front desk wasn't going to help this hopeless situation.

I lay back on the bed and stared at the ceiling. It was time I started accepting the fact that Hazel wasn't coming. That hurt like a motherfucker. And the more it started to set in, the more I just *couldn't* accept it. Losing Brady as a friend was one thing. That sucked, and the way things had ended with us was something I'd always regret. But Hazel was the love of my life.

The love of my life.

Wow.

It felt strange to acknowledge that now—when it was apparently too late. I'd loved Zoe deeply. And maybe it wasn't fair to compare my feelings for Zoe with how I felt about Hazel. They're two different people, and my love for each of them was unique. But I felt like Hazel was the person I was meant to be with. And losing her made me realize just how much I did love her. It felt like she was holding a part of me I'd never get back.

I forced myself up to a sitting position. I must have sat at the edge of the bed with my head in my hands for an hour straight.

Then something happened. A surge of adrenaline seemed to come out of nowhere—an inner strength powered by love.

No fucking way you're giving up like this.

Grow some balls and go get your woman back.

In that moment, I started to gather my things in a hurry, pretty sure I was about to head to the airport and ask for the first flight to Connecticut or New York City.

I wasn't going to give up on us until I had a chance to explain my rationale for not telling her about Brady's cheating. I owed it to her and myself to make sure she understood where I'd been coming from, and that I never meant to hurt her. And if she still couldn't trust me, at least I'd know I'd done everything I could.

I'd just gathered all of my stuff when there was a knock at the door.

I rushed to see who it was.

When I opened, the sight of her nearly knocked me on my ass.

Hazel.

She looked tired, disheveled, and was...holding a kitten?

Why?

I didn't care. I stood there in awe, filled with hope.

Because goddammit, she was here. My Hazel was here.

Still in utter disbelief, my words came out in a whisper. "You're here."

She nodded silently, still clutching the kitten.

What the hell?

After she set the kitten down on the rug, I pulled her into my arms.

I spoke into her hair. "I was just about to leave. Thank God I didn't."

"Where were you going?"

"To Connecticut. To you."

I wiped a tear from her eye. She looked drained.

"What happened to you, Hazel?"

"It's a long story. Can you kiss me first?"

"Fuck yes, I can."

I couldn't take her mouth fast enough, letting out an exasperated breath that she likely felt at the back of her throat. With each second that passed as I devoured her lips, I realized it didn't matter why she was late, why there was a random kitten here, or why her hair looked like she'd been electrocuted.

I was just happy to have her in my arms. That was all that mattered.

As I lifted her up, she wrapped her legs around my waist. And I got the sudden urge to carry her over to the wall.

She worked to unbuckle my pants as I slid hers down. Within seconds, I'd moved her panties to the side and pushed myself into her beautiful, warm pussy. Hazel raked her fingers through my hair as we fucked against the wall in a primal frenzy. As I rocked into her, it felt like I was letting out all of the tension and fear that had built up inside of me over the past twenty-four hours.

When I felt her muscles squeeze against my cock, I let go, holding the back of her head in the palm of my hand to protect it as I came hard inside of her. It was the fastest sex we'd ever had, but probably the most intense orgasm of my life.

"I love you so much, Hazel," I said, panting as I looked down at her.

"I love you, too, Matteo. I thought I'd never get here in time to tell you. And Happy Valentine's Day. I bought you something, but I realized when I got to the airport that I'd forgotten to pack it. I guess today has been one screw up after the next."

I pushed the hair from her face. "There's nothing you could give me better than the gift you just did—your heart. Happy Valentine's Day, my love."

When the kitten meowed, that was my cue to slowly put Hazel down. She escaped to the bathroom as I tucked myself back into my pants and the kitten circled my legs. It still felt surreal.

When Hazel reemerged, I held out my hand, leading her over to the bed. She rested her head on my chest as she started to explain things.

"I missed my flight. There was a huge traffic backup due to construction on 95. So even though I left for the airport several hours early, I didn't make it in time. And the only flight that would get me here at a reasonable hour was one that landed at an airport a few hundred miles away from here."

My eyes widened. "You drove part of the way here? Why didn't you tell me? I would've left earlier and met you."

She sighed. "Well, for one, my phone died on the plane."

"Shit."

"As soon as I landed and got a rental car, I drove to a gas station to get a charger, but after I took off from there, I got a flat before my phone could charge up."

Shit.

"Oh, baby. I'm sorry." I kissed her head.

Getting teary eyed again, she continued, "I didn't want to wait on the side of the road. Since I wasn't that far away from the gas station, I drove back there again on the bad tire. While I was getting it changed, this adorable stray kitten appeared out of nowhere. The mechanic told me the mother had abandoned a bunch of her litter. She was weaving in and out of my legs and actually really helped calm me down, because by that time, I was freaking out." She wiped her eyes. "I couldn't just leave her. So I took her with me and drove off."

"And you drove straight here?"

She shook her head. "That's not exactly what happened. About twenty minutes into my drive, I realized my phone was missing. I assumed I'd left it back at the gas station when I was getting my tire changed."

I cringed. "Hazel, this story is crazier than the entire last three months put together."

"It gets better." She sniffled and laughed a little. "I was never able to find my phone at the gas station, so I drove all the way here with no phone."

"Jesus."

"But when I went to get my luggage out of the trunk just now, there was my phone. I must have dropped it there when I was looking for the spare tire at the gas station."

As soon as she said that, the craziest realization hit. "Holy crap." *Trunk.*

"What?"

"I came to town a day early. One of the things I did to pass the time was visit that psychic, Zara. She told me something that made absolutely no sense until now."

"Uh-oh. What?"

"She told me an apple I'd be looking for was in the trunk of the car. I was thinking red apple, like the fruit. Now I realize she was seeing the Apple phone in your damn trunk."

She chuckled. "It was no more an apple than I am a hazelnut, apparently."

"No shit. This is crazy."

"What else did she say?"

I scratched my head trying to remember. "Something about a bull...like the one that represents the Taurus sign. You didn't stop at a saloon on the way here and ride one of those mechanical bulls, did you?"

Her eyes moved from side to side as she pondered. "You said Taurus? My rental car is a Taurus."

I couldn't help but laugh. "Well, mystery solved."

The kitten jumped onto the bed and landed at our feet.

I placed my hand on Hazel's cheek and stared into her eyes. "I can't believe you're here."

She breathed in deeply. "It took me a while to get to this place—both literally and figuratively. Even though in my heart I knew you weren't keeping that information from me to be malicious, it really hurt."

Her words squeezed at my chest. "I know. What I did was selfish. But I need you to know that I always planned to tell you. If you'd chosen to be with Brady, I wouldn't have let you make that decision without divulging what I knew. But I just..." I paused to gather my thoughts. "I needed to know that you chose me because you loved me and not because you felt betrayed by him."

Her eyes softened. "I would always have chosen you. The choice was made the moment I laid eyes on you again at that bar in New York, when I saw the hurt on your face and realized that I meant as much to you as you'd meant to me. And I've fallen more deeply in love with you each moment we've been together since. I love you so much, Matteo Duncan. I really do."

Holding her close, I spoke into the nape of her neck. "I'm never letting you go again."

"Good. Because I have no plans to go back to Connecticut."

I moved back to look at her. "What?"

She bit her lip. "If you'll have me, I want to come to Seattle with you."

"What about your job?"

Hazel shrugged. "My love was never school photography. I want to follow my love—and that's you. I'll find freelance work. Ever since our road trip, I've been trying to figure out how to build the life I truly want, and being tied down to that business was a deterrent. I'd been thinking about selling it for a while. Felicity and her husband are happy to take it over. She was excited."

Wow. This felt like a dream

"What about Abbott the Rabbit?" I asked.

Hazel looked down and her lips started to quiver. "Abbott...died."

Oh no.

My stomach sank. "What?"

"They think she had a heart attack. They say sometimes a loud noise can startle a rabbit to death. I came home one day and...found her lying there. I still don't know what happened." She began to cry.

My heart broke for her. "When was this?"

Wiping her eyes, she said, "A few weeks ago."

"I'm so sorry, sweetheart, that I wasn't there for you when it happened."

She sniffled. "Thank you. It made these past several weeks apart from you even harder. But Abbott's dying was really the thing that solidified my decision to give up my life in Connecticut. Life is too short to waste it with people you're not passionate about or doing something you're not passionate about. And right now...I'm passionate about doing you."

"Fucking hell, woman. I'm already hard again. Who am I to keep you from your passion?" I placed a long, hard kiss on her mouth before releasing her.

Her lips were swollen when she asked, "Do you think there'll be room for me and Nola?"

"Nola?" I looked over at the small, gray kitty. "Is that the cat's name?"

"Yeah. I figured if we made it here alive, I was going to name her Nola." She smiled. "One of the reasons I brought her with me was I figured a new cat might distract Bach a little. You know, since I'll be taking away his only companion—or at least much of your attention. He hates me as it is. Maybe she'll be a distraction?"

Holy shit.

Zara's other warning now made perfect sense.

Your pussy doesn't want a new friend.

"I'm not so sure Bach is going to be happy."

"Why do you say that?"

I didn't have the heart to tell her about Zara's prediction.

"Don't worry about it. We'll work it out. Everything's going to be fine." I smiled.

Epilogue

Hazel – Ten months later

Matteo and I were planning an early Christmas celebration in Seattle before we traveled to Vail to spend the holidays with his parents.

For two people who loved adventure, we'd lived a pretty settled life over the past several months. Though we kept a jar full of folded-up pieces of paper with different trips we wanted to take written on each, vowing never to lose the adventurous spirit that had launched our union. Sometimes we'd pick a paper randomly out of the jar and take off for the weekend when finances would allow. But honestly we loved our downtime just as much—hanging out at local coffeehouses or playing with our cats. When you're with the person you're supposed to be with, every day is like an adventure. We didn't need to always travel the country to feel fulfilled. Just being together—hanging at the local coffeehouses or playing with our cats—made us happy.

We were blessed to have found each other. Despite the rough start to my relationship with Matteo, I knew in my heart that my time with Brady had existed so I could meet his friend. Maybe that's fucked up, but it's the truth.

We'd opted to stay in Seattle because of Matteo's teaching job. As much as I'd always said school photography wasn't my passion, I ended up getting a photo contract with a local school district here. Only now I wasn't just doing school photos; I'd branched out, shooting more weddings, family portraits, and headshots—and even some local musical acts. Diversifying my offerings gave me more flexibility. I could make my own schedule, and if that meant taking two weeks off to go to Vail with my boyfriend, it was my choice.

Matteo and I had moved out of his studio apartment and found a two-bedroom not too far from his original place. With both of our incomes, it was still affordable to live in the city. I didn't miss Connecticut at all. I hadn't really found myself until I'd met my true love. With Matteo, I didn't long for anything but being with him—I didn't need stability *or* wild adventures. I just needed him. He'd helped me realize that true happiness is simply following your heart. He *was* my heart.

Matteo walked in as I was daydreaming and petting Nola in the living room.

"What are you thinking about?" he asked.

"Just how much better this Christmas is than the last one. It feels fitting that we're going back to Vail soon, too. Like we've come full circle."

He sat next to me on the couch and kissed my forehead. "I can't wait to take you skiing again."

"Yeah, maybe I can graduate from the bunny slopes with more than a day of training this time."

He winked. "I'll make it happen."

I massaged his knee. "My sexy ski instructor."

"I was thinking maybe we should book a night at the hotel where we met," he said. "You know... we might get sick of being at my parents' house for two weeks anyway."

"I would love that. It'll be like old times."

He kissed my neck. "Except now instead of dreaming about sleeping with you while I'm in the next room, I'll get to have you as much as I want."

I gripped his shirt. "And instead of sneaking looks at your shirtless physique, I can have that body however I like."

He moved closer and spoke over my lips, "What do you think would've happened if we hadn't both chosen that hotel? Where would we be right now?"

I sighed. "I hate to say it, but I think I'd be married to Brady. I would've never known he'd cheated on me. I'd be bored and feeling unfulfilled back in Connecticut. And I would've never realized how amazing life could be."

Matteo nodded. "I feel like I'd still be in the funk I was in before we met. I probably would've eventually met you back in New York and wondered how Brady got so damn lucky, though. The thought of you with him now makes me want to throw up."

We didn't speak of Brady much. But when we did, I could tell it made Matteo a little sad.

"Do you ever...miss him?" I asked.

Nola crept up on us and purred.

Matteo pondered that for a minute. "I miss what he and I had before I knew he was a cheater. I don't think he's a bad person, but he damn well didn't deserve you.

I had to lose his friendship in order to have you in my life, so I don't have any regrets."

"I don't, either. Knowing what I know now, I don't even feel sorry for him anymore." I stared off as I rubbed Nola's belly. "I do miss his mother, though. She and I were close. I wrote her a long letter before I moved to Seattle. I never heard back. That makes me sad. But he's her son. Her allegiance will always be with him."

Matteo laid his head on my shoulder. "Have I thanked you lately for giving your old life up for me?"

"Are you kidding? I wasn't really living back then."

The kitchen timer went off, prompting us both off the couch. I'd baked a lasagna for our early Christmas dinner.

A while later, we sat together in our little kitchen, enjoying each other's company while the cats lurked under the table, holding out for our scraps. Thankfully, after a rough start, Bach and Nola got along, for the most part. They had a nightly routine where they'd fight playfully. Of course we had to find someone besides Carina to watch our pets while we were away, because you know I nipped that shit in the bud real fast. No more attractive exes watching Matteo's cats. We now had a nice neighbor, Elias, who'd agreed to check in on Bach and Nola daily while we were away.

After dinner, Matteo stood up from the table and reached for my hand. "Are you ready to exchange gifts?"

I was nervous, but excited to give Matteo his present. It wasn't anything like what he was expecting.

I followed him to the room where he'd been storing my gift. "So, I finally get to see what you've been hiding in the spare bedroom?"

Matteo had told me my present was too big to hide in a closet. So he'd ordered me not to go into the spare room for the past couple weeks. I'd been tempted to peek, but had managed not to give in. I suspected it might have been the treadmill I'd hinted at.

Instead, what met my eyes when he opened the door was the best, most heartfelt present he could have given.

"When?" I shook my head in disbelief. "How did you manage to put this together?"

"It hasn't been easy. I've been sneaking in here to assemble it whenever you had an assignment and I happened to not be working at the same time. The other day when you ran to the store to get your tea, I snuck in fifteen minutes."

It was a Victorian dollhouse, like the one I'd always wanted as a kid. I'd told Matteo when we first met that Brady once bought me a kit, but hadn't built it for me. I never would have imagined he remembered.

My jaw dropped. "I can't believe this. It's amazing."

The dollhouse had three floors, and it was blue on the outside with pink shutters. It was basically a mansion, as far as dollhouses went. As I looked closer, I realized that this was more than your average dollhouse, and not just because of its size. This was personalized.

"The animal on the wall!"

He laughed. "It's a stuffed raccoon, an ode to our time at Wyatt Manor."

I shook my head. "I cannot believe all the detail you put into this."

"Check out the tablecloth in the kitchen," he said.

I covered my mouth. "Oh my God!"

It had pineapples on it, in honor of the sex party we'd attended in Santa Fe.

He'd turned our adventures into a home. It felt like a metaphor for my entire experience with him.

It was a feast for the eyes—miniature furniture with real linens, carpets, lighting. But where were the people?

Then my eyes found the upstairs bedroom, and there they were. The male figurine with brown hair was kneeling in front of the female—a redhead wearing southwestern-style boots. The man's hands were extended, and there was a tiny box sitting atop them.

My heart beat faster as I realized the man was proposing.

When I turned around to look at Matteo, he was already down on one knee with a little box of his own.

My mouth went agape.

"Hazel, we haven't known each other for two years yet, but I can't remember a time without you. You're my adventure partner, my best friend, my lover, and my soulmate. I want to spend the rest of my life with you. Will you marry me?"

He had no idea how much his doing this *tonight* meant.

At a loss for words, I wiped the tears from my eyes. "I love you so much. I would rather die than live life without you at this point. I will absolutely marry you."

I hadn't even looked closely at the ring until now. It was a gorgeous, round solitaire diamond. He couldn't place it on my finger fast enough, and when he did, it felt magical—like my entire experience with him since the moment we met.

Matteo lifted me up and spun me around.

When he put me down, I said, "I'm really anxious to give you your present. Be right back."

My heart racing, I ran to our room to grab the gift bag.

I returned to him in the spare room and handed it over.

He removed the tissue paper, and his forehead crinkled. He lifted out buffalo plaid footie pajamas—a pair for him and a pair for me. His said *Mr. Hooker*, and mine said *Mrs. Hooker*.

Clearing my throat, I said, "I struggled with whether to order *Mr. and Mrs.* I didn't want you to think I was being presumptuous. It was supposed to be a joke. But after tonight, it totally fits, doesn't it? The buffalo plaid is really Christmasy, too."

"Heck yeah! How did you know I've always wanted these?" He winked. "Are we supposed to change into them tonight? Because I'd be down for that. Although, they'll be tough to get off easily when I need you naked." He paused. "Wait. Buffalo? Buffalo plaid. Maybe Zara wasn't referring to your rental car in Louisiana? Maybe this is where she got the buffalo from. Or I guess it was a bull..."

"That hadn't occurred to me. I'm not sure."

My palms were sweaty. He hadn't seen what else was in the bag. The entire point of this was being missed.

"There's something else in there," I finally said.

"Really?" He reached inside. "Oh shoot. You're right."

Matteo lifted out a third pair of buffalo-plaid footie pajamas. He unfolded them and held them up to read the words on the front: *Baby Hooker*.

He grinned. "Sweet! Someday our future baby can wear this."

He wasn't getting it.

I bit my lip as my heart pounded. "Well, if the future's in eight months...yeah."

It took him a few seconds to process.

"Wait, what? You're...you're pregnant?" He shook his head in disbelief. "How?"

"Turmeric." I laughed nervously.

"Huh?"

"Turmeric. I started taking supplements. Heard turmeric had lots of health benefits. Didn't know one of those *benefits* was interfering with birth control."

He blinked repeatedly. "I fucking love turmeric! Gonna put that shit on everything now!" Still holding the pajamas, he wrapped his arms around me.

"You're happy about this?"

He squeezed me tighter. "Of course I'm happy. This is best Christmas gift you could give me."

"I was worried it was too soon."

"It can't come soon enough." An adorable excitement flashed in his eyes. "Be right back. I have to get something."

Matteo walked over to the closet and removed a box from the top shelf. He opened it and took something out. "I was saving this. But I think it's time to bring it out now."

He held up a little baby figurine and walked over to the dollhouse. He reached into the second floor bedroom and took the small box out of the man's hands. He adjusted the guy's legs so he was standing across from the woman. Then he positioned both of their arms out and placed the baby in between them. It was one of the sweetest moments of my life.

Matteo knelt down and placed his cheek on my stomach.

"Hey, little guy or girl. It's your daddy." He looked up at me.

I smiled down at him as tears came to his eyes. It was rare to see him cry, and now I was crying, too.

He continued talking to our baby. "I thought your mom's hair in that Ziploc bag was my favorite keepsake from our time together. But nope. You, little one, will always be my favorite souvenir."

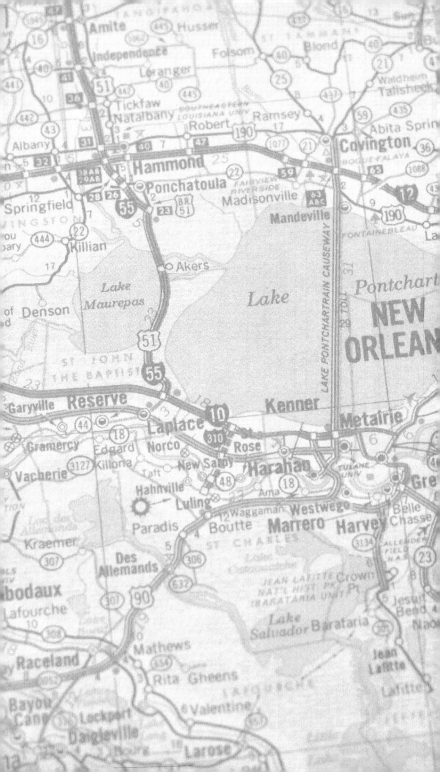

Acknowledgements

We are eternally grateful to all of the bloggers who enthusiastically spread the news about our books and persist even as it becomes harder and harder to be seen on social media. sThis has been a challenging year for all of us: bloggers, readers, and writers alike. Thank you more than ever for all of your continued hard work and for helping to introduce us to readers who may otherwise never have heard of us.

To Julie – We are so lucky to have your friendship, daily support, and encouragement. Thank you for always being one message away.

To Luna – Our right-hand woman. We appreciate your friendship and help so much and are so proud of all you've accomplished this year.

To our agent, Kimberly Brower – We are so lucky to call you a friend, as well as an agent. We're so grateful that you are always with us every step of the way in this literary adventure.

To Jessica – It's always a pleasure working with you as our editor. Thank you for making sure Hazel and Matteo were ready for the world.

To Elaine – An amazing editor, proofer, formatter, and friend. We so appreciate you!

To Sommer – Thank you for bringing Matteo to life on the cover. You nailed it. This one is at the top of our favorite co-write covers ever!

To Brooke – Thank you for organizing this release and for taking some of the load off of our endless to-do lists each day.

Last but not least, to our readers – We keep writing because of your hunger for our stories. We love surprising you and hope you enjoyed this book as much as we did writing it. Thank you as always for your enthusiasm, love and loyalty. We cherish you!

Much love,
Penelope and Vi

Other Books by Penelope Ward & Vi Keeland

Cocky Bastard
Stuck-Up Suit
Playboy Pilot
Mister Moneybags
British Bedmate
Park Avenue Player
Rebel Heir
Rebel Heart
Hate Notes
Dirty Letters

Other Books by Penelope Ward

Just One Year

The Day He Came Back

When August Ends

Love Online

Gentleman Nine

Drunk Dial

Mack Daddy

RoomHate

Stepbrother Dearest

Neighbor Dearest

Jaded and Tyed (A novelette)

Sins of Sevin

Jake Undone (Jake #1)

Jake Understood (Jake #2)

My Skylar

Gemini

About Penelope Ward

Penelope Ward is a *New York Times, USA Today* and *#1 Wall Street Journal* bestselling author.

She grew up in Boston with five older brothers and spent most of her twenties as a television news anchor. Penelope resides in Rhode Island with her husband, son and beautiful daughter with autism.

With over 1.5 million books sold, she is a twenty-time *New York Times* bestseller and the author of over twenty novels.

Penelope's books have been translated into over a dozen languages and can be found in bookstores around the world.

Subscribe to Penelope's newsletter here:
http://bit.ly/1X725rj

Other Books by Vi Keeland

About Vi Keeland

Vi Keeland is a #1 *New York Times*, #1 *Wall Street Journal*, and *USA Today* Bestselling author. With millions of books sold, her titles have appeared in over a hundred Bestseller lists and are currently translated in twenty-five languages. She resides in New York with her husband and their three children where she is living out her own happily ever after with the boy she met at age six.